NEW EROTICA 3

Other titles in the series:

NEW EROTICA 1
NEW EROTICA 2

NEW EROTICA
3

Extracts from the best of Nexus

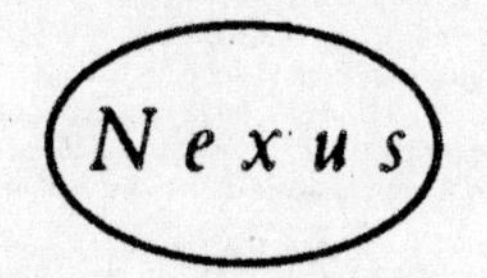

This book is a work of fiction.
In real life, make sure you practise safe sex.

First published in 1997 by
Nexus
Thames Wharf Studios
Rainville Road
London W6 9HT

Reprinted 1997, 1998

Extracts from the following works:

Phototypeset by Intype London Ltd

ISBN 978-0-753-53903-3

All characters in this publication are fictitious and any resemblance to real persons, living or dead, is purely coincidental.

The Random House Group Limited supports The Forest Stewardship Council (FSC®), the leading international forest certification organisation. Our books carrying the FSC label are printed on FSC® certified paper. FSC is the only forest certification scheme endorsed by the leading environmental organisations, including Greenpeace. Our paper procurement policy can be found at www.randomhouse.co.uk/environment

Printed and bound in Great Britain by Clays Ltd, St Ives PLC

CONTENTS

INTRODUCTION

More than two hundred works of erotic fiction have been published by Nexus. With two new titles on sale every month, and an extensive backlist, readers new to erotica – or those wishing to reacquaint themselves with this fascinating genre – might find the choice available from this bestselling imprint a little daunting.

New Erotica 3, the latest in a series of anthologies, showcases extracts from books by many of Nexus's best authors, all of whom have had several books published by the imprint. Also featured is an extract from *Beatrice*, an anonymously – and beautifully-written – early work of lascivious fiction.

With settings as diverse as Victorian Cornwall, a training institute on an exotic tropical island and a dark, magical otherworld, New Erotica has something to appeal to every open-minded reader. Virtually every erotic activity imaginable – from bondage to watersports via depilation and orgies – is featured, and described in the most explicit detail.

All that remains to be said is that we hope you find *New Erotica 3* as engaging and arousing to read as we did putting it – and all the other titles in the Nexus library – together. Enjoy!

HEART OF DESIRE

Maria del Rey

One of Nexus's most popular authors, Maria del Rey, specialises in stories of domination and submission, and invariably flavours her work with a subtle taste of the bizarre. Each of her novels is striking in its originality, with settings as diverse as a lush Greek Island – *Paradise Bay* – and a remote hi-tech community, whose sexually liberated inhabitants enjoy a disciplined alternative life-style – *Eden Unveiled. Dark Desires*, an anthology of Maria's kinkiest short stories, further underlines her versatility and is the perfect introduction to her work.

Maria's characters are always well-rounded and engaging and *Heart of Desire*, a novel with a contemporary setting, centres around Sarah Kowalski, a young actress. Cast as a dominatrix in a forthcoming film, she is determined to research the role thoroughly. She is introduced to the mysterious Dominique, a professional Mistress, who agrees to train her in every aspect of the art and who, as is seen in the following extract, leads Sarah to discover some surprising truths about her most secret desires.

All of Maria del Rey's books are in print. Given that she is a prolific author of stories whose principal themes are erotic domination and the surrender to shame-making but exquisite humiliations, it's not surprising that she has written eight titles for Nexus and many short stories for publications such as *Fetish Times* and *Forum*. Maria is an erotica aficionado par excellence.

'Are you really still interested in doing the film?' Dominique asked after a while.

'Yes,' Sarah said doubtfully, and then said more positively, 'I do want to do it.'

'Then I want you to have a dress rehearsal.'

'I couldn't, not with you.'

Dominique smiled. 'I wasn't offering myself as your victim. I want you to have a session with one of my slaves. It'll give you an idea of what you'll probably be expected to do in the film.'

'With a man?' Sarah said under her breath, quietly horrified by the idea.

'Yes, with one of my male slaves. You'll learn a lot by doing this, much more than you'll learn from reading books or just talking about it.'

'I couldn't,' Sarah said bluntly, unable even to imagine herself as the bitch-queen to a submissive male.

'It's alright,' Dominique said reassuringly, 'I'll be with you. I can show you what to do and how to act. Trust me.'

Sarah stood up and went into the other room, her mind full of doubts and questions. She wished that Eddie had never told her about the film, that she had never met Dominique, that things had been left as they were. It would have been better if the strange feelings inside her had been left dormant, unknown and unsuspected, because now there was no escape. Dominique came into the room, and when Sarah looked up she felt her heart skip a beat. For a moment, the pale young female before her was the Mistress that she had obeyed so willingly in the chamber.

'Why do you do it, Dominique?' Sarah asked earnestly, gazing up desperately, as if Dominique's reply would be the answer to her own confusion. She couldn't understand her at all; Dominique's manner was direct, detached, yet still friendly, still helpful, as if there were two parts to her personality, two sides always on display.

'What do you want?' Dominique snapped irritably. 'Do you really think I've got some neat little answer, a nicely labelled, nicely packaged explanation of why I am what I am? It doesn't exist. Why do you do what you do? Why is anyone the way they are?'

'I'm sorry,' Sarah whispered timidly. She had hoped for an answer, hoped that Dominique had rationalised and explained before, and so would explain it all to her.

'Come here,' Dominique ordered, her voice hard and unyielding. Her face had changed too, her eyes were harder, her lips narrowed. She sat down on the edge of an armchair, her knees together, back straight, waiting.

The room was spinning, and for a moment Sarah felt lost, but when she looked again Dominique was still waiting. She felt many things at that moment, fear among them, but most of all she felt a thrill of excitement, a thrill that was oddly familiar. Without being asked, she fell to her knees and crawled across the room, her heart beating out the journey in rapidly measured beats.

'Pull your knickers down,' Dominique ordered.

Sarah did as commanded. She slipped her hands under her loose skirt and pulled her panties down to her knees, then she looked up expectantly, waiting for the next order. She was wet between the thighs, the desire had speared her suddenly, an emotional switch had been thrown, so that one moment she was cold and the next she was hot. Desire had never been like that before, she had never known herself aroused so easily. In the past, desire had been buried, hidden under layers of inhibition, and it took time to strip those layers away to get to the pure physical response she now felt.

'Across my knee,' Dominique barked, sitting back so that there was room across her lap. She wasn't giving instructions, they were not proper orders but telegraphic codes, ciphers that Sarah instinctively understood and responded to, like a language that she had known in a past life and in which she had suddenly become fluent once more.

She placed herself across Dominique's lap, legs straight, arms out in front of her for balance. Her nipples were hard, jutting against her blouse which was stretched tight, so that even the tiniest movement was amplified, sending trains of sensation through her body. Dominique took the hem of the skirt and pulled it up, throwing it over the waist so that Sarah's backside was bared, her panties still caught up around her knees. Sarah held her breath, could feel Dominique's eyes, feel the way she was regarding the bared backside, eyeing the tight roundness of the buttocks, the darkness that obscured the pink lips of her sex.

The first slap was hard and loud; the sound seemed to hang in the air, an audible expression of the white heat of pain that burned the soft flesh of her arse-cheeks. She had sucked in her breath and held it, fighting back the squeal of pain that was her natural reply to the hard smack on the bottom. 'This is stupid,' she tried to tell herself, 'stupid, stupid, stupid.' She turned slightly, caught the blurred movement of the hand as the second smack fell hard across her backside. This time her cry was loud, as sharp as the stinging pain on her flesh. She tried to move, the third slap stopped her at once.

'Stay still,' Dominique hissed.

It was an impossible order to obey; Sarah's entire body seemed to be aflame, her sex was red and aching, the red heat on her backside somehow merging with the rubbing of her nipples on the blouse and with the desire in her pussy. The pain was intense every time Dominique's firm hand made contact, and yet it was sucked away as pain and returned as pleasure, inverting itself so that what was bad felt good. Sarah lifted herself higher, raising her buttocks to meet the downward stroke, her backside reaching up to kiss the flesh that smacked hers. She could feel where her skin had reddened, all over her buttocks and down at the top of her thighs, and the burning felt delicious. The humiliation was total, as emotionally painful as the physical pain on her behind, yet she sought that too, she sought it as much as she sought the spanking.

'On your knees,' Dominique ordered curtly, pushing Sarah to the ground.

Sarah looked up, dazed; she had become lost in the steady rhythm of her spanking, lost to everything but the pattern of punishment that marked her pale skin. She knelt in front of Dominique expectantly, quivering, the burning of her flesh and the aching of her sex a single maddening sensation. Dominique began to unbutton the blouse, her fingers snapping the buttons off quickly. In a moment Sarah's breasts were bare, her heaving chest open to Dominique's steady scrutiny. The hard nipples were yearning to be handled, to be kissed and sucked, to be pulled and pinched.

'Fuck yourself,' Dominique said coldly, her face revealing nothing of her own emotions or desires, her face as much a mask as the leather that had hidden her expressions when in the chamber.

Sarah reached down under her skirt, pulling it up so that Dominique could see the pussy mound, see the parted pussy lips, see the fingers pressing tentatively into the sex. She closed her eyes and gave herself fully to the sensation, revelling in the pleasure of fingering herself, stoking the fires that burned so hot in the wetness of her sex. It didn't matter that she was frigging herself in front of Dominique, it didn't matter, all that mattered was the purity of pleasure.

She screamed, opened her eyes wide. She looked down in slow motion, down at the finger marks that were dark red on the pale white of her breast. A second hard slap caught her other breast, a bullet of pure pleasure-pain shooting through her body. She closed her eyes, sought her clitty with her fingers, the steady spanking of her breasts adding layers of pleasure. It was too much, too much. She cried out suddenly, overcome by the force that seemed to tear her out of herself, her body froze, back arched and muscles taut. She climaxed, fell forwards, and still her body was alive to pleasure.

Dominique reached out and resumed spanking Sarah hard on the behind, making her climax again quickly, her breasts still smarting as her bottom was tanned once more. 'Thank me,' Dominique ordered, pushing Sarah away after her second intense climax.

'Thank you,' Sarah whispered shakily, her body tingling all over, her bottom and her breasts smarting sharply, the skin patterned red and white with finger marks. 'Thank you, Mistress,' she said again, and this time she felt an added thrill of pleasure, as if the very act of thanking Mistress were a sexual act in itself.

Dominique smiled at last, the look in her eyes becoming softer. She lifted her T-shirt up to her shoulders and revealed her own naked breasts, the nipples standing enticingly on end. 'Thank me with your lips,' she whispered, taking hold of Sarah's hair and pulling her closer.

The next day Sarah entered the room timidly, fully prepared to fall to her hands and knees if Mistress desired her to do so. At the chamber it was Mistress first and Dominique second. Sarah had tried to reconcile herself to the division, forcing herself to accept it, although common sense told her that it was childish to play games. Reluctantly she was coming to understand that common sense and cold rationality were a hindrance to knowledge. Mistress seemed to appeal to something far deeper than that; to something buried in the personality, to somewhere out of reach and out of sense.

Mistress was dressed in a shiny red latex catsuit, clinging sensuously to her body from the neck down to her sharp-heeled red ankle boots. It outlined her body to perfection, clothed it in a sensual red skin that shimmered as Mistress moved. 'Good, you're here,' Mistress smiled. She wore brilliant red lipstick that matched her outfit, as red and as sensuously glossy, making it seem as if her costume and her body were one and the same thing.

'You look beautiful, Mistress,' Sarah said softly, secretly delighted in being able to call Dominique Mistress again.

'Jenny has laid out your clothes.' Mistress pointed to a neatly laid out collection of black garments. 'Remember, you're a Mistress too, keep that in mind as you dress. Think of it as putting on a new personality, it's an armour, a magical armour that gives you power.'

'Yes, Mistress,' Sarah agreed, unable to keep her eyes off Mistress. She hesitated then walked across the room to look at the costume that the maid had selected.

'The slave is waiting down in the chamber,' Mistress informed her, sounding relaxed and confident, positively looking forward to the encounter that she had arranged.

Sarah put her shoulder bag down and gently touched the costume, her fingers lingering for a moment on the cool reflective surfaces. She knew that she had to get changed, but was reluctant to do so in front of Mistress; she wanted time to change by herself, to accustom herself to the look and feel of the rubber. And, more importantly, she wanted time to get into character, to fully become a Mistress herself – powerful, confident, sexual. 'I've brought my own heels, just as you wanted,' she said, stooping down to pull a pair of black high heels from her bag.

'Good, Jenny's picked out some latex stockings to go with them. Now,' Dominique urged her, 'get dressed.'

Sarah turned her back to Mistress and undressed hurriedly, self-consciously aware of being watched. She had been beaten and fingered, had joyously kissed Mistress's heels and yet she was still slightly embarrassed to be stripping naked in front of her. There was an undercurrent of excitement that she felt, a tingling expectation that she might suddenly find herself on hands and knees in abject worship of Mistress once more.

'What are you doing?' Sarah cried, turning to find Mistress standing directly behind her.

'Just getting you ready,' Mistress explained pleasantly. She poured a handful of talc in her palm and rubbed it softly on to Sarah's thigh, the snowy white powder dusting her flesh. With brisk, expert movements she powdered Sarah's body quickly and efficiently, over the thighs and breasts, down the back and over the buttocks. Sarah stood silently, relishing the feeling of Mistress's hands all over her body, a soft fleeting touch that was erotic and yet unfocused, making her feelings of excitement more pronounced. When Mistress's fingers stroked her between the thighs, Sarah shuddered, sighed softly, unable to restrain the evidence of her arousal.

When Dominique had finished, the room was filled with the pleasant odour of the talcum powder, an odour that had always reminded Sarah of bathtime and childhood. She gingerly took the first of the stockings, so soft and shiny, gleaming with a polished radiance, and pulled it on slowly. It slipped over her powdered body like a dream, close fitting, pressing tight against the skin. She put the second one on and then stepped into her black high heels.

'How do I look?' she asked, staring down at herself, hardly able to believe the transformation. Her thighs looked fuller, longer, the skin so pale compared to the blackness that sheathed her; the stocking top was tight, making her flesh bulge a little against the rubber.

'You look great,' Mistress laughed, flashing brilliant white teeth against glossily painted red lips. 'Now the rest of it.'

Sarah donned a pair of tight PVC pants, high cut and tight-waisted, with a zip down past the crotch, studded at the sides with shiny chrome spikes. The top was made of the same clinging fabric, a studded half-cup bra that revealed the tips of her erect nipples, the studs at the sides. She turned to Mistress, the physical transformation complete. Mistress took her hand and led her to a mirror that was covered with a dirty white dust-sheet.

'Is that really me?' Sarah asked when the cover was pulled away and she stared at the cold hard reflection. Her body was accentuated, her thighs were perfect and slightly unreal, a fantasy figurine that made her head swim with excitement.

'Put some of this on,' Mistress suggested, giving her some red lipshine to apply.

In a second, Sarah looked complete, pouting in the mirror, unable to quite recognise herself in the reflection. She looked like someone else, another woman, a woman more attractive, more powerful, more alluring than she had ever been.

'How do you feel?' Mistress asked.

'Weird. It's hard to believe that that's me. I look so different . . . so sexy. It's just a set of clothes, right?'

Mistress smiled and shook her head. 'It's not just clothes. You've invoked something from within yourself, the devil inside, the real you, it could be anything. Don't try and analyse,' she warned, 'just look at her,' she pointed to the reflection, 'and be her.'

'Do you always feel this turned on, when you're dressed this way?' Sarah asked sheepishly, fascinated by the way Mistress's nipples were jutting hard against the tight red latex skin.

'Always,' Mistress admitted, 'but it's not the clothes. It's when I'm Mistress, whenever I assume her character I'm aroused, whether it's in my chamber or in my sitting room.'

Sarah blushed at the memory of her punishment the last time they had met. 'I'm ready now,' she said softly, her heart racing at the sudden awareness that now it was her turn to punish, and that she was a Mistress too, even if only for one day.

Mistress stepped back to take a long hard look at Sarah, smiled approvingly then leant forward and kissed Sarah on the mouth. 'You don't have to ask now, you don't need permission,' she said, her tongue tracing the shape of Sarah's lips, 'if you want something then do it.'

Sarah passed her hand up over Mistress's thigh, her fingers pressing against the impervious covering that turned Dominique's body into something abstractly beautiful. The nipples were hard little points, ringed by circles of light on the shiny red surface, and she rubbed her fingertips across them softly.

'Let's go,' Mistress sighed, her eyes misting slightly, her breath faster and deeper than it had been moments earlier. Sarah kissed her on the mouth again, wanting to enjoy the freedom of being a Mistress, helpless to resist the desire growing stronger and stronger inside her.

Mistress led the way, out into the dingy hallway and then down the stone steps towards the chamber. Sarah stopped at the top of the steps, afraid to start the descent into the darkness. 'Mistress,' she whispered at the top of the steps, waiting for Mistress to stop and look back at her, 'I want to thank you, for this and everything else.'

'There's nothing to thank me for. And today I'm not your Mistress, today you call me Dominique, OK? Especially in front of the slave. As far as he's concerned you are a Mistress too.'

Sarah nodded and followed Dominique, her own heels echoing hard on the stone steps, drawing comfort and encouragement from the staccato rhythm and the hardness of the sound. Dominique pushed the door open and Sarah strode into the chamber, chin up, an unconscious look of disdain on her face. 'I am Mistress, I am Mistress,' she repeated to herself, willing herself into the role, willing herself to assume the attitude and countenance to match the uniform that clothed her body so erotically.

It took a second for her eyes to adjust to the pale light, and another second for her to look away from the whips and chains that turned the chamber into a vision of a nightmare. Dominique touched her on the elbow and Sarah followed her across the room, their heels in unison on the flagstones. She struggled to keep her face impassive when she saw the slave, bound tightly in leather and chains behind the bars of the cage. His skin was dark, glistening, muscles stretched tight against the leather restraints that bound his arms together. He was chained to the bars of the cage, but still he had managed to twist round slightly and was straining to get a good look at the Mistresses as they approached him.

'Well, what do you think?' Dominique asked, barely glancing down at the slave.

Sarah shrugged, her eyes met the slave's; she held his gaze for a moment then he looked away. 'Is he good?' she asked, silently gratified that he had turned away from her.

'Vincent's a good specimen,' Dominique decided without too much thought. She opened the door of the cage and walked in, stepping up close so that her heels were by his face. He strained forward to kiss her boots but he was unable to reach; his neck was taut with muscle and the chains holding him to the cage were stretched tight.

'Is he obedient?'

'Only if chastised regularly.'

Sarah caught him glancing at her again, his dark eyes filled with an intense curiosity. This time he looked at her for a moment longer, challenging her silently. She stepped into the cage, Dominique stepping aside for her, and planted her heels next to his face. He made no movement towards her, instead he turned contemptuously away, a faint sneer on his lips. She turned to Dominique looking for guidance; her heart was beating wildly, she knew that Vincent was testing her. Dominique raised her eyebrows, waiting for a response to the slave's insulting arrogance.

'Let him go,' Sarah ordered, gritting her teeth. She was a Mistress, she told herself, there was no way she could let Vincent's impudence go unpunished.

Dominique did as she was asked, she loosed the chains that held Vincent to the cage and stepped away from him. He rolled forward on the ground, exhaling heavily, his breath misting slightly in the cold dark air. For a moment Sarah watched him lying on his back, looking straight up at the ceiling as he caught his breath. 'On your knees,' she ordered, her voice controlled so that the threat was clear without being too over dramatic.

He moved slowly, lifted himself up on one elbow, and looked at her, a smile forming on his lips, part amusement and part arrogance. Dominique had stepped back and Sarah knew that she was alone The anger came suddenly, overwhelming her doubts and confusions, he was laughing at her, smirking when he should have been obedient and adoring.

'What are you laughing at?' she demanded, stepping forward and smacking him hard across the face. The slap filled the room with its harsh report, her fingers were smarting and Vincent was looking away. She watched him turn towards her, his eyes large and filled with rage, the smile gone from his face. 'Now,' she hissed, 'on your knees.'

He began to lift himself; his arms were still bound together so that movement was obviously difficult, but still there was something lazy about his actions, something deliberately insolent. The second slap was as hard as the first. Sarah clenched and unclenched her fingers for a second, hardly aware of the look on Vincent's face.

'Do you want to use something? A strap or a paddle?' Dominique suggested quietly.

'No, not yet,' Sarah murmured, satisfied now that Vincent was moving as she wanted him. 'On your knees,' she directed coldly. 'I want to see what he feels like,' she explained, glancing back to Dominique.

Vincent obeyed, he managed to sit up on his knees, back held straight, looking up at Sarah with unconcealed hostility. 'Don't look at me,' she ordered. He held her eyes for a moment too long before turning away, his gaze falling on Mistress Dominique's heels. Sarah touched him firmly, passing her fingers over his shoulders, feeling the hardness of muscle under the cool skin. He was strong, good looking in a certain dangerous kind of way, and his passions and emotions were expressed purely and physically. She could feel his anger, feel him fighting against the bonds that wrapped him so securely, feel also the arrogance and the rebellion that seethed within him. He was dangerous, and that single thought made Sarah excited.

'He responds best to harsh treatment,' Dominique remarked impassively.

'Is that true?' Sarah asked him, circling slowly, her fingers trailing his body lazily.

'You're not a Mistress,' he said slowly, his voice was assured, confident despite the restraints that bound him.

'Aren't I?' Sarah asked, grinning. She stepped behind him and grabbed him suddenly, bending down low and forcing his head back with one hand so that his face was close to hers. His breath touched her skin, a hot whisper against her lips. 'Aren't I a Mistress?' she hissed, passing one hand slowly down over his chest and over the ridge of tight flat muscle of his stomach. His prick was hard when she wrapped her fingers tightly around it, hard and pulsing sensitively. 'Why are you hard then, slave? Isn't it because you're enjoying this?'

She released him suddenly and pushed him forward. He could hardly resist; he tipped forward so that his head touched the ground. His back was bent over, the leather bands digging deep into his ribs. Sarah knelt down beside him; she was fascinated by his body, by the pure masculine power that had been tightly reined in and was now prostrate before her. His thighs were thick and powerful and his buttocks were tight and round; she touched him, playfully stroked the soft flesh of his backside. He tensed up as her fingers explored between his thighs, her finger circling menacingly around the forbidden area of his rear hole. She lingered for a moment, looked up and saw Dominique smiling.

'You seem to have silenced him,' Dominique said approvingly. She moved closer, bent down and kissed Sarah on the mouth softly, holding her under the chin while she did so.

Sarah felt Dominique's kiss as an infusion of desire, as if all that she had been doing had been emotionless; the whole thing had had an abstract, unreal quality. She touched Dominique's thigh, stroking the soft rubber skin to feel the firm flesh underneath. 'I want a strap now,' she smiled, turning to catch the look of horror and desire in Vincent's eyes. She took hold of his balls, cradled the coolness in her hand, squeezing very gently so that he held his breath. 'Am I a Mistress, slave?'

He hesitated, the confusion clear in his eyes and on his

lips that quivered with half an answer. 'Yes,' he whispered at last, his voice thin and reedy in the dark quiet of the chamber.

'And what do you want?' Sarah teased, holding him firmly, her fingers encasing his balls and gripping tight the base of his stiff prick.

'I don't know . . . Mistress,' he whispered.

'You want to be punished,' Sarah whispered, delighted that he had succumbed. She was a Mistress, he could no longer deny it, and it felt good. She had been holding back, but now she was aware of the beating of her heart, of the throbbing in her nipples and the wet heat of her sex. The abstract feeling, the feeling of being disengaged, was gone and now she felt powerful, erotic, a Mistress for real. Dominique came back, holding a long black strip of leather, a tawse with knotted strips of leather at one end. 'What do you want?' she asked, bending low to whisper into his ear.

'I want to be punished, Mistress,' Vincent whispered, and he was pleading, looking up at her with begging, crying eyes.

Sarah took the tawse from Dominique, smiling, her eyes alive with an intense excitement. The tawse felt heavy in her hand, the leather strips long and stiff. 'Have I done well?' she asked softly, certain that for once she had fulfilled all that she had to.

'You've been wonderful, much better than I gave you credit for,' Dominique admitted with a smile.

'Thanks. I think I've surprised myself too,' Sarah confessed. 'Now, I think Vincent needs to be taught a lesson.'

She leant across and slowly undid the straps that held his arms together. Each of the four straps burst loose as she undid them, and then he was free. He rubbed his arms with his hands, trying to get some feeling back into his body; the straps had left deep indents on his flesh which Sarah traced with her finger. She stood up and walked lazily round him, he fell on hands and knees of his own accord, assuming a position of reverence that was her due as a Mistress. She stopped at his head, heels planted firmly in front of him. Instantly he fell to licking her black high heels, his tongue wetting the shiny patent leather.

'Enough!' she snapped, passing a happy smile to Dominique. 'Now slave, I'll teach you to question me.' Very slowly she unzipped her pants, unzipping the plastic garment right round so that the darkness of her pussy hair poked through. She squatted down in front of him, knees apart and her pussy exposed to his adoring eyes. 'Suck me,' she ordered, 'and do it well or the strap will bite twice as hard.'

Vincent needed no second bidding. He inched forward and buried his face in the dark groove between her thighs, his mouth and lips kissing her pussy lips. She could feel him breathing deeply, sucking in the pure perfume of her pussy scent. She dug her nails into his back and he moved responsively, his tongue snaking between her pussy lips to lap at the thick sex-honey that was oozing sensuously from within her. The pleasure pulsed through her, his tongue a flame that burned whatever it touched, making her sigh loudly.

'Good, good,' she whispered, edging herself forward so that she was open to him, open to the greedy mouth feasting on her sex. It felt odd to have a man sucking her as she wished, giving her the pleasure as she desired it. She lashed out with the strap, a hard stroke that licked at the rippling flesh of his lower back. It had been unexpected and Vincent cried out with shock and pain, but then he was sucking her passionately, his tongue stroking the walls of her sex.

She beat him again, enjoying the feeling of power and control, the sound of leather on flesh filling the air with all the magic of a peal of bells. He was working furiously with his tongue, sucking and biting, playing on the pussy bud so that she was rocking back and forth into his mouth. She used the tawse again, biting it into his flesh so that his moans were whispered into her sex. The pleasure was reaching fever pitch, she dropped the strap and pinned her nails into his flesh, gripping him hard while she climaxed into his sweet adoring mouth.

Dominique was there to hold Sarah as she stood up shakily, her body sprinkled with dewdrops of sweat, her thighs wet with her pussy cream that dappled the plastic garments and rubber stockings. She looked down and felt a thrill of delight when she realised that her heels were being licked clean by Vincent.

'I don't think you've anything to worry about,' Dominique said softly, kissing Sarah on the lips, 'the film should be no problem at all.'

'The film?' Sarah repeated, too dazed to really think straight. The film had slipped from her mind completely, it was an irrelevancy, something that existed outside of the chamber, and for the moment the chamber was her universe.

'Do you think you can submit to me after all of this?' Dominique asked, pressing herself against Sarah.

'Yes, you know I will,' Sarah replied instantly and without hesitation. She was a Mistress, of that she no longer had any doubt, but for her, Dominique was the ultimate Mistress and she knew that she would submit to her without question.

'But you don't think that today will make you react any differently?'

Sarah shrugged. 'I don't know, Dominique, all I know is that I'm still your slave, no matter what happens.'

'Let's make love now,' Dominique sighed, seeming to melt into Sarah's arms. They locked mouths, kissing passionately, arms around each other, the feel of each other mediated by leather and rubber so that layers of sensation were added to the embrace.

'What about him?' Sarah asked derisively, looking down at the silent slave at her feet.

'Slaves are to be used and enjoyed,' Dominique explained, smiling wickedly. 'Get me the big gag, the one Mistress Sarah and I will need,' she commanded, speaking down to Vincent coldly. He looked up sharply, as if to complain or protest, but the harsh glare from Dominique sent him scuttling across the chamber on hands and knees, his body rippling with muscle tone, and yet leashed by the force of his Mistress's will.

'Is he really a typical slave?' Sarah asked, her voice lowered so that he could not hear.

Dominique shook her head. 'There's no such thing as the typical slave, just as there's no such thing as the typical Master. Everyone has their own history, their own private landscape of desire. Vincent is difficult though, he needs to be reconquered and subdued every time; I think he can never accept the domination as anything but temporary. You've handled him well, and if you can do that then you're genuinely a Mistress.'

'Aren't you afraid of him?' Sarah whispered, eyeing him carefully as he returned, holding something dark between his teeth.

Dominique nodded. 'A little,' she admitted, 'but then the danger is part of the journey. I'd be more afraid not to confront my own desires.'

Vincent stopped in front of the two Mistresses, waiting like an obedient animal for them to notice him once more. His body was bathed in sweat, and he was breathing hard, heaving powerfully. Sarah touched him softly, traced her fingers where she had dug her nails into his flesh. He accepted her touch without complaint, pressing his face into her palm, eagerly accepting her caress.

'Sit up, where I can reach you,' Dominique told him. He obeyed and she took the object from his teeth and showed it to Sarah. 'This is a gag,' she explained, holding it up to the light. It had the shape of two pricks back to back, with a grip of some sort at the join. Dominique pushed one end into Vincent's mouth. He swallowed the plastic prick without complaint, it filled his mouth fully so that his cheek bulged around it. His teeth gripped tightly at the join and then Dominique secured it with a strap that she tied around his head. The second prick emerged from his mouth, a long, ribbed dildo that was the mirror image of the one in his mouth.

'Down, now,' Dominique snapped impatiently. Vincent lay on the floor, arms at his side, legs stretched out, the hardness of his prick jutting out from the dark tangle of hair between his thighs, a hardness that was matched by the dildo projecting from his mouth like some anatomical monstrosity.

Sarah knelt down beside him, took his prick in her hands and stroked it lovingly, enjoying the sensuous feel of it in her fingers. A wet rivulet of fluid poured from the glans, it glistened on his thickly veined rod, a silver river on the landscape of his prick. She leant across him and kissed the glans softly, flicking her tongue over the slit so that she could lap up the almost tasteless fluid that was warm and sticky on her tongue. He sighed softly, tensing his body in an effort to control himself. She smiled, suddenly aware of what it was to have power over a man; he could not give himself to his pleasure, he had to hold back, save himself for her, because her pleasure was paramount. She could lick and suck, torment him wickedly with her tongue, enjoying his prick in her mouth just as she liked, without worrying what he wanted. The joy of it was that what he wanted, what he desired more than anything else, was to serve her, that was all.

She lapped up the fluid from his prick very slowly, tantalised by the sighs that escaped from behind the gag, excited by his squirming and tensing as he fought back the pleasure that she gave him. Her tongue traced a route from the thick hairy base right to the tip, tracing the thick underside of his dark cock with the pink tip of her tongue.

'You want his prick, I take it?' Dominique asked, interrupting Sarah's exploration of the slave's thick hard penis.

Sarah looked up and saw that Dominique was undoing a row of studs around her thighs and waist. In a second she had undone the middle part of her red latex catsuit, exposing a section of white flesh against the red rubber. She looked divine, her body was still clothed in rubber above the waist and from the top of the thighs down, but her middle was exposed, the swell of her buttocks and the fullness of her quim were free. 'Do you mind?' Sarah asked, momentarily distracted by the delicious sight of Dominique.

'Why should I mind?' Dominique laughed, advancing on Vincent with a slight swaying of the hips. 'The penis gag always fills my pussy just as I like it, and I love fucking him this way, I can feel the other prick fucking him in the mouth at the same time.'

Sarah straddled Vincent quickly, she held his cock and guided it to the opening of her pussy, which was wet and tingling with aroused anticipation. She let herself down on his prick, enjoyed the feel of it slipping into the warm velvet sweetness of her sex. She sat for a moment, filled with his hardness, her pussy tight around the shaft that pulsed with his heartbeat against her own pulse. Dominique sat down too, sliding herself down on the rigid hardness that Vincent held in his mouth. Sarah watched, fascinated by the way it entered her, by the way her pussy lips seemed to stretch around the hardness.

Dominique leant across and kissed Sarah on the mouth, their lips entwined while they pressed down hard on Vincent. They began to move together, timing the slow rhythmic dance so that they were penetrated in unison, so that the pleasure was shared, doubled, savoured. Vincent's prick flexed powerfully, rising up to spear between Sarah's thighs as she ground herself down on him. At the same time he moved his head higher, moving the dildo deep into Dominique's sex.

Sarah closed her eyes; all she wanted was to enjoy the feel of Dominique's mouth and Vincent's hardness. The sensations were hard to tell apart, making her catch her breath, hold it, enjoy the frisson of delight and then exhale with the next stroke. She felt lost, dizzied by the rush of energy. She opened her eyes and looked down at Vincent; he was moving in a frenzy, writhing, bucking his hips manfully while his head thrashed from side to side. The dildo was wet with glistening juices, dripping down from Dominique's pussy and into his mouth. He was being fucked too, fucked expertly by Dominique's pussy, and his mouth filled with her essence; an essence that poured down the prick as if it were come that were filling his mouth. Such a clever punishment, Sarah thought before the pleasure overwhelmed her, so clever because it was so confusing for him.

'You're being fucked Vincent! Fucked in the mouth!' Dominique gasped, riding up and down to climax over his face, her pussy slipping easily over the smooth polished surface of the dildo, a polished surface that ran with her come.

Sarah felt Dominique stiffen, felt the breath go from her body as she climaxed in a string of convulsive spasms. Vincent froze a moment later, his body caught mid-position, his hips pressed up against her backside, his face buried deep between Dominique's thighs. He climaxed too, shooting thick wads of juice into Sarah's hot quim. She continued to ride him, to slap herself up and down over the pumping hardness. He recovered quickly, pumping harder and harder until she cried out, gripped Dominique tightly and let herself go to the force of orgasm.

'That was good,' Dominique whispered, rolling off the dildo that glistened with the thick creaminess of her pussy juice.

'I haven't finished with Vincent yet,' Sarah smiled, the words whispered between deep heavy breaths. The words had an immediate effect on him; he moaned softly, turning to look at Dominique with pleading in his eyes. 'It's no good begging, Vincent,' Sarah assured him, a cruel smile playing on her freshly kissed lips. 'I'm going to thrash you again, then I want you to clean my pussy with your tongue. Is that clear?'

Vincent's beseeching look to Dominique was to no avail. 'Mistress commands,' she told him softly, 'and you'll obey.'

CHOOSING LOVERS FOR JUSTINE

Aran Ashe

Aran Ashe is probably best known to the Nexus readership as an author of erotic novels with fantasy settings. His *Chronicles of Lidir* is a bestselling Nexus series and *Citadel of Servitude*, the much-anticipated second book of the *Chronicles of Tormunil* will be published by the imprint in June.

Choosing Lovers for Justine, a dark tale of intrigue within a clandestine, decadent circle of Edwardian society, is something of a departure, but Aran Ashe's often breathtaking descriptions of domination, subjugation, pleasure-pain and sublime perversion are still very much in evidence. Young, lovely and utterly masochistic, the elfin Justine is introduced by her strict guardian, Julia Norwood, to a succession of lovers, each of whom has favoured methods of enjoying her willing body.

In this extract, a letter written by Justine, which reveals in explicit detail some erotic secrets of her rather tragic past, has been forwarded by Julia to the seemingly respectable Philip Clement. Despite the presence of the lascivious Roxanne, Philip cannot resist reading it immediately.

Rarely can one find descriptions of exquisite violation so lovingly described. Aran Ashe's work within the erotic genre has a rare quality in that it is without a trace of obscenity, and is all the more powerful for it. The mythical principality of Lidir is home to both the good and evil; a place where taskmistresses and overlords slake their lust on the flesh of the young initiates of the Castle. The second of Aran's series is the *Chronicles of Tormunil*. Tormunil is a mysterious citadel of erotic mastery from which there can be no escape from its harsh rulers; where every avenue of sexual love must be tested and every taboo broken.

They told me that I was upset, that I was naive and that Rachel had taken advantage – that she had done it with other girls and she was evil and not to be trusted – but I knew that they were worse. They never cared. Every feeling that was good, they said was wrongful. And because I loved Rachel, I was punished.

After that first night we spent together, I was summoned by the headmistress. She had her deputy with her. My bed hadn't been slept in and they wanted to know where I had been. But I kept quiet; I wouldn't betray her; I didn't say a thing. The more they shouted, the more certain I became that they would never get to know. They said they would give me until that night to come to my senses – after that, it would be the cane. It would be the cane every night until I told them where I had been. Perhaps they suspected even then. They found out in the end, of course, but not that way. I never told them. I went away and cried, but I didn't know why I cried, because their threats hadn't frightened me. I cried the rest of the morning and into the afternoon. And that night, they kept their promise. There were two of them there, always two each time, although not always the same two. They asked me again and when I wouldn't speak, they called me names and accused me of terrible things. They tried to trick me into admitting where I'd been. Then they caned me. They made me lift my skirt and bend across the arm of a chair. They took it in turns: while one caned me, the other watched her doing it. Then they quizzed me again – they even asked about my mother, trying to make me feel worse – and then the other one caned me. It hurt me – how it hurt – but I never cried for them. When they had finished, I left them none the wiser. 'Remember – tomorrow night, the same,' they said. 'And every night, until you choose to tell us. And make no mistake, you will tell us.'

I went out into the night – we weren't supposed to go outside after dark even to cross the yard – and I cried then, when I was certain none of them would hear. When I looked up, I could see the light from Rachel's room, and her silhouette on the curtain. I went up there, making sure that nobody saw me. Her door was unlocked and I crept in. And when I closed the door behind me, I felt afraid – that she might reject me now. I couldn't move. She was working at her table. She looked up, then threw her pen down and ran across the room, then suddenly stopped. And it was obvious that she knew. There were tears running down my cheeks again. They wouldn't stop. Rachel touched them. 'You didn't tell them?' I tried to swallow, shook my head, but could not answer. She checked the corridor, then locked the door and took hold of me. 'I knew that you wouldn't . . . I knew . . . Hushhh . . .' She turned me round and lifted the hem of my skirt. 'Oh,' she said. 'Oh – what have they done to you?' Her tenderness made my tears keep coming. They hardly stopped that night.

She unfastened the ribbon and my knickers fell to the floor. She took my skirt off; she was kneeling at my feet and I was still crying. She kept touching the backs of my legs and buttocks where the cane had marked me, and whispering, 'Oh – what have they done?' And I just stood there, trembling. Every time she touched me, I shivered – and I loved it, even though the tears were running down my cheeks. It made it worth all the punishment in the world, just to have her touch me and whisper these things to me. No one else had ever shown me such concern, and no one else had ever touched me in the way that she did. From that moment on, she owned me. I would have done anything she asked, anything at all.

She turned me round and pressed her cheek against my stomach. Then she kissed it. I kept shivering all the time. She kissed my legs; she asked me to open them. I thought that she was going to touch me there; I was aching for her to touch me between the legs and to possess me with her fingers in the way she had done the previous night. I closed my eyes and waited. But it was her lips which touched me; she just kissed it. She took it into her mouth and kissed it, and I was terrified. She kept kissing me there, and I kept shaking and wanting to pull away. It was an awful feeling, that first time – the sweetness of it, and the shame, giving way to the terrible fear that something dreadful was going to happen, that she was pushing me towards something that I could not control. And suddenly it came. I had never had it happen before. I did not even know what it was. I thought that I had wet myself. I stood there, shuddering, with my legs apart, trying to pull back, to lift up on my toes while Rachel kept it in her mouth and touched it with her tongue. I thought that I had peed into her mouth, and Rachel just keep kissing.

But when it was over, I felt so good. I told her what they had said about punishing me again. 'Then come to me,' she said, 'and I shall make the pain go away again.' She unfastened my bodice and touched my nipples. I wanted her to put me into bed again and hold me – even let me freeze, so I could feel her against me, warming me again – but she wouldn't. She said it would be too dangerous now, that we might be found out. She must have seen the look in my eyes – even then, after so short a time together, I was terrified of losing her – because she said to me, 'We will take our chances as they come. Whenever they punish you, come to me.'

And I did. And when I look back on it, that was what made it so exciting: the secrecy and the way that Rachel made those short times last. The next night, when they punished me again, every cut of the cane pushed the feelings of longing up through my belly and to the back of my throat, because I knew that every weal would be caressed by the tip of Rachel's finger. The more marks I had across my bottom, the more concern she would show and the sweeter would be her kisses. Before they had finished caning me, there was a damp patch in my knickers. Half an hour later, I was in Rachel's room, with my bottom bare and my bodice open and my nipples tingling while she knelt between my legs again and kissed me in that special way. She made me hold her head while she kissed me here. She kept kissing it and sucking it, making wet sounds and touching it with her tongue. Then the feeling came on harder than before. I pulled my hand away from her and bit it to stifle my cries.

'Why did you do that?' she asked me. 'I wanted you to hold me when you came. I wanted you to hold my head and press it between your legs. I wanted you to take my mouth and fuck it with your cunny.' Then she laughed because I was embarrassed. But those first few nights, she was kind almost all the time.

On the third night, she made me go naked under my skirt when I went for my caning. I was terrified of what they would think, but I did it. And while I waited to go in, it suddenly occurred to me that they might examine me when I was naked. It became fixed in my mind that this would happen, and the feelings I experienced then were overpowering. The arousal was so intense that it scared me. I stood shaking, with the frightened feelings washing up between my legs: I was swollen and they would see it swollen, but I couldn't help it – and they might touch me. And the feeling was there between my legs, the feeling of wanting to pee. But it was another kind of wetness seeping out of me, and it felt luscious but shamefully wrong.

When I bent across the chair, my heart was racing. They ordered me to pull my skirts up. I heard their gasps; my face was burning, but I felt secure because my face was buried under my arms and against the seat. They called me all the wicked things in the world, all the wicked names they could think of. But they did not make me get up, and they lashed me harder than ever. When they finally let up, the middle part of the cane was shiny and there were splashes of wet on the backs of my legs. But that was the last time it ever happened that way. They never called me back and I never told them anything. They only found out when it was too late.

When Rachel saw how sharply the cane had marked me, she became very excited. She undressed me to my bodice, then kept me standing while she licked my skin. Then she opened my legs and touched me from the back, between my buttocks, just stroking the skin very lightly while I kept my legs apart. She would not let me lie down. Her fingertips kept coming back to the throbbing ridges on my legs and buttocks. She moved to my front and unfastened me. My nipples were hard, but she didn't touch them; she lifted my bodice open so they stood out and she looked at them in the mirror. Then she knelt in front of me, pushed the tip of her tongue into my navel and played with me between the legs until her fingers were wet to the knuckles. She knew what I wanted, but she would not give it; after those first two times, that was always the nature of Rachel's love, to teach me how to plead. Not that night though, because I was too shy to speak things out loud. But over the next few days, I learnt.

When I was wettest, she made me dress and she sent me away with a warning: I was not to touch myself. 'I shall take charge of you, now, Justine. I shall play with you. And I shall decide whether you will come and when and where and how.' She made me kneel and promise. She said that if she were ever to discover, or even suspect, that I had done anything like that, she would never let me see her again. That was the threat, and it was more than enough. 'You can come to me again tomorrow night,' she said: that was the promise that made her threat so sweet a burden to bear. 'But keep your bottom naked for the caning.' I hadn't told her that the punishments were over – I had been afraid to do that in case it might have meant an end to our meetings – but this way, if I kept quiet and did as I was told, our meetings might continue. That was all that counted.

When I lay in bed in the dormitory that night with my legs open and my nightdress rolled up above my breasts, I was imagining her tongue still licking inside my navel, her hand upon my belly, stretching the skin, and the warmth of her lips gradually moving down, toying with me, gently pulling the wetness in between my legs until the ache became a hurt. But when she did her rounds, she ignored me. I could hear her whispering to one of the girls; I saw the sheet move. When the other girl started to murmur, Rachel's hand moved across her mouth, and there were no more sounds. But the sheet still moved and Rachel stayed with the girl until she fell asleep. Then she came to me. She moved the cover down, exposing my breasts to the cold air, and pulled my nightdress down across their tops to trap them, because that was how she liked to see them, tight and exposed. Then she pushed her fingers into my mouth and made me suck them. I could taste the girl and it aroused me. I spread my legs for her, but she wouldn't touch me there. She pulled the covers partly back to leave my breasts exposed. I fell asleep that way. When I woke, she was gone: my breasts were frozen, my legs were still apart and I was hot there and swollen. I felt sticky.

In the morning, when I washed myself, I was afraid that Rachel might disapprove of even this touching. Even the slightest brush of the moist flannel against my skin, I found arousing. It was as if the fingertips touching me were no longer mine.

In the evening, I had to remove my knickers before going into her room. I stood at her door and dropped them. I had never felt so aroused – she picked them up and pressed them to her lips and my legs were quaking – but I was frightened, too, because I had no new marks: all that she would see would be the faint remaining ones from yesterday's caning. I began to tremble when she got me inside and her hand moved up my skirt and her fingers started searching my skin. 'Oh,' she whispered. 'Have you no hurts today that I can tend with kisses? Then why have you come to me without your knickers? You do not need me any more. Perhaps you should go.'

Perhaps she was playing games with me, but it did not seem so then. I began to weep. I pleaded with her not to send me away. She never replied to any of my entreaties, but stood there, looking at me and smoothing her hand over the bareness of my bottom. 'Have you touched yourself?' she asked suddenly.

'No. No!' But the question had taken me unawares and I felt guilty – because I was so aroused and she would be able to tell this if she examined me.

She stared at me as if she didn't believe me, then she undressed me to my bodice, which she left open again, and she made me stand with my legs apart. She went into her bedroom, returned with a cane and flexed it, then whipped it through the air several times. My heart was racing. She kept whipping the cane through the air in front of me. Then she stared round the room impatiently. Her gaze fell on the table. It was a heavy black table with rounded corners and a top which had been polished to a mirror finish. She swept to one side the things that were on it. The table was very large. 'Get on,' she said. 'Lie on it.' She made me bend, face down across it, with my bodice open. But she made me stretch out my arms and bend my knees, so my feet lifted from the floor. Then she caned my bottom, while my hands and breasts and belly pressed and slid against the polished table and the weight of my hips and legs gradually pulled me to the floor. She kept whipping me while I slipped, and she made me keep my legs open. She didn't seem to care where the cane strokes fell. When my knees touched the floor she lifted me up and it began again. She wanted my legs kept wide, she said, so she could see between them – see my cunny tighten when she whipped me. She used that word and reminded me that I was to call it by that name. She made me say it every time the cane whipped down, and she kept caning while I slid until my breasts were balanced on the table and my knees were on the floor. Then she made me stand and turn round while she touched me. She pushed three fingers into me and they came out wet. She made me lick them. While I licked that hand, the other one held me open and played with my cunny, then used the wet to smear about my nipples. Then she sucked them. Then she said that she would cane me in a new way.

She moved me round and showed me the corner of the table, but I did not follow what she meant. Then I saw that the black polish showed a paler stain there, a small oval patch where a cup might have spilled. She said one word – 'Veronica' – and she touched the stain upon the surface of the wood, and smiled, and I was frightened. She said that she wanted me to understand the meaning of that mark. When I looked at her, she put her finger across my lips. Then she turned me so I faced away from her and made me sit astride the corner of the table, with my thighs kept open by the two diverging edges. I had to balance with my arms locked behind my back and my knees bent and the soles of my feet together under the table. I had to balance on my cunny while she whipped me. She whipped only my buttocks, whipping one at first, then switching to the other. Each lash made my legs jerk open. She stood to the side, so she could watch it. 'You cane better than she does,' she said, *whipping the cane down swiftly. 'Come on . . . Come on, Justine. Let it open, let it kiss.'*

I groaned; my feet pressed hard together and my cunny opened; I felt the lips push out and slip against the polished wood and kiss the image that was bleached into the grain. Rachel suddenly pushed me forwards, holding my arms pinned behind me. With my feet still pressed together at the soles, she touched me in between the cheeks of my bottom, touching the entrance, pinching it lightly, and telling me the things she would do with it when next I came to her. She explained that she wanted it kept at all times clean and ready – to be opened, kissed or licked, or filled, as she might choose. Then she made me keep my feet together while she showed me what she would use.

She put a heavy silver serving spoon on the table in front of me. She stood behind me and made me sit up as straight as I could. Then she lifted the open lips of my cunny from the table and took the tip of my clitoris in her fingers. She kept hold of it while she picked up the spoon by its bowl, turned it upside down, wetted the smooth crown of the handle and pressed it against the mouth of my bottom. She began rubbing my clitoris. My legs began to open but she made me keep my feet together while the smooth knob of silver pressed. My clitoris was poking out between her fingers and it kept slipping against her skin. She made me hold my head back. There was a sudden tightness from my belly to my breasts and the feeling came – when the handle tried to enter – that I wanted to pee, and I could not stop this feeling. My bottom opened and the handle of the spoon went in. It felt cold and it kept coming. The feeling kept coming too, like the feeling when she sucked me; my cunny just kept slipping, and my clitoris came wet between her fingers. She made me cry out when the feeling peaked. Then she would not let my clitoris retract. She kept rubbing it while my belly wriggled, but she wouldn't release it. She said that she could feel my arousal through the movements of the spoon. When I gasped, she held my clitoris still while she pressed the handle of the spoon against the front wall from inside. When the feeling came this second time, she held the spoon pressed against me, but kept it still, so the feeling came on slowly, but it came much deeper and it lasted much longer. And I remember that I reached behind and touched her, and her blouse was open and there was naked skin and a nipple that I squeezed and Rachel murmured.

She lifted me down and laid me on the table, on my back, with the spoon still inside me. She placed my feet flat to the polished surface, took the spoon out, turned it upside down and slid the handle up my cunny. Then she sucked me with the spoon in place, with the curve of its handle fitted to my shape. She rocked it very slightly against the front wall of my cunny. The smooth crown pressed against me. When my legs began to move, she slowed the pace of the rocking and she stopped sucking. She made me look at her and move my hips. She lifted the flaps of my bodice aside and touched my nipples. She made me wet them for her first. Then she kissed me again between the legs and the feeling started coming on so strongly that it hurt. My legs collapsed open. Rachel's lips released me. She tried to slow me. She held my cunny lips open for a few seconds, then she licked them. She touched my clitoris with the underside of her tongue; she lifted the spoon against me and I jumped. My legs tried to open wider. I wanted to push my cunny down her throat. When the tip of her tongue touched me again, the feelings took me in overpowering waves. She held the upturned bowl of the spoon and lifted it, and my body tried to snatch it from her fingers. When she slid it out of me, I whimpered; she had made me sore. The table was wet where my lower back had pressed against it.

Rachel lifted me up and held me in her arms. Then she told me I had to go. 'We must be careful,' she said and kissed me. I told her I loved her – how I loved her: she had given me sweet and dreadful feelings that I had never known before.

After that, we always met in secret. We dared not spend too long in one place, least of all in Rachel's study. But our love-making evolved to suit: after a short while, it would be suspended. Rachel would use that word: 'It is suspended,' she would say, and my bottom would be burning, my cunny liquefying, my nipples aching for more. She would touch me very gently, then dress me and I would have to go. And she would warn me no to touch myself, but to keep myself in readiness for the continuation, which might come the next day, or I might have to wait longer, and pray for chance encounters. When these encounters happened, I would already be swollen and aroused, and I would be wet before she touched me. She would devise elaborate games to keep me that way.

On Sundays, she used to make me go without my knickers to mass and sit on the cold stone pew. She would have already caned me and the hot aches would be throbbing across my bottom. And I would have to lift my skirt and move the cushion out of the way and sit on the bare stone seat. Rachel would be behind me to make sure that I opened my legs and made my burning cunny kiss against the freezing seat. Then she would whisper to me where she wanted us to meet. After mass, in her room or in the grounds, she would play with me to keep me aroused. If I climaxed, she would always spank me; I would become aroused very quickly and the cycle would begin again.

On that first Sunday, she left mass so early that people noticed. Afterwards, I ran to her room and found her waiting, but she seemed edgy and excited. She looked at the clock on the mantelpiece, then checked her fob watch – she used that watch many times. She used to frown when she looked at it; in the middle of our lovemaking, she would stop and use it to check my pulse, and I would be gasping, groaning, while she counted; whenever she looked at it, it caused a shiver of expectation to run between my legs. 'We have nine minutes,' she said, 'before they get here to find out why I left.'

I couldn't see how she knew that, but I believed her, and it made it doubly exciting. 'Take your clothes off – everything.' She sat in the chair and watched me until I was naked. 'Seven minutes. Now stand at the window.' I was terrified because it overlooked the quadrangle. For the first time, her hands were actually trembling when she touched me. 'Stand up to it – against it – and stretch out.'

I was shaking as my arms reached up. My nipples touched the glass. Rachel was behind me, watching the scene from over my shoulder. I wanted to look up. 'Look out there,' she said. We were very high up. Two tiny, darkly draped figures moved below; they were joined by several more. A face looked up. 'Stand still,' said Rachel. 'Five minutes.' Then the awful feeling came between my legs; Rachel's hand had slipped between them from behind, supporting the cross that my body made, and her fingers held me open. The middle finger began masturbating me. 'Four minutes.' It kept sliding up and down between my cunny lips; my cunny lips kept sucking it and my open body moved. I lifted up on tiptoes. 'Three minutes . . .' My cunny was wet; it was dripping. Rachel used two hands and my legs bowed out. 'Two minutes – come on . . .' I tried to masturbate myself against her hands. 'One minute.' And it was coming, and I was gasping. But she counted the seconds down slowly, with small wet smacks of her fingers against the side of my cunny lips, until my belly jerked against the glass. Then she took my clitoris in hand and gently rubbed it. When I cried out, she suddenly spun me round, pushed my head down and lifted me on tiptoes, then forced me back until my open cunny pulsed against the coldness of the glass. And she finished me in this position, with my clitoris protruding down between my legs and the lips of my cunny suckered to the glass.

When the knock came at the door, she hid me, naked, in the wardrobe. When they had gone away again, she showed me the marble egg.

Afterwards, at breakfast, it was as if nothing had happened. Rachel sat at the top table. I watched her and felt warm all over; the waves of warmth kept coming. She glanced across at me and again the feeling came. I wanted to touch myself, but could not. When I moved, I could feel the polished marble egg that she had put into my cunny. 'It will keep you swollen,' she had told me. She made me keep it in all that day and it was still inside me that night, when she told me it was time to have me in her bed again.

She made me kneel up with my hips in the air and my breasts on the bed. She spent a long time touching me. She used her thumbs to massage the swelling around my cunny, then she probed me with her fingers. She said she wanted to feel the shape of the egg inside me. But the more she touched, the more I tightened, and it hurt. She wanted me to deliver the egg into her hand while she masturbated me. But every time she touched my clitoris, I contracted and the egg stayed fast. Eventually, she used oil, applying it thickly around the whole *area, opening the lips and dripping it in then rubbing it between the cheeks of my bottom. She kept rubbing the entrance to my bottom with her thumb. She made me squeeze it while she masturbated me. She oiled her fingers and pushed them down into my bottom and coaxed the egg from inside. I felt it begin to slide. She used her thumb to stop it at the entrance, then made me tuck my knees up and squeeze my legs together. Then she took her fingers out of me, oiled her hand again and just kept rubbing it gently from side to side across the protruding egg, across my clitoris, across my cunny lips until my climax came and the force of the contractions squeezed the egg into her hand.*

She spread my knees out across the bed. Then I felt my bottom being oiled again. She oiled it and it kept contracting. Rachel smacked it. Then she held the egg against it and pushed. 'There . . .' she said. 'There . . .' while I murmured and cried and the egg kept slipping endlessly through the ring, with Rachel whispering, 'There,' and my belly shuddering as she rubbed my dangling lips around my clitoris until the mouth of my bottom had closed around her thumb and the egg was now a heavy weight inside me. She turned me over and lifted my legs in the air and I could feel it moving, sliding down inside me. She wanted me to suck her.

It was the first time that she had let me do it to her, but even then, she controlled me. She put my head on the pillow and she knelt over my face. She pulled her drawers down to her knees then over my head, so my head was captured between her legs. Then she made love to my mouth. There was a small stud earring fastened to her cunny; she kept pushing it between my lips and begging me to lick it, to make it move and to bite it. She promised she would fit one to mine, that she would use a needle and a cork to do it, and that when I was pierced, she would play with me and whip me, with the lip of my cunny fastened.

Philip looked at the page. The last lines were scrawled shakily and the rest was a smudge. Then he realised there was a pattern there – two round bulges with wispy outlines, the bulges separated by a narrow gap and, down the centre, a thick straight line. He knew now what it represented.

Roxanne murmured. Her belly moved against his fingers. He wetted them and pressed them up between her legs and suddenly felt them slip. She groaned as they disappeared. She felt hot in there and good, and moist. When he took his fingers out again, he could smell her on his skin. He got up, made her stand, then lifted her on to the large walnut table. Its surface was smooth against her naked skin. He pushed her knees up, placing her feet beside her narrow buttocks and flat to the table surface. Young women were flexible. The distended lips of her cunt projected over the table edge. Her toes curled to the roundness of its bevel, as if gripping. In the half light, she seemed a primeval creature. Her scent was strong, primeval too. Her hair was dark, like Charlotte's. Philip gathered her body slowly. He spread his hands around her waist – he had hands that were strong; they were not too bony yet to touch a girl up to pleasure, he prided himself on that – and he gathered her, sliding his hands up, lifting her breasts, easing her weight up, until he supported her under the arms, then lowering her body again gently. He was searching for something, an intimacy between her body and the smooth top of the table. And he wanted to make it clear to her, by the single-mindedness of his actions, that he would indeed bring about this intimacy – that this intimacy was what he required. Her buttocks spread, her breathing changed, but no, it was not there, not quite. He pushed his hands under her bodice again and rubbed the tips of her nipples. Young women always felt good, so very good: their skin was so soft, their breasts so smooth and warm and their nipples so resilient.

He looked down while he worked her breasts and he listened to her breathing. Her body moved, attempting to co-operate, guided by the urgings of his hands, and her projecting cunt lips pouted, opening and closing like a moving, breathing mouth. And the exhalations of that mouth he found primeval and exciting. He touched it briefly, opening it fully with his fingers and tickling the thick small protruding sticky tongue. Then he took her round the waist again and his hands slid down to complete his purpose. They spread about her buttocks and gently pulled the cheeks apart, forcing her toes to crawl sideways, out along the table. Roxanne gasped; a shudder rippled through her and he knew that she had opened and that her anus touched the wood. He pressed her hips down to make her anus kiss against it like a small round sucker.

He became aware of a noise on the landing outside, but he chose to ignore it. There was only one thing that mattered now – this intimacy. 'Push it out, let it kiss,' he whispered to Roxanne. She moaned while he touched the sticky tongue that lolled so sweetly between the split lips of her cunt. Her breathing had reached that stage of quickness in which she was oblivious of all else. She groaned and tried to push herself against him when his cock touched her naked cunt. It bathed its head against the thick lips, then it thrust and she gave a small half-stifled cry. He held her hips down, hard against the table and thrust up into her again. And this time, he reached the hilt. His balls hung down, suspended against the bevel of the table and between the curling toes that tried to claw a purchase round the edge. He pushed her bodice up, bared her breasts and thrust deep again, deep so that the sticky-tongued clitoris touched his body. And he held her while she whimpered her arousal. He opened her buttocks and held her down and thrust, The small sobbing cries kept coming and his balls were turning wet with her secretions. He held her tightly against him, took her hair and wrapped it round his hand. He kissed her face and ears.

And at the door, his man, who had been roused by the sounds – thinking his master might require something – now watched his master moving against the flexible figure balanced on the table, her belly pushing out between her doubled-up knees, her belly thrusting. He watched the kisses, the caresses and the lifting of her breasts. And he saw the strange and distant expression that was on his master's face throughout the gentle but deliberate twisting of the long dark hair.

The slender figure gasped; the master took his erect cock out of her and knelt. Then he kissed the part of her that pouted most strongly between her doubled thighs. But while he kissed it, he held her round the waist, holding her waist down, hanging on it, pressing her haunches against the table until she screamed. But he kept kissing the pouting place in small quick kisses as it reached out over the edge. At this point, the observer crept away to consider the scène at his leisure in the kitchen.

Philip pushed Roxanne back until she was lying on the table. He stood above her, rubbing her belly, the creases of her legs and the place above her cunt, but he was not looking at her now. His gaze was fixed upon the small moist round mark ingrained into the perfection of the polished surface close to the table edge.

Roxanne was good. Of that there was no doubt. But her hair was long and it was dark, not blonde. And Roxanne was too willing.

He read the letter again when Roxanne was gone, and then again the next morning. He reread the last two sentences many times. But in all those readings he never thought to check the envelope thoroughly. There was a small slip of paper still inside. Eventually it fell out. It said:

You may take Justine tomorrow night, though you might care to postpone: I fear her time of indisposition is imminent. But she is a good girl and I know that you would treat her with consideration at such a time. I leave the decision to yourself. Meanwhile, I shall see to it that she makes herself available, should she be required. – J.N.

THE TEACHING OF FAITH

Elizabeth Bruce

In many Nexus books the presence of a liberated – and, more often than not, gloriously kinky – 'supporting cast' is as important to the naive or jaded central character's sexual progress as is her own inclination for debauchery and perversion. Faith, lovely heroine of *The Teaching of Faith* and its sequel, *Faith in the Stables*, is a case in point. Bored with her rather unrewarding sex life, her life changes when her new lover Alex introduces her to the Chosen – a very exclusive set of libertines who open up a whole new world of erotic possibilities to her.

Here, we find Faith attending her first orgy and keen to prove herself worthy of membership. Her hostess, Lillian, subjects her to some very exacting challenges, then undertakes a challenge of her own for the amusement of the assembled revellers.

Who knows how many secret societies devoted to libidinous practices exist unnoticed among the semi-detached houses of suburbia; how many men and women are indulging in unbridled erotic pleasure behind a facade of cultured respectability? One could be right in thinking that Britain is the home of all things kinky and covert. When something is forbidden, it becomes much more attractive and alluring. In the Faith books, this is indeed the case for the heroine of the title. She knows it hurts, but she cannot resist exploring her new-found taste for erotic punishment again and again.

Lillian was nothing if not thorough. She had been asked to arouse this young woman, so she would do so. If in the process Faith entered a different world to any she had previously known, then so be it. Lillian knew the agenda planned for Faith, as, slowly, she slipped the tassels up one of the lips and back down the other, before moving away downwards towards the soft flesh of the inner thighs. From the reaction so far, Faith would train beautifully as a Pleasure Slave. Alex would be so pleased.

Faith no longer felt ashamed of her reactions; that feeling had vanished beneath the urgent need within. She was gulping air more noticeably, her chest almost heaving, tiny whimpers coming from her in response to the waves of pleasure which were sweeping through her deepest recesses. These waves surged down her hard, out-thrust belly to explode within the inner walls of her vagina, where they added to the musky aroma which by now, she was certain, most of the group could appreciate.

Lillian watched the tension in the inner thighs until she saw the indications for which she had been searching. Suddenly, without any warning, she dropped the scarf, and reached both hands beneath Faith to grasp her stiff engorged nipples. They felt to Faith as though the whole substance of each breast had been filled to overflowing; they tingled and ached with a sensation previously unknown, even in her most passionate encounters. With a determined expression on her face and an almost savage strength, Lillian's thumbs and crooked forefingers closed around them, and squeezed. Hard.

Faith was at the point of release when this sudden unexpected and painful sensation surged through her, bringing her body back up to the vertical; with head thrown back, and eyes closed, her mouth opened in a silent scream of protest to the high ceiling as Lillian crooned into her ear, 'Not yet, my darling. We have only a little way to go, now. Just a little way. I can't let you come just yet. But don't worry; Lillian knows when to release you. Lillian will help.'

Obedient to her mentor's instructions, too shocked by the treatment to protest, Faith lowered herself into the same position again, arms splayed out and bottom raised as Lillian called, 'Simon, my champagne, please! And the ointment in the black tub,' as she took up the scarf again.

Faith waited with the patience of a well-schooled horse as the ends of the scarf were once again picked up and adjusted loosely around her stomach. This time, Lillian slowly moved the scarf up towards and then over her breasts, keeping it slack, carefully adjusting the tension so that, as she moved it, the scarf only just brushed the fine hair on the skin.

The young newcomer groaned again as the fabric finally found her nipples, wondering why, when they had felt so sore a few moments previously, that pain was transformed into a source of heat which seemed to radiate through them. Back and forth the scarf moved, growing gradually tighter until the breasts were enclosed in the soft fabric which was not yet sufficiently taut to distort their pointed cone shape. As Lillian moved the scarf gently across her nipples, Faith's pleasure returned, more insistent than before; she could feel her sex-lips swelling and then something cold and wet dropped on to the small of her back.

She gasped at the sensation, but Lillian's voice was soft in her ear. 'It's only a little champagne, my darling. Would you like me to lick it off?' and before Faith could reply, her warm mouth was applied to the spot between her shoulder-blades where the cold liquid had touched. Lillian's soft, moist, hot tongue followed the trail of champagne down towards where her sacral dimples showed as very faint outlines. Yet all the time the scarf was moving across her nipples, rousing her again.

Faith was moistening her lips once more when another slight splash of the chilled champagne landed, this time lower down. As she gasped, aware of the conflicting tensions within herself, Faith found her voice. 'Please, no! No more,' she managed to gasp; but she was too new to these games, too ignorant to realise she could not yet be released from the delicious arousal. The wanting within her was like an explosion which she could only contain by tensing the muscles in her abdomen into a hard, rounded shape which Lillian noted, nodding to Simon. Had Lillian given way to her plea, the others would have complained. Faith's performance was the reason they were there; to judge it, to sample her, to decide whether she should be admitted to the Chosen. That would never be done if Lillian gave way to the desperate pleas Faith was sending to her, and Lillian knew that, more than anything in the world, Alex wanted Faith to be Chosen.

'Just a little more, my darling. You'll like this, especially,' she said, tipping champagne from her glass on to the base of Faith's spine.

The young woman whimpered softly, then moaned as Lillian drew her finger from the pool of wine on her back, down to the depression which rapidly became the 'natal notch', the groove between her buttocks. Under the slight pressure of Lillian's forearm, for her hand still held the champagne glass, Faith raised her belly a fraction and then gasped as the pool of champagne began to trickle downwards towards her anus. As it found its way, the wine flooded over the tiny hairs there, imparting such a sensation that Faith's tongue poked out, large and round through her permanently-open mouth. To Claire, now thoroughly roused by her husband, Faith looked sufficiently depraved for anyone; she wondered how long it would be before someone displaced Lillian to mount the young woman; she looked as though she would appreciate a hard ride. Would Lillian spank her, first? No, it was too soon for that; she was too undisciplined yet. She had probably never had a spanking before.

As the wine hissed passed her anus, imparting a fizzing, tickling sensation, Faith's groan was even more pronounced. Her deep breathing had become dangerously shallow, the tension in her body and limbs imparting a tremor which most of them knew only too well. Lillian dropped the scarf, swung her right leg over Faith's back then let herself down on to the naked skin, facing her rump.

'There,' Lillian said as Faith gasped. 'Not long now, my sweet, I promise you. You've been very good. Hasn't she been good, Max? So very good.' But there was no answer from the expressionless man who watched.

Max moved to stand behind Faith, looking directly at her rear, watching the muscles of her thighs and crotch carefully. He could see the tiny, pink, palpitating anus and the deep red of her sex, and he nodded to himself as the latter throbbed. He had taught Lillian this technique; it was quite basic and perfectly proper for someone as uneducated in these ways as Faith. It would be a useful introduction to the ways of arousal, and the deferring of satisfaction until the proper time.

Yet that proper time was fast approaching, by the sounds she was making as Lillian worked. When she was more experienced, more trained, Lillian could prolong this with Faith for an hour or more. He had worked Lillian for most of one day before giving her release. He could still remember her high, keening scream as she climaxed.

Faith could feel Lillian's sex on her back; knew it for what it was, knew the heat within it. She could feel the slippery softness of the oily, shiny, open sex lips which gently massaged her spine as the blonde woman bent, gently touching Faith's open sex. Faith groaned instantly with a long, warbling wail of pleasure which Lillian dealt with firmly. With her thumb and forefinger she pinched the delicate, damp skin around Faith's anus, instantly stopping the warble as Faith's flesh retreated from her touch.

'You haven't educated this little opening, have you?' Lillian asked no one in particular. She expected no answer and got none, for she was starting on the last stage.

Lillian felt up beyond the clitoris, pressing the bump she found, expelling one of the 'love balls' which she laid on the carpet between Faith's legs. Then she removed the second, listening to the sound of Faith's reaction before exchanging her champagne glass for the black pot of ointment Simon held out to her. She was glad she had been told about the balls in advance, for it was important for Faith to be mounted quickly after her arousal. Removing the balls at this stage – the last chance of a rest for the young woman – prevented any delays. The balls had done their work, for Faith had been halfway aroused before Lillian ever laid eyes on her.

While Lillian carefully took some of the white ointment from the jar on her finger, her other hand was caressing Faith's right buttock, testing the tension within the smooth contours. Once the ointment was in place, Lillian stepped clear of Faith, crouched beside her and with slow gentle strokes, applied the ointment first to the outer lips of Faiths sex, then, refilling her finger, touched the clitoris lightly, and pressed her finger slowly into Faith's vagina. Just the touch alone would have been sufficient to have started another paroxysm of lust, but the added sensations which were beginning to flow from within her added to the response.

Faith's groan brought Lillian's other hand into play at once, digging a thumb directly into Faith's inner thigh to suppress the pleasure which was sweeping through her. For the third time, Faith's pleasure had been reduced, but the older woman was too experienced to believe that it was permanent. This was just a temporary expedient to stave off the inevitable. Faith's pleasure was going to come sooner or later. Lillian knew that she had done well to hold her this long, but she was unable to work miracles, not without much sterner methods which were totally unsuitable in this context; with a strap she could have prolonged it far more. None of the Chosen would have objected, of course, but it would have frightened Faith, which was not the object of the exercise. Faith was here to be gradually introduced into the ways of the Chosen; to be chosen herself, albeit without her full knowledge.

Dipping her forefinger into the pot again, Lillian smeared ointment gently around the swollen nipples which shook and shivered as Faith's body strained. With another smear of ointment on her finger, Lillian remounted Faith in the same position as before, facing backward. She knew she had only a few seconds before the ointment began to work and positioned herself carefully. Lillian brought her legs round outside Faith's, planting her feet against the inner sides of her widespread knees; her limbs were intertwined with Faith's, holding them securely apart. By that time, Faith no longer cared about her position or the circumstances in which she found herself. All she wanted was release from the dreadful, lustful longing within her. With careful precision, Lillian applied the tip of her finger directly to Faith's anus without penetrating it.

The warmth the ointment imparted had been slowly seeping through Faith's tissues, gradually gathering pace. The young woman's sensations had been battered to the point where she thought that it would be some time before she felt any pleasure again, but suddenly it struck. Immediately the hot, stinging sensation in her vagina and clitoris began, Faith tried to close her legs against it, but found that Lillian was stopping her.

'Tongue out, darling,' the woman whispered to her lovingly, glancing round to where Simon was watching Faith's face. He nodded as, automatically, Faith's tongue extended.

'Now! She's ready for release, Alex!' Lillian called sharply as Faith brought her head up and back, mouth open in a whimpering croon as *Bolero* blasted forth in time to Faith's mounting desires.

Ahead of her, Rupert's erection was firmly embedded in Claire's body, the fair fringe of her short pubic hair offsetting the long, shiny-wet flesh. She could see Claire's abandoned expression, her mouth still open though no sounds were emerging, her eyes now wide and staring, her hands rubbing down the sides of her labia to add manual stimulation to her pleasure. Rupert's hands were on her breasts, the nipples being gently caressed. Claire meanwhile was wondering whether she had ever seen anyone look quite so abandoned as Faith, whose expression of desperate desire made the older woman melt.

Just as Faith felt the air move behind her, before she felt Alex at all, Claire found her voice in a long, low moan of release, her hips working a little, her muscles clenching frantically at the embedded organ. Faith could see the seepage from Claire, running thickly past her anus on to the leather, then she lowered her own head as the first touch of Alex's penis at her entrance took her grateful attention.

Lillian never moved. She remained on Faith's rump while her feet held Faith open and Alex quickly knelt behind the imprisoned young woman, his erection looking too hot to last long. She reached out her arms and, as Alex placed his penis against Faith's vaginal opening, Lillian drew Alex to her, rubbing her breasts against his smooth chest, calling out, 'Your lover, darling! Suck, my darling, suck!'

And Faith sucked; how she sucked! To the stridency of Ravel's music, Alex was drawn smartly within her, his tight scrotum slamming against her clitoris; further pressure on the abused organ brought another gasp from the frantic young woman imprisoned between them. There was no backward and forward movement from Alex at all, for Faith had gone beyond that point. Her vaginal muscles, uneducated as they were, squeezed hard on the invader of her sexual organs. Alex, already kissing Lillian deeply, their tongues fighting like snakes, gave a grunt. Lillian knew what that meant, and slid her body backward to press her clitoris against Faith's spine, still taking her weight on her legs.

While Faith milked Alex's penis, Lillian rubbed her clitoris against Faith's spine, the bumps of the bones alternately pressing and releasing against her. Faith climaxed violently, bucking her back up and down, her voice rising to a scream of sheer pleasure which was torn from deep within her. Even the pleasure Alex had provided that afternoon was as nothing to the extremity in which she now found herself. Prudence raised her head from Colin's crotch, her mouth dripping with seminal fluid, to look in wide-eyed wonder, and not a little jealousy, at the explosive nature of the release.

Claire, her honeypot now seeping her husband's fluids too, looked benignly at the scene before her, whilst Julia simply smiled as Harry replaced his erection in her bottom, took hold of her tiny breasts then sodomised her again. Simon, the odd one out, knelt, cutting off Faith's cries by kissing her; it seemed the best way. He had seen her reaction to the suggestion of fellatio and thought it would be best if someone else took the risk of being bitten first. His erection was complete, so full that it ached. He was looking around for someone in whom to plunge it.

In the hallway, Max smiled as he closed the door on the scene he had done so much to set. Faith was a good choice. If that was how she reacted to Lillian's ministrations, then she would indeed be worth educating. Lillian was, after all, his best pupil, but he thought that with a little care, Faith might just be almost as good. Discipline would be a problem; it always was with someone coming to it so late in life. Yes, the Stables would be best, but getting Faith there without trauma might be difficult to arrange. There would have to be some very careful planning.

As Max closed the street door quietly behind him, Alex withdrew his flaccid penis from Faith's still-writhing opening. Lillian stood up to go with him, laying the length of her body along his, feeling the wetness against her abdomen. Simon spotted his chance; moving quickly in behind Faith, he inserted himself deeply within her before she was aware of him. The young woman had lowered her face to the carpet, resting her forehead on her forearms; her throat was making crooning noises at this new intruder; she was now careless of who it might be, taking such liberties. She wanted a stiff penis within her. She wanted to feel that boost again. Often.

Simon's hands sought and found her breasts and as he began to move within her, Faith moved her body in sympathy with his. If he was mounting her, then Faith was more than willing to be mounted. The ointment on her sexual organs, anus and breasts was firing them up for the occasion and, long before Simon obtained his release, Faith was climaxing gently. Each wave was stronger than the last, though nothing reached the epic proportions of the one Lillian had induced.

In a distant, neglected corner of her mind, Faith thought that she would never let Alex go, and she would worship Lillian. This woman had brought her to a pitch which she had never known existed, and which she would have doubted had she not experienced it. These people might have odd ways; they might seem slightly perverted, to some. But of one thing she was certain. Faith was never going to return to Albert. *She* had Chosen.

Faith became aware of a different mood in the party. Her head felt light and yet thick. As though she had cotton-wool where her brain normally resided; her mouth too seemed full of it. She had lost count of the various sexual mountings, had hardly been keeping score, in fact. It seemed that, no sooner had one man exited her than another replaced him. Yet there had been periods of calm and quiet. Periods when she had lain back on the rug with closed eyes and focused on the semi-dark room around her, listening to the blood pounding around her system, to the liquid slappings of passion all about her.

The men had approached individually; she recalled words being spoken, but nothing of the content. What they had asked, whatever they had suggested, she had complied with. She had lain on her back; she had knelt on all fours; they had penetrated her hot, aching sex with their hot, hard erections. They had climaxed within her after a longer or shorter time, their harsh breathing matching the urgency of their frantic movements. None had offered her anything but the most considerate attention; there was no attempt to force her. Not that she would have objected. Faith felt that any of them could have suggested something much more different and she would have complied readily.

Yet there were other approaches, less direct, less demanding, more insidious. Claire had been first, a hand stealing across her flattened breasts as she lay looking sightlessly above her, adrift on her own cloud of euphoria. A soft, gentle hand which caressed her burning breast, a mouth which nibbled and sucked at her firm nipple, wetting it. It felt so hot to her that Faith thought she must be steaming gently but, on opening her eyes she saw nothing, just the tranquil features of Claire, her lips still encompassing the coral nipple, a vacant look of passionate surrender in her blue eyes, heavy-lidded like a religious statue.

When Claire realised Faith was watching, she smiled, and raised herself to kiss Faith's still-swollen mouth gently, her lips almost as dry as Claire's own; then she eased her hands down Faith's stomach to her pudenda. While Faith groaned softly, only slightly more violently than a sigh, her legs parted automatically before the approach. Claire's fingers carefully opened her wet outer lips and flicked gently against the inner lips, exciting them in an unusual and yet very pleasant manner, before two fingers gently probed her hot, moist passage.

With those fingers placed deep within her, Claire's thumb began a dance up and down the soft external tissue, gently touching without pressure, never remaining in one place long enough to be noticed, yet attracting blood back to the outer lips. The tingling which Faith had felt so strongly, deep within her, began to surge again, starting from a multitude of diverse points. Her breasts contributed a substantial share of the early tingles, the electric threads leading down through her abdomen to unite with those radiating from her clitoris which, despite being left alone, throbbed with desire.

The moisture began to seep again, and Claire's thumb

transferred it from her vagina to her hot, eager and willing clitoris; tenderly applying the juices, she revived the battered little organ. Deep within herself, Faith could feel the wanting begin again; the monster with the apparently insatiable appetite inside her acted as though it had hardly been fed at all.

Claire felt the first tremors in Faith's breasts with her lips, the trickling tension which she recognised from her own desires. In response, she took all of Faith's right nipple into her mouth, sucking deeply, using her tongue to jam the rubbery tissue against her upper teeth, letting the discomfort work on quieting Faith's unappeased monster. It was important – not just to Claire, but to the others – that Faith should not be brought to her climax too soon, for there were others to be satisfied yet. Alex would probably want to mount her again; she knew her husband would.

But Faith was not so easily stilled. Lying back with her eyes closed, her pink tongue poking out from the swollen lips, she tried to quell the ache of desire within her; she was more than happy when Claire kissed her mouth, her teeth trapping her tongue in place. As she kissed her, Claire's restless hand soon had Faith panting again, thrusting her hips forward into the embrace. Albert had been a quick fumble man, followed by an even-quicker mounting. Unable to sustain intercourse for long, he had persuaded Faith by sheer repetition and personality – along with a lack of knowledge on her part – of the myth that this was satisfying sex. Faith knew better, now. Before long, Claire's head vanished between Faith's thighs.

Claire knew what she was doing with her tongue around Faith's vulva. She held open her labia with her fingers while she slowly, carefully and, above all, lightly, caressed the soft, moist, ruby-red skin. The delightful salty taste of the young woman stimulated her tongue to flicker higher, barely touching the glossy skin of the swollen clitoris, then down, changing shape to penetrate the hot moisture of her tunnel. Faith's hips were beyond jerking high against this torture; her exertions filled her limbs with a gentle fatigue which drained her. Though she slowly moved her hips up and down, her autonomic system was sending out uncertain messages which were being reinterpreted by her body. Faith rested her hands in the blonde hair, moaning softly as Claire, misjudging Faith's responses, climaxed, her breath shuddering within her chest.

The young woman, legs apart, eyes closed and mouth opened, arched her back against the sensations which threatened to engulf her perceptions. Her rump lifted off the carpet, balancing her body lewdly on her outspread feet and her shoulders as she offered herself to Claire's insistent and experienced tongue and fingers, her juices spilling over the fair woman's chin. Faith's open mouth, with nothing to fill it, gaped; the swollen lips held apart as much from passion as from fatigue, emitting noises she was sure she had never made before.

Rupert looked over from the bar to where Claire was sitting, half-turning away from Faith's fleecy crotch, chest heaving with her deep breathing as she tried to regain her composure. Claire knew that she was able to arouse both men and women, yet she had never come across anyone so uninhibited as Faith. There was something wild yet terrifyingly innocent about this young woman; something she found difficult to understand. Faith had looked thoroughly attractive and normal when she had arrived with Alex, a little awed by the occasion maybe, but others had been the same before her; Alex had that effect on young women. Yet, once she had been roused, her reserve had fallen from her; she had become as lascivious as any of the much more experienced women present.

Lillian, attracted by Faith's moaning, returned, and her tongue lapped up all the emissions she could get, covering Faith's entire vulva while the young woman tried to regain her composure. Lillian however would have no truck with such weakness and, within a few minutes, Faith's breathing grew faster and deeper. Lillian's tongue was both an energetic, mobile, soft, moist snake which explored deeply into Faith's sex, and a firm, round spear which shot back and forth. At other times it was a broad, waving leaf which scooped the oily, salty fluid from her very walls.

Carefully, Lillian inched her fingers up Faith's buttocks, separating them gently and moving on until, as Faith lifted her hips to her in ecstasy, Lillian slipped a finger into the optimum position. As Faith's lips returned to the carpet, Lillian's forefinger gently pressed against the wrinkled rim of Faith's anus. Faith felt the touch immediately, but found the sensation not unpleasant. Rather, it enhanced the other sensations her body was producing.

This, she thought, must have been what it was like when Alex inserted his finger into her, or nearly. Then, his erection had been within her, forcing her vaginal passage back against her rectum. Perhaps *that* made a difference. She would have to try to find out, but later. Later. Now she was being stimulated very thoroughly and well.

Slowly, fraction by fraction and with gentle care, Lillian introduced her forefinger into Faith's bottom hole; she watched the expression of awed pleasure on Faith's face, and listened to the catches in her voice as a guide for when to push gently, and when to wait. And, like Claire before her, Lillian's tongue was working, moistening Faith's sexual organs, bringing the younger woman to an extremity of pleasure. That was something they all had to get across to this new addition; the fact that sex was pleasure. Sex was fun! Sex wasn't something to be hidden from the light of day; it was not just furtive fumblings in a darkened bedroom. Sex and pleasure could take place in the open, in the light. With friends.

Quite half an hour after Lillian had begun, the pleasure was finally delivered. Lillian's forefinger could be inserted no further; Faith's hips were raised as she whimpered with pleasure. Already the web between her fingers was pressing on Faith's perineum. But Lillian had no desire to penetrate further; bringing on Faith's pleasure like that had satisfied her. That, and the emissions at which she had lapped, with every expression of delight. Faith had been an inspired choice. She was sure Max would agree with her, and that everyone there would give a good account of her performance. Faith had been Chosen.

Eventually, when Faith's head cleared enough for her to see and think straight, she found she was being caressed by Alex, lying with her back to him whilst his hands smoothed over her young body from shoulders to crotch. Her legs were splayed out, displaying her gaping orifice, but so were Claire's and Prudence's. Claire sat on top of Harry, his short, thick erection pressing against her anus. In a few moments, Claire knew, her control over those muscles would be overcome.

Then she would slip on to his shaft and Harry would enter her as he had been entering Julia – as he always entered Julia – who was kneeling before Colin, her mouth around his rising member. Prudence was sprawled on Simon, who held her sex open with two fingers of his right hand; his middle finger meanwhile gently stroked up her cleft, carrying the moisture she was emitting up to her sharply defined clitoris, which stood proud of the surrounding flesh.

Rupert and Lillian arrived with drinks, a concoction in which champagne had been mixed with ginger, lemon, guavas and a couple of drops of a green liqueur Rupert kept well out of sight of Lillian. He usually denied there was such a liquid to be had, though he had desperately importuned Max for it, until finally he had been given a small bottle with the injunction to use it sparingly. Now they handed out the drinks, Claire glad to rise to collect hers, for her muscular control had been slipping and she knew Harry had distended her opening. It wasn't that she disliked Harry, or being sodomised, for Rupert often obliged her like that. It was just the combination she disliked, though it would have been rude to have refused him.

'Lillian said she'd do the beads,' Rupert said cheerfully handing round the drinks, making sure that everyone, including Faith, had one.

If anyone deserved one, Faith did. He would be interested, too, to see what effect it had on her. Max had claimed that, administered properly, it would perk up the most jaded palate and, from the look of exhaustion in her eyes, Faith's palate was the most jaded in the room. But then, most of the party had already enjoyed her.

'She'll never do that!' Alex snorted. 'Not now.'

'Who said I won't?' Lillian asked sourly, turning on him from her prone position on the carpet where she had placed herself next to Simon. 'I could show you a thing or two.'

'I agree; you could,' he smiled. 'But you couldn't do three, now. You're too far gone. You'd be lucky to get them *in*, far less out again.'

'No I wouldn't!' she protested. 'Fifty says I could.'

Before Faith was fully aware of it happening, some of the party had begun trying to organise bets on the outcome, the loud and contradictory conversation making any attempt to understand the proceedings impossible. It was at this point that Faith asked in a plaintive, almost querulous voice,

'What's going on, Alex? Betting on what?'

'Lillian's going to do the beads. I've seen her do five. I've even seen her do seven, though that was some time ago. She won't do three, tonight. Not after the rogering she's had. Two's as much as anyone can expect.'

'Oh.' Faith found the explanation less explicit than the comments which had prompted her questions, but Rupert was already marking names on a sheet of paper.

'Alex?'

'Two.'

'Claire?'

'One.'

'Pru?'

'Two.'

'Simon?'

'Four.'

'You'll be lucky,' Rupert grinned. 'Faith?'

'Six.'

'Six? What do you think Lillian's made of? Brass?'

'Six!' Faith insisted, irritated into sullen obstinacy by

his superior air, though she had no idea what she was doing.

'It's your money! Harry?'

'If Faith says six, I'll go five.'

'Four,' Julia said without being prompted, digging her teeth into Colin's tender shaft so that his howl had to be repeated.

'Three!' Julia smiled at the response. She would keep him aroused like that until Lillian began 'doing the beads', when she would let him release his pent-up seed. That was what he needed to cure his drooping member; lots and lots of mouth massage.

When all the bets had been marked down – Lillian bet seven – the woman lay on her back on the long-haired sheepskin rug on which Faith had been roused and pleasured, her legs spread wide. In one hand she had a bead necklace which Claire had provided. Each white bead was oval, about one and a half centimetres long, and about half that at the widest point. She unfastened the clasp and, with the necklace in her right hand, used her left hand to open her sex, unable to resist running her soft fingers up and down her swollen, blood-engorged sex lips. After she was calm again, while the tension in the room mounted, Faith – who was still lying on Alex in a position where she could clearly see every detail of Lillian's anatomy – was suddenly surprised to see the woman introduce the ring of the clasp into her vagina then, shifting her grip to the first bead, push gently upward.

To Faith's mounting amazement, Lillian slowly introduced the beads one by one, not moving quickly, but steadily pushing them, one after another, into her vagina and, after the first three or four, twisting the beads as she pushed.

'Why is she twisting them, Alex?' Faith whispered.

'The string is securely knotted, so they're held rigid. As she turns the beads, the string turns too, and further up, they move. Remember the balls? Remember how you felt? Lillian's feeling that right now.'

'God!' Faith gasped softly, her heart going out to the

gasping, flushed woman who was nearing the end of the string, and pressing the beads within her much more slowly.

When she stopped, Simon knelt between her thighs and passed a leather thong through the ring-clasp at the protruding end of the necklace, drawing it through until the knotted end prevented it moving any further. Once done, Lillian pushed the remainder of the necklace deep within herself until she came to a stop, her breathing too deep to continue. Then Lillian released her hold on the thong, placing her hands beside her hips and pressing down while she cleared her mind, trying to ignore Simon.

Simon opened her outer lips and laid the thong up her cleft and across her clitoris before closing them together again, pressing them tight, holding them like that until Lillian tapped his hand. Immediately he withdrew, moving away from her as Lillian took charge. She paused for a few minutes to allow herself to regain normality, her eyes closed, not looking at anyone. She took the free end of the thong in her right hand and tugged it gently, holding her lips closed with the fingers of her left hand all the while.

The thong slipped across her clitoris but she held it away at an angle, so that it made no contact until Alex called, 'Clasp in sight!' which made her stop and recover her composure.

'She's going to pull that thong and bring the beads out again across her clitoris,' Alex whispered in Faith's ear. 'And she'll count them out while she's doing it. She can't stop; she has to keep pulling, so there's no chance of a rest in between them to give herself a break. And she can't just rip them out quickly; Lillian has to bring them out slowly, one by one. She thinks she'll get to seven before she comes, but she's too aroused to make three. Your fifty pounds is as good as lost.'

'Fifty pounds?' Faith asked, wondering what he was talking about. Who had said anything about fifty pounds?

'Yes. Your bet,' he answered. 'You bet fifty pounds she could get to six. Remember?'

'Yes. I . . .' She paused. 'What if she reaches eight?'

'Anything above six means Lillian wins,' he said sourly, shaking his head, 'but she won't.'

Faith's eyes grew large and round as Lillian's right hand began to move steadily while, if anything, her left held her sex even more tightly.

'One!' Lillian said with smiling confidence as the first white bead slipped wetly into view.

'There goes your bet, darling.' Rupert hoisted his glass to Claire, who shrugged, her breasts wobbling provocatively.

'Two!' Lillian's voice was a little more strained as the second appeared and Alex sighed, shaking his head. He had guessed wrong again.

'Three!' Lillian had found a new confidence; the announcement upset Colin, who was on the verge of spilling his seed into Julia's mouth.

'Four!' Lillian's confidence was waning again, the catch in her voice a sign that her pleasure was being brought on quickly so that, 'Five!' sounded shaky, even to her, but her hand never stopped the same, relentless pressure until, 'Six!' Lillian's hips jerked upward, her head tipping back as the waves of pleasurable pressure broke within, and she surrendered to the sudden desire inside her. Without waiting, she began to move her hips up and down in a parody of love-making, as she continued to remove all of the beads. Simon knelt to kiss her mouth while Claire fastened her lips around her left nipple and sucked hard.

When order was restored, Rupert looked around and into Faith's languorous, half-open, heavy eyes, smiling at the sated young woman who had previously performed so beautifully.

'You win, Faith. What made you choose six?'

'Alex said he'd seen her do five and seven,' Faith answered slowly, thinking carefully about the words, unsure whether she was speaking, or dreaming she was speaking. 'I just took an average.'

'You bastard, Alex.' Rupert looked at him in surprise. 'You might have told me!'

'I didn't think she'd make two,' came the unworried answer, and they both laughed.

EMMA'S SECRET WORLD

Hilary James

Appearances can be deceptive. Outwardly vivacious and apparently content with married life, blonde, pretty Emma is, in truth, the ultra-submissive slave of the elegant Ursula. A confirmed lesbian, Emma's Mistress is easily one of the most cruel, cold and ruthless dominatrices ever to wield a cane within the pages of a Nexus novel. Consequently, *Emma's Secret World* – the first book of the Emma series – soon became a bestseller.

Bored in her husband's absence, Emma is drawn into the clandestine world of lesbian domination and, despite her determination to rebel, finds the thrills derived from submission and punishment far too addictive to give up for very long. The fifth Emma book, *Emma's Humiliation*, will be published by Nexus in May.

In this extract from *Emma's Secret World*, Emma, enrolled by Ursula in a training institute deep in the French countryside, is being schooled in the art of pleasing a woman. That her tutor is a man – the huge and terrifying Achmet – makes the experience even more humiliating for her.

Surrendering every dignity of adulthood may not seem like every woman's idea of fun but Emma is not like other women. In order to gain the necessary masochistic pleasure she craves from total subservience to a Master or Mistress, Emma willingly puts herself in situations which would seem alien – and very painful – to most people. Often forced to dress much younger than her years, Emma has to learn that upsetting her elders and betters will only result in tears and terrible pain! Hilary James has created a series which is one of the most imaginative and powerfully engaging accounts of one woman's journey of erotic submission Nexus has had the privilege to publish.

Days later, Emma knelt down on the hard cobbled floor of the dungeon. She longed to put some straw under her knees, but she knew that she was not allowed to do so. She had been beaten by Achmet for doing so. The straw had to remain beautifully clean and fresh-looking for the directress's inspection.

Once she had made the mistake of thinking that she could lie down on the straw – and had been beaten for that too. She knew now that she had to push back the straw and lie down on the cobbles.

Once she had similarly made the mistake of assuming that she was intended to relieve herself on to the straw. She would not quickly forget Achmet's anger when he discovered what she had done. Nor would she easily forget the humiliation of being taught by a repulsive man how she was always, and only with his prior permission and under his personal supervision, to perform into a bowl as he stood over her, his dog whip in his hand.

'Go on! Hurry!' he would scream, raising his whip, until she had learnt to perform to his satisfaction.

As she now knelt, she put her mouth over the strange little rubber teat at the bottom of a special plastic container that hung on the wall. It contained a sticky liquid with a strange taste. It was no good, she had learnt, just sucking the teat. The thick liquid had first to be coaxed down into the teat and then out of it by a mixture of heating it with her mouth and tongue and then sucking it hard through the tiny hole at the end of the teat.

It was all very tiring and exhausting, but she knew that she simply had to empty the container, drop by drop, before the timer rang. She glanced at the timer – one hour to go. She looked up at the container – it still looked so full. The graduations on the side still showed ten. That would mean ten strokes from the awful bamboo carpet beater that Achmet used for more formal beatings.

Desperately she applied herself to the task of licking and sucking each little drop of the sticky liquid out of the container. She knew that Achmet would sweep into the room as soon as the timer rang, the carpet beater in his hand. He would glance at the amount of the liquid remaining and then take her out into the passage to be beaten with the same number of strokes as shown on the graduation.

She longed to use her hands to squeeze the wretched stuff down into the teat and on to the floor. However, she knew that the internal television camera in the comer of the dungeon would be trained on her. If Achmet, perhaps alerted by one of his colleagues watching on a remote screen, saw her cheat by using her hands, he would, she knew from bitter and painful experience, drag her out into the passage for an extra beating.

Each time she was beaten she had to stretch out over a special table in the passage. Achmet would quickly secure her ankles wide apart to two of the table legs, and then make her reach forward so that her wrists could be fastened to the tops of the legs on the far side of the table. The table top was polished from the wriggling of innumerable girlish bellies as they writhed under their trainer's chosen instrument.

Through a slit in the door of her dungeon she had seen some very pretty young women from the adjacent dungeons being flogged as she waited her turn. With the slit closed she had also heard many more floggings. She did not know which was more terrifying – watching a poor girl being thrashed or having to listen to it. Each brought her to a new peak of fear and panic.

She had seen how some of the other huge trainers used

a carpet beater, like Achmet, whilst others preferred a wide rubber paddle. Both left no clear weals, just generally reddened areas. In both cases, she knew only too well, having the girl strapped down over the table put her into the ideal position for chastisement. The man could readily apply his carpet beater or paddle to the girl's bottom, to her back, or to the lower part of her thighs.

Emma had lost all sense of time. She had no idea how long it was since she had awoken to find herself locked naked in the cellar. She had no idea whether it was day or night, for there were no windows in the dungeon and the electric light, controlled from the passage, was never switched off – just as the television camera's little red light never ceased to flash, showing that it was switched on and watching her.

All she knew was that every four hours the wretched timer would ring and Achmet, or, if he was sleeping, one of his equally cruel colleagues, could come in and check the plastic container, before frogmarching her out to be beaten.

She had learnt to keep her eyes lowered to the ground in the presence of the trainers. Once she had dared to raise her eyes to Achmet's in a furious gesture of defiance. Immediately she had been taken out and flogged yet again. Now she kept her eyes demurely down at all times. She did not even dare to raise her eyes to the television camera.

If she slept between Achmet's inspections, then she risked being beaten for not emptying the plastic container of its sticky contents. However her tongue and lips were now becoming more adept and she found it less tiring to use them for an hour or more at a stretch. Indeed, she found that she could now empty the wretched container in about two hours and then, keeping a close eye on the timer hanging on the wall, snatch a little sleep.

Periodically, all the girls were taken out of their dungeons and made to line up for feeding time. Emma longed to speak to them, but if a girl said one word to another girl she earned a beating there and then. So Emma had no idea who the other young women were. Indeed, she was not supposed to know, for security at the so-called school was very tight. They all seemed very pretty and, like her, had been reduced by their trainers to a state of utter abasement. There were usually three or four girls in all, but new ones would be periodically added and others disappeared never to return.

They had to stand in line, their eyes dutifully lowered, while the trainers inspected the naked bodies in each other's charge, calling out lewd comparisons. She had felt utterly degraded from Achmet's callous and appallingly intimate handling. But to be prodded and felt by his colleagues was even worse. She was, she realised, being reduced by fear and shame to a new level of submissiveness and obedience. She could not believe that Ursula, her beloved Ursula, could have condemned her to such a terrifying regime. Was it because of Henry?

When a gong was rung, the line of girls would have to run across the passage, kneel down on all fours, with their hands flat on the floor, and thrust their heads deep down into a trough containing a sort of watery porridge. Any girl who did not put her face into the horrible mixture had her head pushed down by the trainer, and got a stroke or two across her back or bottom from his dog whip.

They had to stay like that motionless, scarcely able to breathe. Then, when the trainers were satisfied with their submissiveness, the gong would be struck again. This was the signal for feeding time to start. As this was all the food that they were given, Emma soon learnt to guzzle and gobble hastily, and get as much of the tasteless mixture down her throat as she could before the gong was rung again, marking the end of feeding time. They would then have to kneel up instantly. Occasionally the gong was rung for the third time because a girl had been seen to raise her hands off the floor to try surreptitiously to scoop more food into her mouth to ease her hunger. As Emma had learnt the punishment for this was to be immediately fastened across the table and given a dozen strokes. She now slurped and guzzled like the other girls and kept her hands prominently flat on the floor.

When the gong rang again, the girls had to crawl back to their dungeons, trying as they went to clean the horrible sticky porridge off their faces and out of their hair. They knew that to use the clean straw for this would bring down the wrath of their trainers, yet again.

Emma now had no bodily secrets whatsoever from Achmet. When he came into the dungeon she immediately had to assume the position of what she learnt he called 'presentation' – lying on her back with her hands down between her raised knees, and gripping the outside of her ankles. It was impossible for her to close her legs in this position and it was, perhaps, the most humiliating position that a woman can be ordered to take up. He would then kneel down and inspect her. If he thought, rightly or wrongly, that he had found the slightest sign of her having touched herself, then she would be immediately ordered out to lie over the table, and be given ten strokes.

Ursula could not have known, Emma told herself, just what appalling things they would do to her in this school. She simply could not have had any idea, she kept telling herself. But then the nagging doubts kept coming back. Supposing it was all being done on purpose – to put her off men for life, and ensure her faithfulness to Ursula?

She was now far more submissive and obedient than before. The awful degrading beatings by Achmet, the constant fear of another and of hearing her companions constantly being dragged out of their dungeons to be beaten in the corridor, stretched over the same table as she had been stretched, had made her far more humble and servile. She would do anything to avoid another beating, she kept telling herself, as she degradingly presented herself, lying on her back with her legs parted and raised, as soon as she heard Achmet's key in the door. Had Ursula sent her here, she wondered, to have any sign of recalcitrance beaten out of her for ever? Was this all part of what Ursula and her cruel woman friend had so laughingly referred to as having her 'professionally trained'? Would it enable her to keep Ursula's interest? If so, then she did not mind so much. Certainly Achmet had put her right off all men!

It was all indeed part of what the directress had described to Ursula as a short, sharp, shock. It lasted only a week, but to Emma it seemed like months. Months of degrading humiliation. Months of sucking and licking at the ghastly teat until her tongue and jaw ached and ached, as she drove herself to empty the container – or at least get it nearly empty before the timer announced Achmet's return.

Unknown to Emma, Achmet, pleased by the degree of obedience and submissiveness that he had succeeded in instilling into her, had recommended to the directress that she was now ready for the next stage of her training – a recommendation in which the directress, who had been monitoring Emma's progress on her television screen, concurred.

Suddenly and unexpectedly, the door of Emma's dungeon was flung open by Achmet. He stood there in the doorway – a terrifying figure, impatiently tapping his dog whip against the palm of his hand. He was now smartly dressed, Emma was astonished to see, in a well-cut blazer and white trousers. The incongruity with her own abject nakedness was even more humiliating than when he had just worn that dreadful loincloth. Hastily, Emma flung herself on to her back on the floor in the degrading 'presentation position', hoping to assuage the fearsome man's temper by this show of complete subservience. What had she done, she wondered? Had the television showed her touching herself for a brief second? She was shivering with apprehension as she gripped her ankles and displayed herself, like a bitch on heat, to the huge man.

'Up,' he barked. 'Inspection!'

She jumped up and stood in front of him in the second position he had taught her: hands straight down to her sides, fingers straining downward, shoulders back, legs apart, knees bent, pelvis thrust forward, chin raised, head straining right backward and eyes fixed on the ceiling. It was the position in which he and his colleagues had often kept her, whilst sitting comfortably in front of her as they examined her, or compared her with one of the other girls, when they were ordered to stand in silence and in the same position alongside each other. It was a position in which the girl had to strain every muscle. She tried to stop herself from shivering at the thought of more strokes from the ruthless trainer, as she stared up at the ceiling whilst he slowly walked round her.

Then suddenly she felt a canvas hood being thrust over her head. She could see nothing. She felt a rubber ball, all part of the hood, being thrust into her mouth. It must have had a strap attached to it at the front of the hood for she felt it being buckled behind her neck and then seconds later another strap, closing the bottom of the hood, was also fastened round her neck. She was in complete darkness. Terrified, she raised her hands as if to pull the hood off. Instantly, Achmet gripped her wrists and she felt him slip manacles on to them. They seemed to be joined by eighteen inches of chain. She could no longer reach the front of her body. Now she was terrified of suffocating. But there were two little holes below her nostrils and she found that she could breathe quite easily.

She was then frogmarched out of the dungeon and along the passageway. Her naked feet felt the stone floor giving way to a carpet. She heard the noise of a heavy door being opened and shut again. She heard several men calling out to Achmet. They were making obscene remarks about her naked body. She felt herself being pushed into a lift and then being taken down a passageway with a linoleum floor. She was stopped. There was the noise of something metal being lifted. She was made to step up on to a platform and then kneel down on all fours.

Then she was thrust into something. There was the metallic crash of something being closed behind her. She felt a hand reach for her and turn her round, then her own hands being released. She felt Achmet's hands busy with the fastenings behind her neck. She felt him pulling the combined hood and gag off her.

Suddenly the hood was off. She could see! She saw Achmet's hand withdrawing as it gripped the canvas hood. It was withdrawing through some widely spaced iron bars right in front of her. Indeed, through the bars she saw Achmet's face only inches away. He was standing in a passageway. She saw him slide what looked like a double-glazed window in front of the bars. She heard it close with a click. She found herself gripping the thick bars – her fingers could touch the double glazing just a couple of inches beyond, strong and unbreakable. Achmet's grinning face was now at the other side of the glass.

She looked round. She was in a little cage. It seemed to be one of a line of cages on a raised platform. There was a similar cage on each side of her. In each cage there was another naked girl. Excited at having contact with another female she turned to put her hand through the bars at the side of the cage to reach out and touch her neighbour. But there was another strip of double glazing between the bars of the two cages. She called out. She saw the mouth of the pretty girl, kneeling in the next cage, open and close. She could hear nothing. She looked up at the top of the cage, some four feet above the floor. Beyond the bars was more double glazing. It was like being in a fish tank – an hermetically sealed fish tank. In the back of the cage, some three feet from the front, was a little ventilation blower and a grill to let out the air. Otherwise, she realised, she was indeed in a sealed cage.

The cage's length along the passage was only some five feet. Its depth back from the passageway was only three feet, so that she would have to lie down curled up. Otherwise, as it was only four feet high, she would have to remain kneeling or crawling on all fours. She looked down. She was, she saw, kneeling on a piece of thick rubber, underneath which she could feel the bars that formed the floor of the cage.

In one corner, adjacent to the passageway, were two hinged plastic bowls. Being hinged, she realised, they could both be refilled, when the double glazing was slid back, without the need to open the small barred central door to the cage. One of the bowls contained water, the other just a few coloured dog biscuits. Anything, she thought, was better than that awful porridge, even dog biscuits, and she could certainly use the water to clean herself up.

In the opposite front corner of the cage, the thick rubber mat had been cut back to disclose a sand-covered tray under the thick bars that formed the base of the cage. The tray could be readily slid out from under the bars from the passage, when necessary, by simply sliding back the double glazing. The sand covered tray reminded Emma of similar trays that were used by well-trained cats. She blushed as she realised its purpose. Achmet would be able to check her droppings daily.

'Look!' suddenly she heard Achmet's voice. The double glazing had been closed and the voice came from a little speaker attached to the bars across the top of the cage. She saw that Achmet had been speaking into a microphone on the front of the cage, in the passageway.

Achmet now moved to the front of the cage on her right. It held a pretty girl with lovely long black hair. She saw Achmet switch on the microphone in front of her cage. She saw his mouth opening and closing, but she could not, of course, hear through the double glazing that sealed her own cage. But immediately the girl crawled over to the mirror hanging down from the side of her cage. On a shelf below it was a hairbrush, a comb, lipstick, powder, eye make-up, and a set of rouge.

As Emma watched, the girl began to wash and comb her hair and then to make up her face.

Emma had noticed a similar mirror and make-up shelf in her own cage. After the complete absence in the dungeon of even a comb, she was thrilled. Eagerly following the example of the girl in the next cage she reached towards the shelf. It had everything she needed, even soap. Hesitating, she glanced through the bars of her cage towards Achmet. She did not now dare do anything without his prior approval. She saw that he was smiling at her instinct to make herself look as attractive as possible. He nodded his head in approval.

Delighted, Emma washed her body and her hair, powdered herself all over and made up her face. Achmet watched her as she did so. It was humiliating, but she knew that she had no bodily secrets from this terrible man. Twice his voice on the little loudspeaker interrupted her.

'Look!' he said simply. She followed with her eyes as he strode to the next cage door. She saw his mouth open to give an order. The pretty kneeling girl turned towards Emma's cage. She held up her breasts. Emma saw that her nipples were painted the same shade of red as her lipstick. Ursula had often made her do the same. But that was not all. The whole areola of her nipple had been outlined in black. It gave a bizarre and erotic look.

The man smiled again in approval as Emma painted her nipples scarlet and outlined them in black.

The second time he called out 'Look!' the girl had tried to kneel up in her cage with her legs wide apart, facing Emma. But the cage was too low and she went back on to all fours and turned so that her buttocks were facing Emma. Apparently at a word of command from the man she parted her legs. Emma saw that the girl's body lips were painted bright scarlet too. This was also something that Ursula had made her do. But what was new was that the whole of the girl's mound, like her nipples, had been outlined in black.

Again the man smiled in approval as Emma copied the girl next door. The cage being too low to enable her to kneel up properly, she had to do it awkwardly lying on her back with raised knees, and using the mirror to guide her hand.

She had noticed that the girl in the next cage had the number '16' painted in black on her forehead and on her right breast. She had seen the number '10' on her bowl. Was that her number, she wondered? Was she just Number Ten?

As if he knew what was going through Emma's mind, Achmet now slid back the double glazing on the front of

Emma's cage. He beckoned her to crawl forward. He made her press right up against the iron bars. Emma saw that he had a black waterproof marking pen in his hand. She was going to be marked with her number! She shivered with fear. He made her press her forehead against the wide gap in the bars. She felt him writing something carefully on her skin. Then he made her thrust her right breast through the bars. He lifted it up with one hand, held it steady and then carefully wrote on the skin above the nipple.

Then he roughly pushed her back and closed the double glazing. Shocked by the suddenness of it all, Emma glanced in the mirror. There on her forehead and on her breast was the number '10'. It made her feel like an animal.

Nevertheless, thought Emma, even though she was locked in a cage like an animal with her most intimate bodily functions closely and degradingly watched and controlled by a hideous brutal man, and she may just be Number Ten, but, thanks to a wash and make-up, she felt a new woman. Indeed she could not help thinking what an excitingly pretty girl was staring back at her in the mirror, with her painted face, nipples, body lips and number. She could not help thinking that if Ursula could only see her now, painted like a whore and with a new submissive look in her downcast eyes, she would be quite unable to keep her hands off her. She blushed at the thought. Perhaps this awful training was worthwhile after all. She would go through anything, she knew, just to keep Ursula's interest.

Although no word of explanation was given to Emma, she was in fact now in the second phase of her training. The short, sharp, shock was over. She would, however, sleep, eat, rest and defecate in her cage, like an animal. The degradation and humiliation that entailed was calculated to ensure that she remained submissive and obedient throughout her training.

Emma was now going to spend several days under intensive training, getting herself ready to be offered to the rich female clients who used the school as a discreet lesbian brothel. She would be used to supplement the girls that the directress kept permanently on offer. Masked to hide their identities, the large number of these clients and the wide variety of their sensual demands combined to form an essential part of the training offered to those clients who, like Ursula, sent a girl here for 'professional training'.

Achmet was looking forward to the generous tips that a well-trained and properly humble Emma would soon be earning him from delighted clients – quite apart from a share of the high fees that the directress would charge clients for her use.

Indeed, it was only a few minutes after Emma had been marked with her brothel number, that the directress herself came to inspect the inmates of the cages. Emma recognised her and longed to scream at her, protesting that Ursula would never have agreed to the horrors that her little girl was being made to suffer. But with each cage hermetically sealed against sound, what was the point? She saw that as the directress and Achmet and several other trainers paused before each cage, the girl inside would start crawling round and then brazenly display herself in the position of 'presentation'. She saw that the directress, like the men, also carried a dog whip which she used to point out to the trainers those parts of the anatomies of the caged women which pleased or annoyed her.

By the time the directress arrived at her cage Emma was a bundle of fear, all thoughts of protest completely banished from her mind. Instead, all she wanted to do was to please this strict woman dressed in a long black gown who so impatiently tapped her dog whip against the palm of her hand as she gave orders to the trainers regarding each girl – orders which of course, thanks to the double glazing, the girls could not hear.

Hastily Emma showed off her beautifully slimmed down and sleek body, crawling round the tiny cage, and then, as she had seen the other girls do, she raised her breasts with her hands through the bars of her cage so that the painted nipples touched the glass of the double glazing. Then she lay back and degradingly offered her prettily painted body lips in the position of 'presentation'. She knew she must hold this position until the directress moved off to the next cage.

Emma saw that the unsmiling directress was gesticulating towards her with her dog whip as she discussed Emma with Achmet, who was nodding his head respectfully. It was indeed probably fortunate that Emma could not hear their conversation. Even though she could not understand voluble French, she might have followed enough of the gist of what was said to have given her sleepless nights.

'Well, Achmet, I must congratulate you on the degree of submissiveness you already seem to have instilled into this girl. Her mistress will be delighted.'

'My people have a saying, madame,' smiled Achmet, pleased at his employer's praise, ' "control a girl's natural functions and you control the girl, but do not spare the whip" '. It is the mixture of these two that has broken the girl's independence of spirit. Now all that she thinks of is instant obedience, unthinking and unquestioning obedience to whatever order is given to her, just like a well-trained soldier.'

'That's just what her mistress wants. That is what she is paying for – in addition, of course, to the expertise which we will now start teaching her. Has she learnt to suck and lick for long periods, Achmet?'

'Indeed, madame, she can now lick and suck for hours on end!'

'Her mistress mentioned two other points. Firstly, the girl is used to playing with herself, and her mistress wanted us to try and stop this. Secondly, she wanted us to get her figure down to that of a young girl, whilst keeping her breasts well developed, of course.'

'Madame,' replied Achmet obsequiously, 'her intake of solids has been greatly reduced and provided she is not allowed to get at food during the remainder of her time here, then I think your client will be pleased with the result.'

'But those dog biscuits, what about them?' asked the

directress pointing to the half-dozen remaining dog biscuits of different colours in Emma's food bowl. Emma had already snatched a couple of them. She felt half starved after only being fed on the watery porridge when in the dungeon.

'They're just to make sure she gets some vitamins and a little protein,' replied the man knowledgeably. It was not for nothing that he had been in charge of the women used for putting on exhibitions in a nightclub-cum-brothel. 'They are really intended for bitches feeding their puppies, but they are also excellent for keeping a woman's breasts nice and plump whilst she is losing weight.'

'Achmet,' laughed the directress for once, 'you know so much about women's bodies!'

'And as regards her mistress's other requirement – that we make her frightened of masturbating when alone,' said Achmet with a smile, 'should I start introducing her to the frustrating delights of our electrified belt and gloves?'

'Yes,' agreed the directress. 'But of course only when she is in her cage and alone. There is no need for her to wear them during her training sessions.'

'Of course, madame,' bowed Achmet. He enjoyed using this technique on a sensual and passionate girl like Emma, especially since so much of her training would arouse her and make her long to seek relief once she was back in her cage.

'You can have her all day for another few days, Achmet,' said the directress in an authoritative tone. 'After that she'll only be on instruction in the mornings. In the afternoons she will start being available to my clients, and again in the evenings. She'll sleep in her cage of course – unless the client spends the night here and wants to keep her with her. But I discourage this; it tends to give the girl ideas above her station and to undo all our good work. It's much better for a girl, when she's being made to behave like a whore, to be sent back to her cage after she's been used by a woman.'

She looked down at the prettily pouting body lips that

Emma, lying on her back, was now so degradingly displaying.

'I presume you will be starting to exercise those, now. A girl needs a lot of practice if she is to be capable of pleasing her mistress for a long time with both her face and body lips. I know you've already made a good start on her face lips, but a woman likes to feel her girl's juices against her own lips for a long period – even if she does not allow the girl to climax.'

'Madame, Number Ten's special training will be starting immediately.'

'Excellent,' said the directress, passing on to the next cage. 'Now this other girl was found by her mistress actually kissing a young man. She was thoroughly thrashed, of course, but she's been sent here by her outraged mistress not only to make men repulsive to her, but also to make her look repulsive to men. So not only must you treat her as degradingly as possible, but you are also to shave her head completely and keep it shaved. Her mistress wants her to be completely bald with a shiny pate. She'll be just as effective between her mistress's thighs, but she won't find so many men keen to kiss her in future!'

Ten minutes later a horrified Emma saw the pretty girl in the next cage being made to put her head through the bars of her cage. Achmet put a piece of wood behind her neck to stop her from trying to pull her head back again. Then slowly and methodicaly he cut off all the girl's beautiful long black hair with a pair of scissors whilst the girl was weeping with despair. Then he ran some electric clippers over her head and finally settled down to shave her whole head very carefully. To match the bizarre effect, he shaved off the girl's eyebrows as well and polished her bald cranium with saddle soap. When the wretched girl saw her shiny bald head and absence of eyebrows in the mirror of her cage, she screamed and screamed.

But, of course, no one heard her behind the double glazing of her cage.

Emma was pulled to the post, facing it. A heavy belt with

a ring at the back was fastened tightly round her belly. A loose strap was then passed round the smooth, well-worn post and fastened through the ring at the back of her belt. Then Achmet fastened her hands behind her back. She could now move easily round the post, but could not move her belly more than six inches away from it.

A ring was painted round the post level with her hips and another just above her knees. Her task was to use her beauty lips to oil all round the post, between the two red circles, and then polish it with her belly. But no oil or polish was supplied. She would, she knew, have to use her own oily juices.

She knew from experience that she could reach the top ring by standing on the tips of her toes as she inched her way round the post. To reach the lower ring she would have to bend her knees until she was in a crouching position.

The worst part was getting her juices running so publicly, for not only was Achmet watching her performance closely, but four other girls were similarly being made to polish other posts on the little raised platform. The embarrassed girls' bellies were level with Achmet's eyes as they strained and wriggled against their posts. Only by a mixture of wriggling against the post and thinking of Ursula, or Henry, did Emma think she'd become sufficiently wet. But then, to her horror, she found that the most effective stimulus was Achmet's little dog whip. It did not have to be applied very hard for her to be ready to start rubbing her oils into the smooth wood.

Perhaps most humiliating of all, Achmet had shown her how to get her oils on to the wood so that she could then start rubbing them in. She had learnt to lean right back in her harness and to raise her feet around the post, so that her body lips were in direct touch with it. This would enable her to deposit a little of her oil into the wood so that she could start spreading it over and around the post, repeating her little trick again and again to deposit another few drops on to the dry wood. It was a long and tedious process to ensure that all the wood between the rings had been covered properly with her oil – and before Achmet was satisfied that she had done a good job.

Then came the equally long and tiring process of polishing the oil well into the wood, so that it all shone beautifully.

'Gently, Number Ten,' ordered Achmet in his heavily accented English. 'You just rub it round and round with lower belly, very gently until the wood begins to shine. Round and round and up and down, and thrust your belly in and out, in and out.'

Like the other girls, Emma had learnt to do a sort of belly dance, or Hawaiian hula-hula dance, her hips and buttocks thrusting and shaking wildly in a completely uninhibited way, as she desperately tried to spread the oil and polish the wood.

'You pretend post is your mistress, Number Ten,' encouraged Achmet, his dog whip raised menacingly to drive home his point. 'You pretend you trying to give pleasure to mistress with your beauty lips. Then you polish post very nicely. You try and make post cry out with pleasure – just like mistress. And you keep going on and on, until I satisfied. You not rest until then. You keep going on and on. You frightened of whip. You not dare stop for one second, no matter how tired. Your belly muscles getting ready to give pleasure to mistress for long, long time.'

There was a long pause whilst Emma continued to cavort and press her lower belly against the post, slipping up and down as she alternately bent her knees and moved her feet a little forward so that she could grip the post more tightly between her thighs.

'Wood too dry here, Number Ten!' It was the remark that she most dreaded. She felt his hand come down over her bottom and between her legs, checking whether she needed the stimulus of his dog whip to produce more oil. 'You beg me beat you.'

'Please, sir. Please beat me again,' came the shamed voice of Emma.

Three times the dog whip descended. Then the huge

man's hand again examined her. She was soaking wet! It was extraordinary how a beating never failed to have that effect.

'Now up! And spread it!' Achmet ordered.

Obediently, the now deeply blushing Emma leant back in her harness, and fastened her legs round the post, giving little wriggles of excitement as she felt her oil dripping, drop by drop, on to the wood.

'Ten more minutes!' came the voice of Achmet as he proudly strode up and down the line of horribly ashamed young women, each wriggling in a mixture of delight, fear and concentration on the task in hand. It was just the sort of mixture that would most appeal to Ursula, a steady mixture of continual wriggles, writhes and what American striptease artists would recognise as good, old-fashioned grinds. 'Ten more minutes and then we see which girl has polished her post best and which deserve a beating for not trying hard enough.'

That was enough to provoke gasps of fear from the four girls as they each applied themselves even more frantically to their task.

This was the first exercise that they had to do in each morning, afternoon and evening training period.

MEMOIRS OF A CORNISH GOVERNESS

Yolanda Celbridge

Saucy sex and discipline in a Victorian setting is without doubt a favourite Nexus turn-on. From Yolanda Celbridge, author also of the contemporary *Maldona* series, comes a light-hearted trilogy which chronicles the adventures of Miss Constance Cumming – the Governess – each book a stirring blend of whimsy, wantonness and whipping.

In this first book of the series, *Memoirs of a Cornish Governess*, Constance accepts a position in the household of an eccentric, port-loving lord and lady and soon finds her niche teaching local gentlemen and ladies the meaning of discipline, while adding new strings to her own sexual bow. As strict and stern as she is young and voluptuous, Constance gleefully and expertly employs all manner of Victorian instruments of punishment and correction, not least the intimate restraints and other weird and wonderful devices supplied by Mr Izzard's Wimbledon pharmacy.

In this extract, the Governess, aroused by her first encounter with the Sapphic, masochistic, Miss Chytte, and eagerly anticipating the next, has summoned her young charge, Freddie Whimble, to her room.

Yolanda Celbridge's books have – so far – fitted into two separate series, both devoted to the unique chastisement of bottom flesh! In the Maldona series, the complicated Punishment Rulebook is applied with enthusiasm, and the physical upbraiding of miscreants is part of day-to-day life in the world of Mistress Jana and her devoted lovers and servants. With the forthcoming final book in the series – *The Castle of Maldona* – rounding off the adventures of Jana, and the Governess settling down to a life of relaxed rudery in *The Governess Abroad*, we're expecting Yolanda to provide us with a new series very soon. Rumour has it, her next story will feature a Victorian bad girl!

'Come on, Freddie, my sweet,' I whispered, tweaking my nipples to a tingling hardness. 'Let me have that great engine inside me, splitting me and spurting your hot spunk in my womb.'

Such talk excites men, or men's vanity. In no time he was rampantly stiff, and I knelt to present my arse to him. Then I showed him how to fuck me, doggy fashion, as I had seen demonstrated in my book. He performed superbly, clasping my breasts roughly with one hand while diddling my clitty with the other. I heard him roar as I felt the spunk jet inside me, and then I spent too, with his head sunk on to my perspiring back. It was quite delicious, the doggy position, but I had an appetite for something sweeter still, sweeter because forbidden . . .

I let him lie beside me, and he kissed my breasts as I cradled him in my arms, as though I were his Mama. I tickled his balls, and said that I thought there must be another lot of sperm to be emptied from them, so that I could replace his restrainer. He assented with a glum mutter.

'Well, now, Freddie. your cock is pleasingly stiff again, and you are going to fuck me in the bumhole.'

I was rather nervous, for my academic knowledge of this unusual act was about to be translated into reality, which I hoped would not be painful.

'Does the idea frighten you or dismay you, Freddie?'

'Mistress,' he cried, 'I long to fuck you in your sweet bumhole, for that is your desire.'

I resumed my doggy position on all fours.

'First, Freddie,' I ordered, 'you are to kiss my arse-bud – my anus. I want to feel your tongue well inside me, so stretch my buttocks tight as a drumskin.'

He stretched my buttocks quite painfully apart, and got his tongue into my arsehole to a depth of about an inch, which was enormously ticklish and exciting. I frigged my clit gently, then playfully tightened my sphincter muscle and squeezed his tongue, before forcing it out like a stool!

As his tongue slipped out, I had the most exciting tickling sensation, and I longed to feel the same with his fat penis. I was still nervous – his cock seemed so huge to fit into that small place. But I guided him towards me, helping the engorged member towards the opening of my arse-slit.

I cried out as he pierced my anus with his cock. I experienced a sudden sharp pain, and then he was all the way inside me, fucking me very hard. The pain gave way to a lovely sensation of warmth and bursting fullness.

With my sphincter, I squeezed his cock as hard as I could, matching the tensing of my muscle to the forceful rhythm of his thrusts.

He was kneeling behind me, hands resting on my buttocks, I made him remove one from my bum and guided his fingers to my clit, which felt so stiff and excited! I had not realised that arse-fucking – together with the stimulation of my clit – could be such ecstasy! I felt so totally, wonderfully, in the thrall of that ruthless giant cock!

'God, Freddie, fuck me, fuck me in the arse until I burst!' I heard myself squeal. 'Feel how tight and juicy I am for you. Better than any boy . . .'

'Better than anything, Mistress,' he moaned. 'Yes, squeeze my cock like that, it is so good . . . squeeze me till my spunk shoots into your lovely hole!'

I made him withdraw all the way out of my anus at each thrust, then tickle my arse-bud with his glans a while before plunging fiercely all the way into me. In this way my pleasure was prolonged maddeningly, as though – I am almost ashamed to admit – I were stooling again and again . . .'

'Spank me, Freddie!' I cried in a frenzy of painful joy. 'Make my arse tingle as you fuck me, please. Oh please!'

Then I felt a rain of heavy slaps on my buttocks, stinging red-hot, such was the muscled force behind them. To have his strong arms beating me was thrilling, and my clit throbbed; my belly heaved, and I lost control of myself and released a flood of my water! It splashed our thighs, all hot, and at that moment he cried out that he was going to spend. An orgasm shook me with its hot sweetness, and I cried out as though in torment:

'Yes, Freddie, sweet boy, fuck me and spend all your hot spunk in my bum, you cruel lovely beast! How you hurt me with your spanking, but don't stop, spank me, fuck me, please, tan my bum till she is as red as my cunt, all hot and swollen. Oh God yes . . .'

His fingers mercilessly frigged my clit as I felt his hot creamy jet spurt into my tripes, and then his spent cock slid from my anus with a delicious tickle, and we fell exhausted.

'Mmmm,' was all I could think of to say, or rather purr, and I kissed him on the mouth, my tongue searching for his.

'Gosh,' he said at length, 'I must have spanked you awfully hard, Mistress. I am so sorry if I caused you discomfort.'

I felt my arse, which was burning to the touch, both on the skin outside, and the sore anus hole inside. I glowed with pleasure.

'You silly boy,' I said, stroking his hair. How could he guess what I felt? The power of my spend as his hand cracked across my bottom had startled, even frightened me. God, I had needed that. For so long I had needed to be beaten!

After a while, I disengaged myself and told him it was time to retire to his own room.

'I think that your lustful thoughts will be quiet

tomorrow, for I fancy I have well-emptied your balls for a while. But you will put on the restrainer just to be sure.'

I fastened the cock ring tightly, and then handed him my yellow satin bloomers, well-stained with my love excretions.

'Put these on, slave,' I commanded, once more the stern mistress, 'and do not wash your cock or balls until I give permission. Discomfort will teach you obedience.'

'Yes, Mistress,' he chirped joyfully, and obeyed.

I went to bed, but my mind was in such confusion that sleep would not come. The moon gleamed balefully, like a new shilling. I got up and inspected my arse in the mirror, marvelling at the livid red palm prints I had received from my sweet slave, who had spanked me with such fervour – knowing that I took his blows as avidly as he dealt them.

My marks seemed to be a reminder of the tenderness and lustful passion we had enjoyed; a testimony of love imprinted on the flesh, which is also a teasing foretaste of enjoyments to come. My arse still glowed. Impulsively, I took my silver hairbrush and dealt myself twenty fierce slaps, until it burned anew. Only then could I achieve a happy sleep, my whole body bathed in the love of life. My arse-fucking and my spanking had awakened in me desires which I had only dimly imagined before. I thought of Miss Chytte's voluptuous bottom writhing under my own blows; of her flushed lips and bright eyes, that fascinating mannish bosom, and wondered what would happen on our next meeting. Had she been right? That she and I were alike, were sisters?

To be fucked in the anus, I thought, and to be beaten – whether spanked or flogged with a whip – is to experience pleasure in utter degradation and humiliated submission. One is helpless, twisting in torment, yet feeling a damnable joy. It is the joy of freedom. The soul is removed from all constraints of dignity, of the self, and experiences the blissful scream of freedom, when all the cares of grown-up existence are removed; there is only the crack of the whip on bare skin, the thrust of the cock in our intimate and most private part, the anus.

I realised that from being the teacher, I was becoming the taught.

Punctually at two o'clock the next day, Miss Chytte admitted me to her apartment. She wore a robe of black satin which buttoned from her neck to just below her mons, and was daringly slit at the side, giving a tantalising glimpse of her firm bare legs, which were without stockings or, as far as I could tell, panties of any kind. I was wearing only a loose blue blouse under my grey silk jacket, which I removed, saying that she must feel very hot in such formal attire.

'But I never wear underthings, Miss Cumming, which keeps me cool.'

'How very progressive, Miss Chytte,' I said, gravely.

'Practical too – you must try it, Miss Cumming.'

'Ah,' I smiled, 'you are never short of new things for me to try, are you, miss? But let us to business. You have a nice shiny shilling for me?'

She produced the coin but when I reached for it, she snatched her hand away.

'Give me it, Miss Chytte,' I said. 'I will not be trifled with.'

'You must take it,' she answered simply. I grabbed her arm, but she resisted, and in a moment we found ourselves wrestling on the floor. I was slightly the stronger – or at least she let me be – and soon had her pinioned to the floor, her skirt having ridden up around her waist to reveal her naked thighs and minge. She had quite a silky, shiny forest of very lustrous thick hair, which was curiously straight, not curly like my own mink, and I longed to stroke it. But I prised the shilling from her grasp instead. We were both panting from our exertions.

I released her and stood over her exposed body.

'You are naughty, miss,' I said with a smile.

'Will I be punished, then?' she whimpered.

'Yes.'

'Not the cane! I cannot bear it!'

'The cane it is, miss, on your bare bottom.'

'Naked! No, no! The shame of baring my bottom for a flogging is more than I can endure.'

I put the heel of my boot squarely on her exposed cunt, and pressed quite hard.

'I want you completely stripped, to increase your shame. Undress for me, Miss Chytte.'

I released her and she stood, feigning terror, then unbuttoned her dress until it fell away from her body and she stood before me nude. I noticed that the nipples which crowned her taut little breasts were already stiff with excitement. The nipples, even in their quiet state, were a curious and lovely shape, not flat but domed like twin cupolas of a cathedral, and were deliciously out of proportion with the slim breasts they capped. But what surprised me was that they had been pierced, allowing two gold rings about three inches across to dangle from them. Well, I thought, if a lady may wear earrings, why not rings in her more intimate places too?

'You like my nipple rings, Miss Cumming?' she said slyly. 'Perhaps you would like me to pierce your own nipples, so that you may adorn yourself thus.'

'How insolent you are today,' I said. 'You shall do no such thing. Get up, you wicked girl, and I shall tan your arse until you plead for mercy!'

'Please,' she begged, 'I cannot bear the cane! I am innocent, a stranger to the lash! My poor bottom would sting so! Do not be cruel, miss, I implore you.'

I was thoroughly enjoying our little play.

'Oh,' I sneered, 'so you are a crybaby? Well, I think it is not worth chastising such a wilting violet, a cringing thing that would faint at a drop of cold water. You may dress again, Miss Chytte, for I see you are so sunk in self-pity as to be quite unworthy of correction.'

'No, wait,' she cried, as I turned to leave, pretending a great imperious scorn. 'I do deserve punishment, and I'll take it, miss, I promise.'

'Not from me, you snivelling ragwort,' I sneered. 'Find

some fool with hands of silk and a whip of feathers, for that is all you can bear. I come from a harsher school – why, one touch of my hand and you would quake with fear. Your rings would jangle like bells!'

'Let me prove otherwise. Touch me with your hand, Miss Cumming, please, touch my bare bottom and make it tingle.'

'How, then? A spanking? Is that all?'

'Hard, miss. Make my arse all red and glowing as you spank my naked skin. Put me over your knee, sweet Mistress, and make my naughty bottom writhe and jump as you chastise her.'

I pretended to think.

'Hmmm . . . very well, Miss Chytte. I will sit here, on this French high-backed chair, which seems quite admirably suited for the job. You will please bend over my knee.'

'Please, miss, may I first visit the commode?' she asked, her face all flushed with excitement. 'I am bursting to go, really I am.'

I saw that this was another artful part of our game.

'Certainly not,' I snapped. 'You are a big girl and must control yourself, miss.'

'You are so cruel! How can I hold it in?'

'Enough complaining,' I ordered. 'You will position your upper body between my legs, bending your waist over my left thigh. Yes, that's right.'

I rolled my dress up to near my waist, and felt her soft skin slide against my thighs.

'Head right down, now, and legs slightly splayed. Good.'

I then placed my right foot firmly on her neck, grinding her face into the rug, and I could feel her shudder with anticipation. I stroked her bottom rather absent-mindedly, and I trembled myself, for I longed to smother that gorgeous pair of creamy globes with hot kisses, or cruel whip-strokes. I let my fingers wander in the crack of her arse until they found her anus bud set out very prettily like a little wrinkled hillock, and I began to tickle it.

'Oo!' she squealed in delight, her voice muffled by the carpet.

'What a hairy little hole you have, Miss Chytte,' I said gaily. 'It is quite uncouth. And look how the little scoundrel stands up so cheekily.'

I wiggled my thumbnail inside her anus, and slowly slid my thumb in up to its hilt. She squeaked again in evident delight and squeezed her anus muscle around my thumb so tightly that I could not take it out, and her buttocks began to writhe in a voluptuous dance around her filled anus.

The palm of my hand was beneath her squirming pubis, and my fingers pressed against the lips of her quim. I could feel her luscious thick mink, soaked in her oily love juice, and with my fingers brushing her clit, which made her shiver, I raised my free hand and delivered a mighty slap to her bare arse.

'Mmm!' she gurgled. 'Oh, yes!'

My slaps rained thick and fast, as hard as I could make them, until her bottom was all pink and squirming like mad. Her pubis, soaking wet, pumped on my probing fingers as fast as a piston.

Her whole body shook as I vigorously spanked her, and there were indeed little tinkles as her nipple rings clashed daintily together!

My hand grew sore from the spanking, but I did not care, for I was on fire with desire for that lovely squirming arse, glowing hot and red for me. Her bottom and my hand were partners in a quickstep of delight, as she jerked her bottom up to meet my downward slap in a beautiful mimicry of fucking.

But I wanted to see her arse dance in earnest, and for that it would have to be the cane. Before I told her of my decision, she cried out and slammed her pubis hard against my hand, trapping my fingers in her oily slit, and began to grind fiercely with her hips, whimpering uncontrollably.

I wondered if the patrons of the teashop downstairs could hear their proprietress crying out in the ecstasy of a spend!

Gradually Miss Chytte's spasm subsided, and I desisted

from the spanking, letting my hand rest on her burning bottom. I released her neck from my foot and she twisted her head up to look at me with a beaming blush. She panted, as though from running, and I could not help returning her smile, finding it impossible to maintain my play-acting role as implacable governess.

'Enough, miss?' I said.

'No, Mistress,' she gasped, and I was pleased and excited.

'You see I am no wilting violet. Now *you* must prove your mettle, Miss Cumming. I require a sound whipping, with my Chinese snake.'

'Chinese snake? I have never heard of such a thing.'

'Well, you will soon see,' she replied, stretching her body with catlike grace, but making no move to get up from her submissive position.

The prospect of further labour excited rather than deterred me, but I was jealous of Miss Chytte for having enjoyed an orgasm while I was left wet between the legs and itchy with lust. I could not wait for this Chinese thing to appear, whatever it was. Keeping one hand between Miss Chytte's wet thighs, I kept the other, still smarting from her spanking, between my own thighs and began to rub my clit. My half-hearted attempt at discretion did not deceive my host and she purred in approval as she felt my body tremble.

'Don't mind the chair,' she said impishly. 'It has been wet before.'

But I scarcely heard her, as I could feel myself grow hot from the desire building inside me.

'Wet,' I sighed, 'how nice, Miss Chytte, how nice to be . . . wet.'

At that moment there was a knock on the door, and I jumped.

'You're late!' barked Miss Chytte.

The door opened, I heard a tinkle of tea things, and looked in confusion as the maid, Prunella, came in, bearing a silver tray.

'I'm sorry, ma'am,' she said rather petulantly, looking

blankly at her employer's flushed naked bottom as though such a sight were perfectly normal.

Miss Chytte leapt to her feet and reached for her robe, while I attempted to hide my confusion by smoothing my dress decorously over my knees and removing my glistening fingers from my quim. I was rather annoyed at this interruption of my pleasure. What had Miss Chytte meant by late? Had she known, or arranged, that Prunella would interrupt us?

I was not long in finding out.

Prunella looked at me with a sulky *moue* on her bonny, handsome face, but with sparkling inquisitive eyes. I realised I was very flushed in the face, and the knowledge made me blush still more.

'Do not get up, Miss Cumming,' said Miss Chytte formally, as she smoothed her hair and robe. 'I promised to show you my Chinese snake, so I will fetch it.'

'You said *I* could have it today, ma'am,' complained Prunella with a curl of her wide red lips.

'Be quiet, you cheeky girl,' snapped Miss Chytte, and I could not tell if her tone was serious or mocking.

'You are late with the tea, you have interrupted us, and now you are cheeky into the bargain. Oh, you are a muddle today. I think you know what to expect!'

Prunella raised her eyes in mock astonishment, and sighed. Then she resignedly lifted up her short waitress's skirt to reveal her naked minge, unencumbered by panties, and blessed with a fine thick forest of pubic curls.

'Shall I bend over the sofa, ma'am?' she asked in a matter-of-fact tone.

'Not today, Prunella,' replied Miss Chytte with a wicked gleam in her eye. 'Miss Cumming, as you see, has just taught me a very expert lesson, and I think she will apply the same care to your naughty bum. No, wait, a better idea is for you to continue her private pleasure with your nimble tongue, while I attend to your errant backside. Please remain seated, Miss Cumming.'

I did not know what was happening. My heart fluttered as Prunella's ripe body knelt before me. Miss Chytte lifted her waitress's skirt right over her back, to reveal two ample white buttocks, prettily framed by the black straps of her garter belt. Prunella's hair cascaded over her face, which disappeared under the hem of my dress.

I was quite mesmerised as I felt her strong country hands creep up my calves to my knees, which she gently parted, then over my thighs to my wet panties. There was a tug as they came away from my waist and were pulled down around my ankles.

I was intoxicated with desire and anticipation, and stared helplessly at Miss Chytte who was grinning mischievously. She held a flat leather strap of about three feet long, whose end was split into ribbons, rather like a very large bookmark. Her robe was open to below her breasts and she did not bother to cover her nudity.

Prunella's head was under my skirts, her hands holding my knees apart, and I saw the bump of her head moving towards my mons.

'Hurry, ma'am,' came her muffled voice from inside my dress, 'there are customers waiting.'

At once, I jumped as I felt sucking lips and a probing tongue in my wet slit. I swallowed and gasped, for a shudder of pleasure convulsed me as that sweet, rude girl expertly tongued my throbbing clit. My hands clasped her head, stroking her, and I moaned out loud.

At that moment, Miss Chytte lifted the strap and began to beat Prunella's raised buttocks. Her vigorous lashes made a juicy whacking noise, but I do not suppose they can have been too painful, for Prunella took a good dozen or more without flinching, or even seeming to notice. But the spectacle of her bare arse being beaten excited me so much that I could not contain myself any longer. Her sweet, rough tongue rasped on my tender clit until I cried out in a heaving spend, my eyes feasting all the while on Prunella's plump buttocks bobbing under the lash, their tops glowing prettily like two red mushroom caps.

'You naughty, naughty, girl!' cried Miss Chytte as she delivered the final lash. 'I hope that will be a lesson to you.'

I heard Prunella grunt non-committally.

I lay back, exhausted with pleasure, and Prunella disentangled her hair from my wet inner thighs. She replaced my panties on my mons, which was soaked in love oil, and eventually her head re-emerged from under my dress. She stood up and stared at me quite blankly, as though at a cow she had just milked, but with the hint of a pout on her glistening lips, which she licked with evident satisfaction. Then she curtseyed to both of us and impassively departed.

'I promise I won't be late tomorrow, ma'am,' she said as she closed the door.

'She is a good girl,' said Miss Chytte. 'She is always late. Now, perhaps you would like to pour us a nice cup of tea, Miss Cumming, while I fetch my Chinese snake, in preparation for further games?'

I poured tea and listened to her shuffling in her bedroom. When she returned she was barefoot, still wearing the same robe, with no sign of any snake.

'Where is this snake?' I asked.

'Why, here, for I am wearing it,' she replied, and let her robe fall away from her breasts. I saw that she was now wearing a sort of lustrous black bodice which came to just below her breasts, between which a snake's head peeped out! It was about the size of a pear, with a shiny red tongue, and a strange little collarette of rosebuds; the whole garment apparently being made of silk.

'This,' announced Miss Chytte, 'is the only undergarment I wear.'

My curiosity whetted, I leaned over my teacup and saw that it was not a woven fabric, but a coil of thin tubing that wound around her belly in a spiral. We stood up, and Miss Chytte threw aside her robe, and stood naked but for this curious garment, which evidently served as bodice and panties at the same time, for her mons was covered in a thin strip of the fabric not enough, though, to conceal her forest.

She fiddled with the top of the bodice and released the snake's head. Then she stood on tiptoe and twirled around until she had unwound about three feet of the heavy black tubing, which was evidently the silken body of the 'snake'.

'Take this,' she said, handing me the snake's head, 'and I will dance for you, miss.'

I held the silken snake's head and watched entranced as Miss Chytte pirouetted around the room, whirling in a strange ballet until half of the snake's body lay coiled on the carpet, and she stood breathless in the middle of the room, her face as red as her smooth, flushed bottom which I had so recently spanked.

The snake's tail was nowhere to be seen, until I realised that it was hidden inside Miss Chytte's vulva!

She laughed, and picked up the coils of shiny silk.

'A snake with two heads, you see. The Chinese are very ingenious. Squeeze him by the throat, and you will be amused.'

I did so and found that as I squeezed, the fat tongue flickered back and forth quite grotesquely, as though it were a little penis thrusting!

'Imagine what he feels like inside,' she said. 'A silken snake with a silken tongue, that is also a silken whip with a vicious backbone. You will please wear the snake's head inside you as you whip me with his body, Miss Cumming. I suggest you make yourself comfortable by removing your skirts and panties.'

My heart pounding, I was quick to strip off my nether garments and stood in only my blouse, stockings, garter belt and boots, as she took the snake's head from my hand and deftly placed it against the lips of my cunt.

I gulped, and with my own fingers parted my swollen lips. I felt the snake's head glide into my oily slit as smoothly as a gondola cleaving the waters of Venice. It was not smooth and hard like a man's penis, but lumpy, scaly, yet soft at the same time.

Miss Chytte gently unbuttoned my blouse and knotted the lower half beneath my breasts, making them thrust upwards.

'I think we must give our snake room to entwine your belly,' she said softly. 'And now let us dance.'

It was the strangest dance I had ever known. We both whirled languidly as the snake was uncoiled from her body and gradually covered me. With every motion of my dancing thighs, I felt the darting tongue tickle me deliciously, as though that silken thing were alive inside me, and the stiff rosebuds of the necklace rubbed maddeningly on my tingling stiff clit.

At last I had my own black bodice, and Miss Chytte was quite nude, with about six feet of the silken strand left between our bodies. She halted her dance, and plucked the snake's second head from inside her vulva, then kissed it and pressed it to my own lips.

'There is the tip of your lash, Miss Cumming,' she whispered. 'Please whip me well with him.'

I followed her into the bedroom, admiring the swaying curve of her bottom, which I knew she was rolling to entice me, with the desired result, for I felt intensely lustful towards her. Games and charades are so useful in fanning love's flames!

I expected her to lie down on the bed but she ignored it. Instead she indicated a sort of stool, about waist height, with splayed legs beneath a padded leather seat, with straps and buckles at the foot of each leg.

'This is a very valuable antique, Miss Cumming,' she said. I believe it was once used by the Sisters of Mercy in Salamanca, in Spain, at whose nunnery the daughters of the nobility went to be educated.'

'Used for what?' I asked.

'Why, it is a flogging-horse.'

On Miss Chytte's instructions, I set to work to fasten her properly to receive punishment.

A golden chain was attached to each of her nipple rings, then stretched over her belly and tightly across her slit, across her anus and up her back, where it was clipped to a tight golden collar around her neck. A second chain stretched from her nipples under the flogging-horse to her braceletted ankles, and finally looped back to her nipples.

As a result of this chaining, the slightest movement was impossible without causing severe discomfort.

'I have never been chained so expertly before, Miss Cumming,' she said dreamily. 'Why, the metal caresses me.'

'Let's see how you like the caress of the whip, you slut!' I cried rather daringly, but she shivered with excitement at the taunt.

'Oh, it shall be a caress, miss,' she cried. 'Have *you* never dreamt of being flogged by a silken whip? Its touch as light as a butterfly, or as hard as steel, for all is in the mind, a dream of pain, an ecstasy of pleasure.'

'I . . . I am not sure,' I said, confused by the luscious tickling of the snake's head in my wet cunt.

'I am sure, Miss Cumming, for I think I know you. Now please lash my bare bottom with the snake, as hard and as often as you like. How I love it when he strokes me!'

I began to beat her, with long lazy strokes, and the harder I stroked her, the more my body swam with pleasure. I watched as her luscious arse became diffused with a gentle pink, that gradually deepened into a fiery red.

'That is lovely and warm, Miss Cumming. I think my bottom has been well seen to. Please let her glow for a while as you attend to my back. Chained in the position of the rising sun, my arms and legs stretched out like the cross of St Andrew, how often I have dreamt of being a sailor, whipped at the mast. The position of the rising sun is the position of the dawn, of submission to the kiss of the lash, the helplessness of the naked self before the vast universe.'

I thought this very pretty, and I knew that position, for that is how I would stand to worship my moon goddess, Selene. Miss Chytte rapidly gave me new orders. A line of rings hung from the ceiling, whose purpose I now understood. Now, Miss Chytte's legs remained fastened to the flogging-horse, but she was forced to stand upright, on tiptoe. Her nipples were attached by one chain to the ceiling rings, and her wrists by another, so that her arms were forced strenuously up above her head. Her body assumed a 'V' shape, of lovely and perfect symmetry which was embellished by the rippling of her back muscles as I flogged her.

'God, God, it is good!' she moaned. 'Whip me, miss, oh whip me hard, purify my body with your lash.'

She began to writhe in a sinuous rubbing of her pubis against the leather of the flogging-horse, and I realised that she was masturbating, teasing her clitoris until with a frantic jerking of her hips, she cried out in the convulsion of a spend.

'God! I am spending, it is, oh God, so sweet, do not stop, flog me, beat me please, beat me, sweet miss, make my skin burn with your rod. Oh flog me, hurt me, yes, yes . . .'

Her spasm subsided and her voice died down to a sob. I laid aside the whip and released her from her bonds, and we embraced lovingly.

Suddenly I realised I wanted to visit the commode. And it looked as though Miss Chytte had the same purpose.

'After you, miss,' I smiled with exaggerated politeness.

'No, after you, Miss Cumming,' she gasped, then snorted in amusement.

'Oh, it is not necessary to be so formal. We can go together!'

And she led me to her capacious bathroom, where twin floor-level commodes *à la turque* faced each other.

We both squatted naked and did our business, holding hands and gazing at each other with dreaming eyes. To complete our toilette she handed me some pink paper, and our lips met.

'Oh, Miss Chytte,' I gasped, 'I don't know what to say. I am all wet for you between my legs. My cunt is quite overflowing, or so it feels. What a luscious body you have! I must taste it, miss!'

All thoughts of impropriety at being naked and lustful with another woman had now left me. I felt giddy with desire for her sweet body, flushed and burning from my whipping.

I led her to her chamber and laid her on the bed. I lost

no time in clasping her to my body in a fervent embrace, with my lips full on hers, and my tongue probing her mouth in a passionate French kiss.

For a minute or two, we were locked in this passionate, silent embrace, our breasts pressed together and my thigh between her legs, rubbing her. Then I disengaged myself, and moved down the bed. I forced her thighs apart and kissed her on the cunt, as fully and firmly as I had kissed her lips.

'Oh, Miss Cumming,' she sighed, 'I knew . . . I could feel your aura . . . The way you whipped me: you are one of us!'

My tongue found her clitoris and flickered over the swollen thing.

'Turn round, miss,' she begged. 'Sit on my face as you lick my cunt.'

I did so, adopting the position known as *soixante-neuf* and soon her nose was pressed against my ticklish little anus bud while her tongue busied itself with my own clit. I was flowing with juice, which she lapped up with grunts of joy. I wiggled around on her face, tickling my anus with her pretty nose, which was very thrilling. I squeezed it playfully with my sphincter muscle, and in this way we both achieved a hot spend. I clasped her bottom and kissed her cunt with all the passion I could muster, as I would kiss a lover's face.

We had time to repeat the operation, but with a slight variant: this time I sat upright, so that my whole weight pressed down on her face, and while she continued her tonguing of my clit, I pushed my foot between her thighs and rubbed her clit with my bare toes. At the same time I took hold of her nipple rings and pulled them up as hard as I could, stretching her breasts until she squealed in pain and pleasure. I thought it amusing that she should take a whipping without protest but should complain at a simple tension of the breast skin.

Her hands were free, and with them she spanked my bottom as I straddled her face. It was lovely! Hard, ferocious even, her stinging slaps reddened my bottom and made me quiver. After a while of this sport, we both achieved another orgasm, after which I said it was time to go and, to her displeasure, got off her face.

'Oh, I wish you could stay there, sitting on me and diddling my clit all afternoon, miss,' she said. 'I knew Miss Cumming, that you belonged with us, the disciples of the poetess Sappho. Cannot we women pleasure each other more expertly, with more tenderness, than cruel men?'

'I cannot see the tenderness in the flogging I have just given you,' I laughed.

'Oh, but it *was*! It is so lovely to be helpless in your power, miss, to feel myself your slave.'

'Slaves must pay a price for their slavery,' I said crisply, as I dressed. Miss Chytte still lay half swooning on the bed of our pleasure.

'Name it,' she said.

'First, there is the matter of my shilling.'

'Take it from my purse.'

I did so, then said:

'Those nipple rings – they are gold?'

'Twenty-four carat.'

'I think I will have them.'

'They are yours, Mistress,' she said. 'A good ounce in weight. You will wear them?'

'I will think about it,' I said briskly, as I detached the rings from her big stiff nipples. 'I am not yet a disciple of Sappho, more a curious party.'

I bent down and kissed her lips, then her nipples, and then her cuntlips, in farewell.

'I must be off to tea at the vicarage!' I said brightly.

'No!' cried Miss Chytte. 'I mean . . . watch out for him. He is a bad man.'

'The vicar? Surely not! Well, *au revoir*, my little slave.'

'Be careful, Mistress. It is I who, of all in this place, am your true friend.'

MELINDA AND THE MASTER

Susanna Hughes

The prolific and bestselling Susanna Hughes, who debuted for Nexus with the Stephanie series, specialises in stories of decadence, bondage and subjugation with sophisticated and often exotic settings. The first book in the Melinda series, *Melinda and the Master*, finds its beautiful, submissive heroine loaned for a year by her husband to a rich and powerful master as part of a business deal. Dressed for depravity, Melinda is introduced to a world where bondage and kinky sex are part of everyday life and takes to it readily. When her year is up, will Melinda be able to surrender her new identity so easily? And will her master even allow her her freedom?

In this extract, Melinda is humiliated both in public and in private, by her new Master and Mistress and their imposing female staff, and comes to realise just how compelling the pleasures of bondage and submissive sex can be.

Melinda is a girl who likes the sophisticated side of life. She also relishes surrendering her liberty to cruel masters and mistresses who live a pampered existence as Europe's wealthy, sexual elite. Whether tied up in a chateau to the south of Paris, or made to perform at an orgy in a lavish villa decorated in the style of Ancient Rome, Melinda is determined to give others a lot of pleasure while pleasuring herself. *Melinda and the Master* was the first book in the series. Susanna went on to write another four Melinda books, rounding off her adventures in *Melinda and Sophia*.

Lying, just as Marion had arranged her, on the table, Melinda felt so turned on that she began to wonder if it were possible to come without moving. She wanted to moan so badly, she had to clamp her lips together. Her whole body ached for a double release. Release from the invisible bonds that held her so tight, so she could roll and writhe and squirm and abandon herself to pleasure; and release from the sexual tension that stretched every nerve and sinew in her body as tight as piano wire.

'Well, gentlemen, that seems to conclude our business for today. Thank you for your time.' There was a hum of conversation, a scraping of chairs, the sound of papers being tidied away into briefcases. 'Please feel free, gentlemen,' the Master said, indicating Melinda.

One of the men who had his back to her sauntered over to her, as though she were some curiosity in a museum. he stood by the edge of the table, looking down at her. Two more men soon joined him.

'Beautiful body,' the first man said.

'Great.'

A younger man approached. 'Can we touch?' he asked, obviously new to the proceedings.

'I wouldn't,' the first man advised, looking back at the Master who still sat at the head of the conference table.

Melinda held her head to one side, not moving to look up at them. In her eyeline now were the flies of their trousers. She would have given anything to be touched.

She would have given anything to have been able to reach out, unzip one of those flies and delve inside.

Eventually, all twelve men stood around looking at her.

'So what is your opinion, gentlemen?' the Master's voice boomed out.

Various comments filled the air. 'Beautiful.'

'Exceptional.'

'Such lovely legs.'

'Odd pubic hair, so fine.'

'She's wet, you know.'

'Those nipples are hard, too, really hard.'

'Yes, I think she is exceptional. And what is more remarkable is that she is quite untrained.' The Master had risen. Two men made way for him to stand by Melinda's head. 'Aren't you, child?'

It was a question. Melinda was slow to realise she had to answer. 'Yes, Master.'

'Quite untrained. A natural talent.' He extended his hand to the fine fleece of her pubic hair. He teased out individual strands, pulling it up until the flesh from which it grew was stretched into tiny pyramids. It felt like being stung by a nettle.

His hand made no firm contact. How she yearned for him to slip it down between her legs. Couldn't he feel her heat? Couldn't he feel her body throbbing, the engine of her sex turning over like a car idling, but stationary? Didn't he want to propel her forward? But all he did was tease out her hair, like a spinner teasing out the wool, rolling it between his fingers now, forming little clumps of twisted hair.

'Well, lunch I think,' he said firmly. His hand left her. He walked away. The men followed, talking among themselves. The young man was the last. Checking they all had their backs to him, he leant over and cupped her breast in his hand, squeezing it hard. The action was so sudden and so unexpected, Melinda only just managed to suppress a moan.

Quickly the man caught up with the others at the door.

As they filed out, Melinda could see Marion had gone too. She was alone in the vast room.

Another test, she knew. There would be a camera somewhere. Someone would be watching. She had to remain as she was. No one had told her to move. The performance must continue.

Her body ached. The table top was hard. Her weight rested on her buttocks and her shoulders. There was an ache in her neck from holding her head to one side, and the leg Marion had raised was cramped and painful. Even the welts of the stockings seemed tight and uncomfortable on her thighs. But Melinda did not move. The engine of her sex continued to throb, her mind and body full of anticipation. Was this like the raffle at the house last night? Would one of the men be allowed to come and use her after lunch? Perhaps while they all watched?

Or, better still, perhaps the Master would walk through that door. Perhaps that was why she had been brought down here. To satisfy the Master. He had seen her last night, seen her body and her attitude. He had, she was sure, watched as she was being fucked. It must have aroused him. Surely he wanted her, his latest acquisition?

As she lay prone on the table, she was convinced that was the explanation, that all she had been asked to do was a prelude. She was here to satisfy the Master, to satisfy the craving she had created in him.

Out of the corner of her eye she could see the clock. An hour passed. She waited.

She heard the door open. Her whole body tensed. Ready. Only too ready.

But it was not the Master. It was Marion.

'Get up,' she ordered. Melinda obeyed instantly though her limbs needed some coaxing to resume activity. Marion picked up the shoe that stood on the table and dropped it on the floor, indicating that Melinda should put it back on. 'This way.'

Melinda was unsteady on her feet, the blood rushing back into the leg that had been raised. But she was not downhearted. Marion was taking her to the Master. She had to be. She even stopped her to brush out the hair that had been flattened by the table top.

'Poor cow,' Marion said. She could see what was written on Melinda's face, her excitement, her anticipation. The back of her hand caressed Melinda's cheek. She trailed her finger over her lips. 'You wanted it so badly, didn't you?'

The disappointment registered immediately. Melinda's heart sank. She was not being taken to the Master.

'Follow me,' Marion said.

It was another crisis point. Melinda stopped by the door as Marion walked through it.

'Do it,' Marion snapped.

Melinda looked at her. She felt strange, ill almost, as though all her sexual frustration had turned to poison in her body. Mechanically, she walked forward. Once again she seemed to be seeing herself from on high, watching this near-naked woman trudge through the door, her unsupported tits quivering from the movement of walking, her nylons rasping against each other as her thighs met.

She saw herself standing by the lift in the anteroom. She could not form thoughts. She could do nothing but tell herself to obey.

It had been deliberate, of course. Another lesson. It was as though the Master had reached inside her, found all the levers and pulleys that operated her psyche, and used them to reduce her to nothing, to what she felt now: bereft, empty, totally alone and undesired. Untouched. Unwanted. It was all part of the plan.

It was only in the lift that she realised she had not been given her dress back. Was that part of the plan too? Were they going to make her walk through the streets naked? Or did they think she would rebel at that? Another test.

The lift doors opened. Marion led the way out, but did not head back in the direction of the door out into the passageway. Instead, she headed through another door and down a long corridor, at the end of which a half-glass door opened on to a loading area. The Jaguar waited, the chauffeur standing by the open rear door.

Marion took Melinda's hand as they crossed to the car. Two men were loading a truck. They stopped and stared, open-mouthed.

'You have been very good, the Master will be pleased,' Marion said comfortingly.

Why doesn't he want me then? Why doesn't he take me? Melinda wanted to scream out. She said nothing.

They got into the car. The chauffeur looked at Melinda's nakedness, his eyes lingering on her breasts and loins. The leather seat was cold against her flesh.

'Get on the floor,' Marion commanded. 'Lie on the floor.'

Melinda slid off the leather and on to the thick pile rugs. They felt soft and warm.

Marion had taken a silk blindfold from her bag. She leant over and fitted it around Melinda's head, pulling it down over her eyes.

'That is your reward,' she said.

And it was true. The blackness behind the mask was welcome, anonymous, healing. Melinda lay on her side and curled herself into a foetal position. In the darkness she faced no further humiliation, no more eyes that devoured her but did nothing. No more disappointments, no more torments. For the moment at least, she was, like the darkness, featureless.

Her thigh had come to rest against Marion's foot. She could feel the leather toe and the nylon on top of her foot. She had thought Marion would draw her foot away, but she did not. Instead she seemed to press it forward. Or was that just the movement of the car? It didn't matter. To Melinda it felt good, almost too good to be true. Contact. Touch. Human touch.

Melinda had been taken straight back to her cell. Without removing the blindfold, she had been told to lie on the mattress while her hands were cuffed to the wall and the cold metal block chained between her legs. The stockings and shoes had been stripped away.

Whereas before she had welcomed the blindfold, now it was a curse. It turned her mind inward, allowing her to do nothing but listen to the pulses and rhythms of her body, allowing her to see only mental images. There was nothing to distract her. Had she not been prevented physically, she would have been unable to stop herself from masturbating. Her sex throbbed almost painfully for some attention, some relief. But, of course, they knew that. That was the point of this morning's exercise. And why she had been so effectively prevented from even the slightest contact with the part of her body that would bring her release. The metal block chained between her thighs allowed no contact. No amount of squirming and writhing of her body could bring anything to bear on her swollen clitoris but the unpleasant rasping harshness of the upper surface of the metal. And with her hands cuffed above her head any sexual fulfilment was simply impossible.

The greater the need they created in her, the more they denied her the means to satisfy it. Or so it seemed.

Time passed. She tried to think of anything but sex, but that was impossible too. She thought of last night, of that big hard cock buried deep in her throat, and immediately wished she hadn't. Involuntarily, she'd pushed her sex down on the metal block and been rewarded by a cold stinging pain for her trouble. But her mind was not deterred. Image after image filled the darkness behind the blindfold, like pictures on a cinema screen. Graphic, inescapable. The hands reaching out to feel her body at the dinner table; being whipped by Cybele; lying naked in front of all those men; their eyes looking down at her, the younger man cupping her breast . . .

Eventually she must have drifted off to sleep. She had no idea for how long.

The lock on the cell door springing open woke her. Hera walked in, carrying a tray of food. Without a word she uncuffed Melinda's hands, and peeled away the blindfold. She leant against the wall and watched as Melinda ate. As soon as she had finished, she made her lie down again and cuffed her hands back to the wall. She did not replace the blindfold, however, and, after she'd gone, the lights in the room remained on.

Melinda looked up at the video camera, wondering if she was being watched, but though the camera was pointed at her there was no way of telling whether it was operating.

Hours passed, or perhaps they were only minutes.

The cell door opened again. This time Marion entered. She was wearing a high-cut white silk teddy under a matching white negligée which was undone at the front. The teddy's lace panels were cut in a deep V-shape over Marion's breasts, revealing glimpses of their ample proportions. Its cut at the top of her legs was so high, it almost reached her waist, making her long sculptured thighs seem even longer. A dark growth of pubic hair nestled under the translucent white silk.

Marion unlocked the bathroom, the handcuffs and the metal block.

'Use the toilet if you need to,' she said, and stood watching as Melinda peed.

'The Master wants you,' she said.

Melinda's heart leapt. *Wants me! Wants me!* She could hardly believe she had heard correctly. But she stopped herself short. This was probably another game, another exercise in disappointment. The Master might merely want to see her, as he'd seen her this morning. She must not allow herself to get excited. Her needs, she reminded herself, no longer counted for anything.

Marion stood with the handcuffs still in her hand. Without another word she clipped Melinda's wrists into one cuff, then walked behind her, pulled her other wrist round into her back and locked them together. Coming back to face her again, she took a loop of fine gold chain from around her neck, spread it between her fingers and lifted it over Melinda's head. In the middle of the chain was a small key, the key to the handcuffs. It rested between Melinda's breasts.

The red high heels Melinda had worn this morning had

been left in the cell. Marion told her to put them on. There was something different about Marion's manner. Before, she had been cold, and then almost sympathetic. But this time she was surly, almost angry, as though full of resentment.

They walked through the house. Marion mounted the sweeping double staircase and Melinda followed. At the far end of the landing was a set of double doors, panelled and painted white. Marion knocked once.

'Come . . .' It was the Master's voice, but it sounded distant, only just audible.

Marion opened the door and pushed Melinda forward. She did not cross the threshold herself, but closed the door as soon as Melinda was inside.

Melinda found herself in a small hallway. There were two doors, one facing the double doors and one at the far end. She did not know what to do. If she turned her back she could probably turn the handle of the door with her cuffed hands. But is that what she was required to do? Without orders she was lost.

She heard the distinct thwack of a whip, and a responding but heavily stifled moan.

The inner door opened. Melinda recognised the leather uniform and boots, but not the face. This woman was short and plump, but like Cybele, looked powerful and strong. Her hair was a reddish auburn, and her large eyes, too large for her rather small face, were green. The silver brooch pinned to the black leather leotard was inscribed: SELENE.

She gripped Melinda by the arm, her strong fingers whitening the skin, and led her through the door. The Master's bedroom was massive. Large windows were covered by heavy white curtains. The floor was carpeted in a rich oatmeal long pile, the walls lined with a creamy silk fabric. Everything in the room was a shade of white or cream: the counterpane of the large double bed, the upholstery of the large sofa and the two soft comfortable armchairs. Only an occasional table, in front of the sofa, and the television mounted on the wall opposite the bed, were not. Both these items were black.

The Master was sitting in one of the armchairs. In front of him, on his knees, was a naked man. As Melinda entered, the man was lowering his head to the floor and the Master was wrapping his white cotton robe around his body.

'Get your forehead down.' Cybele stood alongside the naked man. She raised her booted foot and rested it on his neck to ensure her order was obeyed.

The man's buttocks protruded obscenely in the air. From the red welts that criss-crossed his backside, and the whip in Cybele's hand, it was obvious that the man had been subjected to a severe lashing. What else he had been made to do Melinda could only guess.

'Get him out of here,' the Master said in a tone of voice Melinda had never heard him use before. Apart from the cotton robe, he was naked.

Cybele and Selene literally dragged him to his feet. Melinda recognised his face immediately. It was the young man in the conference room who had squeezed her breast. Was this his punishment for that? Had the Master seen it on a video camera as Melinda had suspected?

They dragged him out of the room. His cock was erect. From the marks across his belly and thighs it looked as though his front had been subjected to the same treatment as his backside.

The Master turned the full force of his gaze on Melinda. He beckoned her over to his chair. She stood in front of him, her hands locked behind her back, her body exposed to his stare. His eyes roamed. She felt them as surely as if they were hands, on her breasts, on her navel, delving into the apex of her thighs. Then up again, up to look into her eyes. She felt all their power, hypnotic, impossible to resist, just as she had felt them that first evening as he had greeted her at his front door.

'Kneel,' he said, his tone altogether different from the one he had used before.

Melinda obeyed, but slowly. It was not easy to kneel without using her arms for balance.

'Closer,' he said when she was down.

She scrambled forward on her knees until she was inches from the Master's naked legs. Her heart was in her mouth, her excitement coursing through her nerves.

The Master leant forward, looking into her eyes. It was the closest she had ever been to him. The power of his eyes was overwhelming. She felt as though she could drown in them, drown in oceans of steely blue. He stretched out his hand and stroked her cheek lightly. Melinda had to resist the temptation to turn her head and kiss his fingers. His touch was intoxicating. Her heart was beating faster and faster. She begged with her eyes and her body. 'Take me,' she tried to express without words. 'Please.'

She dared not look into his lap. She looked only into his eyes.

He relaxed back into the chair. 'You pleased me today, Melinda.' It was the first time anyone had used her name in the house. 'You excited me a great deal. You are an extraordinary woman. Your obedience . . . your . . .' he searched for the right word, 'passivity. Perfect. So perfect. I don't think I have ever come across such a perfect example. You want it very much, don't you?'

It was a question. She was allowed to respond. She tried to cram all her emotions into the two words, 'Yes, Master.'

'Good, good.'

He got up. As he did, the front of his white robe brushed Melinda's face. He walked behind her. She dared not turn around without being ordered to.

'I want you to do something for me, Melinda.' He did not have to ask. He only had to command. 'Get up now, come over here.'

She got to her feet with difficulty and turned round. He was standing by an open door. She could see a bathroom beyond. He beckoned her forward as he'd done before.

The bathroom was walled in white marble. It was lit brightly, much more brightly than the bedroom. One whole wall was a mirror. Melinda had only glimpsed herself briefly in the mirror in the dining room since she had entered the house. The sight of herself now, naked but for the red high heels, her breasts thrust forward by the position of her arms, was a shock. It did not look like her. It looked like someone else, a stranger. She even seemed to move differently. Her hair and make-up were different. It was another person.

The Master came up behind her, wrapped his arms around her and embraced her, looking over her shoulder into the mirror in front of them. Contact. Real contact. At last. Melinda felt herself melting around him. With her arms cuffed behind her, her hands were pressed into his groin. She thought she could feel his cock.

'Child,' he said quietly, then released her. The moment passed.

She swayed back, almost losing her balance without his support.

He took the key from around her neck and quickly sprung the handcuffs open.

'Do they hurt you?' he asked solicitously.

'No, Master,' she lied.

'But they must do. I can see the marks on your wrists.'

She wanted to say that it wasn't important, that she'd do anything for him, anything. She knew she must say nothing.

'So good,' he said.

Her hands hung by her sides. He sat in a white Lloyd-loom chair by the bathtub.

'Run a bath,' he said, his hands pressed together in an attitude of prayer, the tips of his fingers touching his lips.

Melinda reached over to the mixer taps. She felt his eyes on her buttocks as the water gushed into the tub. He said nothing else until the bath was full.

'Get in now,' he said as she closed the taps.

She obeyed.

'Does that feel nice?'

It felt wonderful. She hadn't had a bath for three days. Her body was flushed pink with the heat of the water.

'Yes, Master.'

'Good. Wash yourself.'

Uncertainly she reached out for the soap. There was a shelf alongside the bath. She took the soap and a large natural sponge. She soaped herself quickly and rinsed the lather away with the sponge.

'Do you know what I want you to do for me, my dear?'

'No, Master.'

'Your hair. I want you to shave your hair.'

Despite the hot water Melinda went cold. He wanted her to shave her head. She went cold not because she was horrified at the request, but because she knew she would do it instantly, without question.

The Master went to a small bathroom cabinet. He extracted a shaving bowl and brush and a tiny razor its blade no more than an inch wide. He set them down at the side of the bath. It was only then that she realised he meant her pubic hair.

'Use these,' he said.

She hesitated. She hadn't the slightest idea what to do next.

'Stand up.' A note of irritation had crept into his voice at her hesitation. He took it for disobedience. 'Don't disappoint me now.'

She picked up the shaving brush and bowl of shaving soap and stood up. The water cascaded off her body. Dipping the brush in the soap she worked up a lather. She transferred the lather from the brush to her triangle of pubic hair, painting on a thick foam.

'Good.' He sat down again, pulling the chair nearly to the edge of the bath and leaning forward.

Melinda picked up the tiny razor. She had no qualms about what she was doing. Her body did not belong to her any more. She was only concerned to do a good job. This was what he wanted. All she wanted was to please him, to earn more praise, to be perfect. She wished he had asked one of the women to shave her, someone who knew how to do it well. She had never done this before.

The razor cut a swathe through the white lather. After several passes most of the lather had gone, and with it her downy fleece of blonde hair. She looked in the mirror, not to see herself, but to check on the job she had done. There was still hair down at the apex of her thighs. Soaping the brush again she put one leg up on the side of the bath and painted more soap down between her legs.

The Master's eyes were rooted to her sex. She looked into his lap, but could not tell whether he was erect. The folds of the cotton robe hid any tumescence. She hoped this was the prelude for him, the ritual that would incite him to take her, the first man to enter her slick, hairless cunt.

Carefully, she stroked the razor over the crease of her sex. She had to bend double to see what she was doing, her leg up, her crotch open. She scraped away at the lather.

The Master let out a tiny, almost inaudible moan.

Melinda reached for the sponge and rinsed away the rest of the lather. She was hairless. It was only now, now it had gone, that she realised how much her pubic hair had covered. Without it, the lips of her sex were clearly defined. Even standing with her legs together, the crease of her sex, at least the first delicate folds of it, was clearly visible. She stared at her sex in the mirror. Now she looked as she had looked as a child.

The Master got up. Melinda could see a clear bulge in the robe. But she could sense too that his mood had changed.

'Dry yourself. Then come into the bedroom. Quickly.' The kindness had gone from his voice. He walked out of the bathroom.

Melinda hastened to obey, taking one of the large bath towels and hoping his mood change was not the result of something she had done. She towelled between her legs, feeling, for the first time, the lack of hair. Her big, puffy labia felt different. She did not look at herself again in the mirror. She slipped back into the red shoes.

In the bedroom, the Master was pacing the thick carpet. The bulge in his robe had disappeared.

'Get over here.' He indicated the bed. What had she

done wrong? His eyes looked at her with anger. 'Lie down on your back.'

She obeyed. The counterpane had been turned back, and the cream-coloured sheets were silk. He came and stood beside the bed, looking down at her naked body. She felt more naked now, the final cloak of modesty shaven away. Her body pulsed. It was a pulse she recognised. Her sex was moistening.

The Master sat on the edge of the bed. *Please touch me, kiss me, take me. Do anything to me*, she wanted to scream. Every nerve in her body ached for contact, wanted her to wrap herself around him, plunge her head on his cock. Make him want her. Every nerve ached for release. The more his eyes looked at her, the more she wanted to touch, to hold, to have.

'I should have had you shaved. You shouldn't have shaved yourself,' he said almost to himself. 'You must do it every morning,' he said to her, 'every morning without fail. Is that clear?'

'Yes, Master.'

Involuntarily, she felt her body inch towards him. It was as though he were a giant magnet pulling her to one side.

'Use this,' he said. From the drawer of the bedside table he took a black dildo. It was a perfect replica of a cock, complete with balls, every detail moulded in hard black plastic. He tossed it on to the bed between her legs.

Oh no, no, she wanted to scream. *Not that. Of all things don't make me wank. Do it to me. Have me tied and bound and spread. Let Marion do it. Or Cybele. Cruel and hard. But not by my own hand, don't give me freedom again. Please, please.* Her eyes begged. This time her hesitation *was* rebellion.

'Melinda. You will obey,' he said.

She saw not anger in his eyes, but sadness. She had displeased him. Immediately, she took the dildo in her hand and scissored her legs open, bending her knees. She had made a mistake. She was thinking of herself, of what she wanted. She wanted not to masturbate, she wanted not to do it for herself. That was wrong, that was her mistake, because it no longer mattered what she wanted in this world. She no longer existed. It was as simple as that. That was what she had forgotten.

Brutally she jammed the dildo up into her cunt. There was no resistance. Her sex was wet. She pushed it up using both her hands, right up until she could feel it at the neck of her womb and the balls were hard against her arse.

This was what he wanted. That was all there was. She would do it because he wanted it, do it as well as she could.

She pulled it back again and felt her body gush with juices. With no subtlety or gentleness, cross with herself for her stupidity, she rammed the dildo to and fro, on the river of her excitement. She had to be excited, she had to excite herself because he wanted that. He wanted to see that.

Using one hand to manipulate the dildo, she ran the other up to her breasts. With all her might she squeezed each breast in turn, then used the long nails of her thumb and finger on her nipples, pinching them hard, so each had a crescent-shaped impression etched into the tender flesh. She wanted to feel the pain, wanted to punish herself.

She repeated the punishment as the dildo reamed into her cunt. But her eyes never left the Master, never stopped watching him as she saw his eyes roaming her body. This was what he wanted.

There was no longer any inhibition. What she was doing suddenly felt like nothing she had ever done before. It was different. It was not an act of freedom, but of submission.

She was coming. All the frustrations of the day were concentrated in her sex. The hard, big dildo filled her cunt. Her breasts and tortured nipples, her clitoris, every nerve in her body, strained for release. The Master's eyes, cool, detached, unblinking, watched the dildo as it sawed in and out of her labia, its shaft glistening with her juices. The first kick of orgasm jerked her body, rolling her eyes closed. Then, instantly, she was falling; falling into a deep black, endless abyss where she could feel only sensation and all conscious thought was gone. Her body was tossed from side to side as the dildo pressed, for the last time, deep inside her.

She lay, eventually, completely still, her hands at her sides, her legs still open. Slowly, inevitably, the dildo slid out of her cunt. The motion jerked her body in an involuntary spasm. She opened her eyes.

Marion stood by the bed. She was taking off her negligée, her long, very black hair flowing over her shoulders. Under the white silk teddy, her body looked exquisite, soft and rich and ripe.

'Leave us,' the Master said, not looking at Melinda. His eyes were fixed on Marion.

Melinda struggled to sit up, her body still lost in the feelings of orgasm, her nerves not coordinated with her muscles yet. Marion was kneeling on the carpet between the Master's knees, her hands caressing his calves.

'Now,' Marion snapped at Melinda. She smiled. It looked like a smile of triumph.

Melinda scrambled off the bed. She headed for the door. She tried not to look, because she knew what she would see, but out of the corner of her eye she saw Marion unwrapping the robe, and her head descending into the Master's lap.

She ran through the bedroom door. Cybele and Selene were waiting. Cybele closed the inner door while Selene cuffed Melinda's hands behind her back. Melinda felt the tears welling in her eyes, but tried to blink them back. The cold metal cuffs were welcome. She strained her wrists against them, wanting to feel them bite into her flesh. She was an object. She should have no feelings. She was there to be used, and she had been. What else did she expect?

Melinda counted the days. Since the evening with the Master, five days had passed. Each day had become routine. She would be woken in the morning by one of the three leather-uniformed chatelaines who would bring her breakfast and supervise her shower and toilet. A razor, shaving bowl and brush had been put in the bathroom, and each morning she shaved. It was necessary. Her pubis sprouted bristles with surprising regularity. They felt different from the fluffy softness Melinda was used to; harsh and wiry. She had become more adept at shaving as the days passed and now her sex was completely smooth, all the little crevices shaved clean, too.

After breakfast, Melinda was given a cotton bra to wear to support her breasts and taken to exercise. The regimen was strict. Each exercise was timed, and she was not allowed to stop until the chatelaine announced her time was up.

Another shower followed. In the afternoon, she would be taken to a solarium. As she was not taken outside, its tanning effect was necessary to maintain her summer colour. Clearly the Master did not want her developing a prison pallor.

The rest of the time she was given a menial task to perform – scrubbing the floor of her cell, or cleaning the bathroom – or left alone, her hands cuffed to the wall, the metal block between her legs.

After five days, Melinda was beginning to lose hope. In some way she had offended the Master. From considering her his favourite, from seeing her as 'perfect' he had, for some reason, lost interest in her. Even the camera in the cell wall seemed to bear testament to his displeasure. Not once had Melinda seen it move. The Master was not watching her anymore.

Neither was Marion. She did not see Marion either, in the days since being summoned to the Master's bedroom.

The only parts of her day that were not predictable were the beatings. They were never done at any set time, nor in any set pattern except that it was always two of the chatelaines together. They were never alone. Some days they would chain her to the wall, her breasts against the plaster, her hands chained so high above her head that she was forced on to the very tips of her toes. In this position they would whip her, alternating their strokes, one standing on one side of her body, the other opposite; her arse assailed from both directions. They never counted the strokes. Sometimes when it was over, they would twist her round to face them, then kiss her, bite at her nipples, penetrate her sex, pinch and maul her.

Then they would leave her. They knew the pain created a need in her body. They would leave her chained to the wall, the metal block placed between her legs, her body stretched, her nerves aching for the relief it would never be allowed to have. Having created the need they left her unable to fulfil it.

Once, after they'd turned her round, Hera and Cybele had lain on the mattress and made love. They had not slipped off their uniforms, just pulled up their skirts and unfastened the studs of the leotards between their legs. With no preliminaries, Cybele had climbed on to Hera's body and positioned her sex above Hera's face, while her mouth had plunged on to Hera's sex. They had lapped eagerly at each other's bodies, squirming and writhing with the pleasure they created, glancing occasionally at the helpless Melinda, smiling tauntingly at her as if to say, 'Don't you wish you could join in?' She did, of course. They knew that. They knew she would have done anything to feel what they were feeling. To be touched. To be had. Instead, all she could do was hang by her hands and watch and listen. Listen to their screams of joy as their bodies exploded in each other's mouths, trembling out of control.

At night, her body ached most. Not from discomfort. Not from the chains that held her or the marks of the whips. It ached for sex. Here in this cell, naked most of the time, waiting for the door to open, there was nothing to do but think of sex. For the first two days they had filled her mind with sexual images she could not forget. But then they had allowed her some release. Now she was allowed nothing. Five days of frustration reinforced by constant attention to, and provocation of, her body and her mind.

It was deliberate. She knew that. All part of a plan. She hoped it was the Master's plan for her. Not just routine. That it was all designed by the Master to make her feel, to make her what he wanted her to be. Not routine. Not what they did to all the women he had trained. Just the same old routine because he could no longer be bothered with her, because he no longer cared. Not that. Please, she prayed at night, when such thoughts plagued her most, please not that.

WITCH QUEEN OF VIXANIA

Morgana Baron

Variety is, according to the proverb, the spice of life, and the Nexus imprint is always looking for new twists on favourite sexual obsessions. *Witch-Queen of Vixania*, and its sequel, *Slave-Mistress of Vixania* are, literally, sexual fantasies yet, other-worldly though Morgana Baron's characters may be, they have more than enough in common with real-life masters, mistresses, slaves and fetishists when sexual and disciplinary matters come to the fore to keep fans of more traditional erotica very happy.

In this extract, the evil Queen Vixia, fearful that her immense power will be wrested from her, resorts to using dark and perverse sexual magic against the rebel Brod. His fleshly diversions with the impossibly servile – and even more agile – Oania are about to be interrupted, but it would seem, in the most pleasurable way.

We've had lots of feedback from the readership who want to know when Nexus will continue the adventures of Vixia and Brod, which began in *Witch-Queen of Vixania. Slave-Mistress of Vixania* is now published and there may be a third book in the series. Sword and sorcery stories with added sex are difficult to get right, but Morgana's knowledge of the genre is impressive and her text sparkles with mystery and magic. She has also written a contemporary erotic novel for Nexus entitled *Rue Marquis de Sade*, which features two sisters: one sweet and sensual, the other sadistic and beautiful, who vie with each other to qualify for their inheritance.

Withdrawn from her own body, for the sake of its sanity, Vixia's Spirit hovered, and watched over the preparations.

Armed with enlarging glasses and fine silver tweezers, Priestesses plucked from Vixia's skin every last tiny body-hair. When they were done, more Priestesses bathed the golden form with soaps and oils. Then they scrubbed it with a fine grit made by grinding the shells of minute sea creatures. When they were finished, every trace of dead skin had been scoured away. Vixia was pristine, pure, and ready to be debauched. Her pale yellow body was covered with steaming cloths, that the pores of her porcelain-fine skin be opened up.

Temple Virgins brought in the pieces of Vixia's bridal raiment, and laid them beside her. The Priestesses shed their robes, and donned protective aprons and gloves. Honey from the Magic Bees was heated in copper vessels, and mixed with the essence of wine made from that same aphrodisiac honey. Although the women worked with averted heads, and held cloths to their faces, the steam of the brew that they prepared brought fiendish lights into their eyes, and many of them walked with thigh rubbing thigh, and twitchy urgent gaits.

The foaming yellow potion was ladled on to the inner surface of each piece of glossy black fabric, and spread to cover every part. Removing the cooling cloths from Vixia's body, they put her boots on her feet and legs, and smoothed the supple leather up to her groin. Next came the gloves, which were formed so finely that once they were fitted, the cuticles of Vixia's nails could be clearly seen. The gloves, too, were long, and stretched even up to her shapely shoulders.

Lying on a black onyx slab, with her limbs encased in a black that was equally glossy, Vixia seemed but a torso, a statue formed from gold, that depicted the very epitome of depraved female beauty.

The hood and mask were one piece that drew down to cover her eyes, leaving only her nose and mouth bare. Her body, even though uninhabited, began to twitch as the magic lotion soaked through her skin, into the hot slow stream of her already tainted blood.

The breastpiece of Vixia's bodice was thicker than the other parts. Inside each perfectly formed cup, rings of flanges accepted her flesh, but having accepted, gripped. Each slow breath massaged her breasts, squeezing subtly from base to nipple, and again, and again, so that the proud spikes engorged more and more, pumped with each inhalation and milked with each breathy sigh.

The seams of the bodice overlapped in the middle of Vixia's back, and when they met, they sealed, never to unseal. When the ordeal was done, and if Vixia survived, she would have to be cut out of the garment, and a new one prepared.

Vixia the Spirit, drifting in arched shadows, felt a tugging from her corporeal form, drawing her down. 'Be quick!' she commanded, though none could hear her discorporate voice.

The last garment was readied. The shape that was to cover Vixia's loins was more than a mere covering. The crotch of the garment was fitted with two hollow spikes, formed from the hardened resin of a tree that grew in the Bee's Valley. One spike was no longer than a man's hand from wrist to fingertip, and slender. The second spike was half as long again, and twice as thick. Warm liquid was poured into each priapic container, before they were introduced into Vixia's most intimate orifices, before and behind.

And then the last garment was sealed in place, and nothing was shown of the Witch Queen save her cruel lips.

With deft speed, the Priestesses stretched out Vixia's encased limbs, and clamped wrists and ankles into the padded manacles that were riveted to each corner of the slab. A broad leather strap was passed across her body, and fixed down. A resinous bulb was inserted between Vixia's teeth, and tied in place with strong thongs. The Priestesses, almost in flight, left Vixia alone.

Vixia's Spirit catapulted down, back into her body – and into a cauldron of lust.

Blind, deaf, and sealed hermetically from all outside sensation, Vixia was wracked with desire. Her body bucked, and writhed. Had her limbs not been constrained, she would have torn her own skin to shreds. Had she not been pinned down by the encircling strap, her arching would have snapped her spine. Had her jaws not been kept apart by the hard black gag, her teeth would have ground on each other, even unto shards.

Her hips juddered on hard stone, driving the rubbery spike deeper into her anus with each thud. Her thighs twitched and her labia squirmed, seeking to suck more of the vaginal impalement into her depths. Her heartbeat became normal, and then fast, and then a fibrillation that would have burst the organ of any lesser woman. Vixia's lips sucked great draughts of air around the hard ball, pumping her chest – and each pump brought more divine prickling agony to the screaming tips of her engorged nipples.

Three – six – nine orgasms, all within moments, carried Vixia to a plane of lust higher than mortal woman knows, but it was only the beginning.

Wracked, grinding, screaming into the darkness, Vixia sweated. Each bead of perspiration dissolved yet more of the essence of honey, and soaked it back into her pores. Each quintessential droplet lifted Vixia higher. She became 'Vixia' no more, but just a living *need*. Her throat thirsted for the savour of male spending. Her coynte, her clit, her vagina, her womb, her arse, her nipples, all hungered!

While at that lofty peak, in an ecstasy beyond ecstasy, Vixia spasmed. Her vagina squeezed. Her rectum clamped. Her jaws bit. The impaling cylinders were compressed, and squirted. The bulb between her teeth jetted ichorous nectar into her mouth. Soaked in the potion, within and without, even the marrow in Vixia's bones demanded and begged.

Elsewhere, elsewhen, elsehow, a thing that was nothing, and everything, felt her need.

And Havoc went to her.

And Havoc entered her.

Havoc went into her mouth, and her coynte, and her anus, and into each of the twenty-seven intricate orifices of her soul.

And what had gone before was as dew on an ocean, for congress with that Aspect lasts an eternity, bringing need upon need, but never satisfaction.

The woman was a strange creature. Brod had offered her a felt cloak for her back, and boots for her feet, but she'd insisted on going naked, except for the iron collar. She'd claimed that going unclad was fitting for a captive, and a slave. What was more, she had insisted on carrying their pack, even though it bowed her down while it would have been no burden for him at all. When the way grew steeper, she had still refused all aid.

'My Lord . . .?' she began.

'I am no "Lord",' Brod interrupted. 'My name is Brod.'

'Lord Brod,' Oania continued, 'must we continue on this path?'

'What? Did you not tell me that yonder mountain pass is the way we must go? And does not this valley lead almost directly to it?'

'A longer path might be safer, Lord Brod.'

'In what wise, "safer"?'

'We near Holy Ground, Lord Brod. Land sacred to The Whore Goddess, Sloona.'

'Are you not in Havoc's service? And is He not mightier than Sloona?'

'I have renounced Havoc, Lord Brod. I was raised in the service of Sloona, in Her Aspect as Concubine and Body-Slave. I was sold into the Temple of Havoc but recently, and am now returned to my true faith.'

Brod scratched his head. The world had become full of puzzles. Women were enigmas. Religion was a tangle. Life had been so much easier when he had been with the Hermit. Except for the itch, of course. It was a curse that the women, who he needed to assuage his needs, brought with them such headaches. 'I see a cleft ahead,' he said. 'It might even be a cave. We will camp there for the night, and you may inform me of your womanly fears.'

It was indeed a cave, a high thin slot in the rock, that receded into darkness. The air within was dank. The cavern's pinkish walls ran with moisture, so Brod made a fire at its opening, and spread fresh bracken to make beds.

'Might there be creatures within?' Oania asked, shivering.

'Cave-bears? I see no spoor, nor do I smell their musk. A pity! If we must climb into mountains, it might be cold. The hide of a cave-bear would make cloaks for us both, and warm boots besides.'

Oania prepared their simple supper, and scoured Brod's wooden platter after they'd eaten. She poured wine from a skin into the brass-bound horn that Brod had received as a parting gift from Leiala, took it to where he sprawled, and knelt by his side to present it.

'Will you bind me before you ravish me, Lord Brod, or after?'

'Ravish? Bind?'

'Am I not your slave, Master Brod? And is it not fitting that a slave, when not about her chores, should be kept strictly tethered, lest she flee? We have little with us, in the way of cord or thong, Lord Brod, but a sufficiency for my ankles at least? And mayhap my thumbs?'

'You said, "ravish"?'

'A Master may use his slave's body, for his pleasure,

either bound or unbound, my Master. If bound, then the female is reduced to a mere toy, to a simple yielding instrument. On the other hand, unbound, some slaves have training in certain arts, and that might please a slave's Master.'

'Certain arts?' Brod asked, his interest beginning to show.

Oania dared to lay a soft hand upon Brod's hairy thigh. 'As I told you, Lord Brod, I was raised to the service of Sloona, Harlot and Hetaera. My training is in the pleasing of men, in all its forms. I can bring a man to his brink, my Lord, and keep him there for as long as it shall be his wish, using hand, or mouth, or coynte, or arse. I am skilled in the revival of slaked lust. My body is supple, that I may bend to my Master's will, no matter what his desire.'

'Supple? How mean you?'

'Would you have me show you, Master?'

Brod settled back into the bracken. 'By all means.'

'Might I have a little wine?'

'Of course you may.'

Oania stood, and dribbled a few crimson drops from Brod's horn on to her right nipple. Smiling down into Brod's eyes, she held the horn aside, and, with her free hand, lifted up her breast as she bent her neck, and so sucked the wine from her nipple.

'I've seen that before,' Brod snorted. 'Often.'

'And this?' Oania asked, tilting the horn once more. A dribble spilled between her breasts, and ran down her slender midriff, to pool in the depth of her navel. Oania bent her head once more, and lapped up the stain from between her breasts. She followed the glistening line, licking as she went, and coiling her body, so that eventually her tongue delved into her navel, and lapped there.

'Er – no,' Brod allowed. 'And if you can . . .?'

'Indeed, yes, My Lord.'

She lay down on her back, across from Brod, and lifted her knees. 'If my Lord would pour?'

Brod scrambled to her. 'Er, where?'

'For now, over my clit, and it please my Lord Brod?'

With a trembling hand, Brod slopped wine over an already engorging ridge. It spilled in two thin streams, following the creases of Oania's groin.

She rolled her body once more, licking the length of her own supple form, down to her navel, and to the lower curve of her belly. Without using either hand to pull herself, she dipped low enough that she nuzzled into her own sweet coynte.

Brod endured the lascivious slurping for a dozen heart-beats before he leapt to his feet and tore off his loincloth.

'A moment, my Lord,' Oania said. 'A supple wand bends two ways, my Lord. If you will permit . . .?'

She unrolled and knelt up. Brod reached out to her breast, but she was bending again, this time backward. Brod was torn – he so wanted to touch, but there was a fascination in her movements.

And she bent yet further, and further again, until her hair brushed the ground between and behind her knees. Still she folded. Her face appeared between her knees, between her thighs, and at last the back of her neck was tight up against her own groin.

Bracing herself on her knees and the palms of her hands she looked up at Brod and gasped, 'If you will hold me, my Lord Brod, in this position my mouth is yours, and my coynte. It would honour me if your cock . . .'

She said no more, for Brod had knelt before her, wrapped his great hands about her hips, and surged into her coynte. A woman less skilled might well have failed the onslaught, but Oania was well trained. The fit was tight, but not impossible. Brod pulled her to him, until he was sheathed to the hilt. Oania reached out and grasped his thighs, so that she might pull her head just that little further forward, and be able to . . .

Brod gasped. In his time at the inn he had enjoyed congress with one woman while the other had laved his swaying scrotum with her mouth, but he had never dreamed that he might ever enjoy those two sublime attentions simultaneously, from just one woman.

He withdrew, slowly. Oania's tongue licked the underside of his cock as it unsheathed! The ecstasy was so great that Brod froze, but Oania did not. She pulled on Brod's thighs, rocking on the fulcrum of her bended knees, and then pushed, and pulled, and . . .

Brod didn't move. He didn't need to. She – the wonderful slave-bitch – was fucking him! And her mouth – she nibbled and licked and sucked so avidly that his cock scarcely knew which pleasurable torment it craved the most: mouth or coynte.

Faster she rocked, and faster. Brod felt the pressure build. The vein beneath his cock was pulsing, and it was so close, so close.

And Oania pulled back, snatched up with one hand, and brought Brod's erupting, fountaining, jetting cock to her mouth. The plum had grown too large for her lips to encompass, but she could press her mouth to its puckering eye, as in a kiss, and *suck* the boiling jism out of him.

Brod fell on to his back. Oania, in a spasm of joy, uncoiled with a leap, and coiled again still standing, so that her arse was presented to Brod with her face between her thighs once more, grinning at him upside-down.

'Now all three paths to Paradise are presented,' she smirked. 'My Master's choice?' Her fingers pulled the cheeks of her arse wide, presenting a tight-clamped rosebud, that relaxed even as Brod stared at it. The thumbs of those same hands tugged the puffy sweetmeat that bulged backwards between widespread thighs, and exposed the slick-pink inner surfaces. Oania's tongue flicked its own subtle invitation as her mouth formed an 'o'.

Brod took a step, torn with delicious indecision.

Deep within the cave, something grated.

Oania uncurled. 'What . . .?'

Brod said, 'A rock moves. That is all.'

'It sounded like the creaking of some gigantic gate, or the swing of a cyclopean door.'

Brod laughed. 'A door? But who . . .?'

Three figures stepped out of the cave's depths. Oania

fell to her knees and pressed her forehead to the ground. 'O Sloona . . .'

'No, child,' the centre one said. 'We are not the Aspects of Sloona. We are but succubi, from the Nether Regions, and formless until summoned.'

'But . . .?'

'Our mission is but the pleasure of those who summon us, my child. What other forms would we take, than those most pleasing? Your desires are writ large, child. Your lust is firstly for this man, and secondly for the Goddess whom you serve. The man is here, and now is come the forms at least of One who is Three, and for whom you have lusted since but a maiden. Are you not happy? Is there anything of our shapes that is less than your dreams?'

Oania stared at the three elementals. The one who called her 'child' was shaped as Sloona the Mate. Of middle height, she had tousled brown tresses that reached down to the small of her back. Her age appeared to be that of a young matron, mature enough for motherhood, yet lusty and wise. Her breasts were formed for suckling, yet still proud and firm. Her waist was between sturdy and slender, and her hips flared dramatically, so that strength and voluptuousness were happily married in her form. Pure love radiated from her soft brown eyes, but that purity was spiced by a broad streak of carnal lickerishness. The nature of Sloona the Mate was that of the ideal spouse, or sometimes the perfect lover of women. Loyal was she, and supportive, but still playful and always ready for bawdy romps. Sloona the Mate took equal pleasure in the giving and the taking of carnal joy. She wore a robe that, if gathered and fastened, would have been modesty itself. It was instead loose, and open at the front from throat to thigh.

To her right stood Sloona the Mistress. Half a head taller than her sister, she seemed taller yet, for on her feet were glossy black leather boots, with heels so high that her naked thighs were tensed for balance, and her midnight hair was drawn up through a golden fillet, into an inky plume. There was a choker about her throat, matching her boots, but spiked with bronze prongs the size and length of sabre-tooth tusks. Apart from boots and choker, and the short whip that hung on a thong from her wrist, she was naked.

The Mistress's eyes were black, and luminous, and imperiously slanted beneath vicious brows. Her skin was white as moonlight, smooth as still water. Her form was slender, but her breasts, tipped with nipples like chips of black coal, were jutting globes, as if they had been formed for the body of a much larger female.

The third succubus, in the form of Sloona the Slave, stood a modest pace behind her Sisters. The shortest, and most slender of the three, had pale blonde hair that cascaded down behind her knees. Her head was bowed, as if in shame at her nudity, but she was unable to shield herself, for her wrists were bound behind her and her arms were tethered to her sides. The softness of her tender skin was grooved by cords that encircled her a dozen times. Each one pulled cruelly tight, so that diamonds of raised flesh bulged between their crossings. The wicked bonds furrowed the natural creases of the Slave's groin, and held back the helpless one's shoulders, so that she could neither close her thighs' forced parting, nor relax her shoulders. They too were pulled back, lifting small, childlike breasts as if to offer their delicacy to the most vicious fingers.

Oania was moved to pity, and to lust. Untied, the Slave would surely be left marked by those bonds. Such welts would call for the comforting of a tongue's caress. Oania licked her lips. Much as she craved that gentle task, there was also a part of her that lusted to pull the cords tighter yet, and cut deeper into that luscious soft innocence.

'Would you have us change our forms?' Sloona the Mate prompted.

'Why are you come to us?' Oania asked.

'For your pleasure,' the Slave whispered.

'For *my* pleasure,' the Mistress snapped.

'That we might all enjoy each other,' the Mate said.

Oania took one faltering step. The Mistress cracked her whip against the side of her boot. 'Here!' she ordered.

Brod scratched his head, uncertain whether or not this was some subtle magical attack, or an unwelcome interruption of his enjoyment of Oania.

But the Mate was at his side, drawing him down onto the bed of bracken. 'Toy with my breasts, please, Brod,' she asked, 'and we will watch the sport even as we dally together.'

Brod found himself sprawled upon his back with one arm wrapping the Mate's buxom body and one large-nippled breast nuzzling into his palm. The Mate's legs were spread; one covered his thighs with its humid warmth. A hand, capable but soft-skinned, half-encircled his cock, and stroked it gently. If this is an attack, he thought, then I am defeated. He cupped the fulsome breast, squeezed gently as his thumb found its peak, and stroked.

The sound of whip on flesh pulled his gaze to Oania and the Mistress. Oania was on her knees before the regal one, her face burrowing avidly. The Mistress had bent her knees and parted her thighs, lewdly. One hand tangled in Oania's hair, drawing her close. The other hand wielded the whip, slashing it down behind Oania, and urging her efforts with blows across her buttocks.

Oania writhed her arse backwards, welcoming the sting. She thrust her face forward the harder with each blow, as if she sought to spike her tongue to the Mistress's very core. The Mistress bucked at Oania's face, spreading her coynte's lips wide across willing cheeks. Just when it seemed to Brod that the Mistress must surely reach her straining climax, the Bitch-Goddess wrenched Oania's face away from its treat.

Oania writhed against the tugging, stretching out her tongue and mewing piteously.

'Be still!' the Mistress commanded.

Oania obeyed, yet still gazed at the puffy and drooling lips that she craved with abject longing. The Mistress released Oania, and turned partly towards Brod and the Mate, so that her sex was exposed fully to them. Brod felt his cock twitch at the sight. In his young life he had seen but five coyntes, and none of them had been formed quite like this one. The lips of the coyntes that he had pleasured, and tasted, had all been tight. The Mistress's coynte-lips, however, hung loose, like engorged curtains, bracketing a slot of such lividity that the flesh seemed almost to glow. Above that gaping wound, riding a mound as bulbous as a young girl's breast, was a ridge as thick and as long as a maiden's middle finger. The length of clit that had emerged, sucked out from beneath its hood by Oania's avid lips, was one joint of that maiden's finger, but pulsing and angry, and smooth as wet satin.

The Mistress jerked Oania's head around, so that it was sideways on to Brod.

'Take this,' she ordered Oania, handing her the whip. The handle of that cruel instrument had been formed into the shape of a cock. Understanding the command, Oania took the whip, and fumbled its bulbous knob between the Mistress's gaping flesh. The Mistress jerked down. The head of the whip disappeared into soft humidity.

'Deeper!'

Oania obeyed.

'Your mouth,' the Mistress barked, 'make it small.'

Oania pursed her lips, leaving just a narrow gap between them.

The Mistress took a two-fingered grip on her own clit, and rubbed, much as a man might masturbate. Incredibly, it grew still longer. The Mistress directed the miniature cock into the gap between Oania's lips, commanded, 'Grip,' and began to fuck Oania's face.

Brod groaned. The Mate turned in his arms and put a soft palm to the back of his neck. 'Kiss me, my darling,' she said. 'Kiss me, and pluck at my nipple, if it please you.'

Brod's mouth found the Mate's, but he did not close his eyes. Beyond her he could still see the obscene exhibition of Oania having her mouth ravished while thrusting the whip upwards into the Mistress's eager slot. With a warm mouth on his, and a hot wet tongue probing and sporting; and a firm breast in his hand, while a hand stroked so very gently at his manhood . . . With so lewd a lesbian coupling before his burning eyes – what greater pleasure could there have been?

And then a moist softness engulfed his great toe, and a squirmy slithery thing slotted itself between that toe and the next. Sloona the Slave, still tightly bound, was kneeling at his feet, and worshipping him with her mouth.

The Mate, feeling Brod's reaction, pulled back, and smiled down at the grovelling Slave. 'Shall we use her, for our pleasure?' she asked Brod.

'What? How?'

'If you will leave this to me, my love?'

Brod nodded, speechless. His ears were full of the intoxicating gobbling sounds that came from Oania's voracious mouth, and the sharp squeals that told him that the Mistress too, was being well pleased.

The Mate rolled Brod on to his back, and bestrode his massive chest. With a playful grin, she pinned his great forearms above his head, and said, 'You are my prisoner, my love. Let me see to your pleasure now, and later you must serve me in like fashion. Is it agreed?'

Brod nodded again.

The Mate sat up to throw off her robe, and bent forward once more, dangling one luscious breast above Brod's mouth.

'Suckle on this, my love.'

Brod obeyed, sucking one large brown nipple as deeply into his mouth as he could. His lips encircled a third part of the Mate's breast, and his tongue flickered its erotic message across the pulsating nub. The Mate writhed her body, sliding the open heat of her coynte across Brod's skin. She twisted, drawing the treat from his mouth, and lifted it on her palm to his eyes.

'You see, my love? See the marks of your passion? My teat is engorged to bursting, and grooved by the gnawing of your naughty teeth.'

'Did I hurt you?' Brod apologised.

'Such a delicious pain that the other craves its fair share,' the Mate assured him, and thrust her second breast into his eager mouth. 'Bite me, my love! Nibble and suck, sweet man. Your pleasure excites me more than you can know – see!' She took his hand, and drew it down to where her wetness was scalding his skin, and rubbed the splay of her coynte feverishly across his open palm.

Brod fumbled, and felt his fingers slip into her.

'Yesss!' she hissed. 'Make me ready for you! Open me wide.

Bouncing on his stabbing fingers, slapping his face with the swing of her breasts, the Mate made a signal behind her, to the Slave.

Brod felt the slurping mouth leave his toe, and the sudden shock of night air on his wet skin. The Slave humped her body forward, awkward without the use of her tightly-bound arms, and wriggled until her own core was above Brod's foot. With an urgent slithering motion, she squatted lower, rotating her slender hips. Brod's toe felt new heat; it was more intimate than before. The Slave grunted as she thrust down, impaling her tender young coynte.

Brod pushed his foot up and crossed the other one over, so that while one toe fucked the girl, the other was able to rub up against her clit.

A strangled gasp made Brod turn his head. The Mistress and Oania had completed their former sport. Now Oania was kneeling on all fours with the Mistress riding her back, facing Oania's uptilted arse. Those luscious quivering globes were criss-crossed with fresh welts, but it was not the bite of the lash that had brought the cry to her lips. The Mistress was using the handle of her whip once more, in urgent buggery of a victim who sobbed with each deep stabbing – sobs of joy.

Brod's cock, already erect, reared yet higher, and slapped the rear of the loving Mate. The Mate wriggled back, and hissed over her shoulder to the Slave, 'Be of service, girl, or there'll be no whipping for you this night.'

The Slave bowed down, without disimpaling herself, and drew the tender pink points of her breasts in a subtle caress across the skin of Brod's iron thigh. Her mouth found the base of his cock, between his arse and his dangling scrotum, and kissed it wetly.

The Mate shimmied back, still kneeling, until the head of Brod's cock nudged at the gaping maw of her coynte. Then she thrust. Half of his length entered that boiling tunnel. The Mate braced, and pushed harder. Brod's foreskin was peeled back. The naked bulbous head slithered over smoothness and soft corrugations, and pushed aside fleshly barriers, until Brod's manhood was engulfed entire.

'You are big, my man,' the Mate gasped. 'I am bloated with the breadth of your weapon. You are so deep within me that my waist is thickened around your girth. Hold fast, my love, and we shall bring you to your climax.'

'Hold . . .' But she covered his mouth with her own, smothering his words and thrusting them back with her probing tongue.

Brod tensed. The Slave was rocking now, stroking as much of his manhood as she could reach, with the flat of her tongue. The Mate stabbed her tongue into his mouth in a lascivious rhythm, and squeezed her vaginal muscles in counterpoint. Her coynte was milking him. Her breasts swayed, drawing lines of fire across his chest with their turgid points. The Slave lapped, and her nipples also drew their erotic pictures on his skin. Two coyntes convulsed; one about his toe, and the other around the thickness of his cock. The squealing of Oania's delight assailed his ears. Brod felt that he *had* to thrust – he *had* to . . .

But he didn't have to at all. The sucking strength of the Mate's preternatural vagina drew the seed up from out of his balls, without his moving. Boiling, the sweet sensation gushed up, and up. Brod felt the liquid explosion as his jism burst forth into the very deepest recess of the Mate's spasming and writhing vaginal passage.

The tension slumped out of his body. Relaxed, his head rolled to one side. Across the clearing, in the flickering firelight, Oania and her unnatural Mistress were still in erotic congress. Oania was resting all of her weight upon her shoulders, with her body uplifted. The Mistress bestrode her. Each woman had her legs spread in the manner of forked branches, and the forks were interlocked. The Mistress held Oania's ankles, and writhed down, grinding her coynte against that of her victim, flicking her engorged giant clitoris against the smaller, but no less engorged, clit beneath her.

Brod's cock, which had flopped against his thigh like a defeated python, stirred. The Mate lifted herself up, reversed, and squatted over Brod's face. Likewise, the Slave turned herself around, presenting the cordbound globes of her young haunches for Brod's caress. Two mouths nuzzled at Brod's weapon. Brod knew what he must do. He pulled the Mate's rear down to his mouth, and sucked a bruised and enpurpled coynte-lip into it. His free hand fumbled, until his fingers found the sites of both of the Slave's nether orifices. Gentle with the Mate, vicious with the Slave, Brod mumbled coynte, and stabbed two fingers each into the anus and coynte of the submissive one.

Come the dawn, while a weary Brod slowly buggered the still-bound slender arse of the Slave, the Mate conjured up a fine repast for their breakfast. Brod, Oania, the Mistress and Mate, all fell to, with an appetite. The Slave was fed at the others' whim; sometimes receiving titbits from their fingers, or from their mouths, and sometimes being forced to delve with her tongue for grapes that had fallen between the lips of a coynte. When they were done, the Mate smeared the grease from the silver platter along the length of Brod's cock.

'What is this?' he protested. 'My ladies, I am not immortal. I doubt I can serve again, not without some rest at least.'

'There is no time for rest, sweet Brod,' the Mate said. 'My Sisters and I have communed, in our fashion, and have a confession to make to you.'

'A confession?'

'Aye. We were sent to you, not by chance, but at the request of one who would do you harm, to delay your journey. Brod – for more millennia than you could understand, it has been the pleasure of my Sisters and I to lie with mortals, male and female, for our own amusement. In all that time, never have we coupled with one so mighty, nor so satisfying. We are overcome by pity, that so fine an instrument of lust might be destroyed, in part by our hands. This meal must be our farewell. Whatever your quest, we wish you well of it.'

'But why . . .' Brod indicted the slick length of his cock.

'As part of our farewell. When we arrived, we spoiled your coupling with your slave. She has decided that she will serve us, in our Infernal home, for the rest of her days. Do not deny her this, we pray you, Brod, but give her to us willingly.'

'But she is my only guide . . .'

'No need of guide, Brod. March towards the morning sun, and you will reach your goal. Trials beyond the bearing of normal men await you, Brod, but we feel that you will prevail. Perhaps – when your battle is won, you might find time to visit us once more, and tell us the tale of it?'

'Willingly, and by then my cock will be revived, mayhap.'

The Mate grinned. 'It is fitting that you and your slave exchange gifts, at this parting. Oania?'

Oania reached up to her throat, and loosened her iron collar. 'More bonds await me, Brod,' she said. 'Heavier, and more restricting. Take this, in remembrance of me, your willing slave.' So saying, she clasped the iron circle about Brod's forearm, which was as thick as her neck, and so well fitted.

'But what can I give you in exchange?' Brod asked. 'I have nothing but my staff and the cloak I wear.'

'A fitting gift for a parting slave,' the Mistress smiled. 'Bow down, Oania.'

The Mate urged Brod to his feet: Oania knelt before him, her face upturned beneath his limp cock, as if awaiting a kiss. Sloona the Slave, in her turn, knelt behind him.

'I have no strength left,' Brod protested, as he felt the Slave's hot wet tongue-tip probe at the knot of his anus.

'You will come, just this once more,' the Mistress snarled, and slapped his right buttock with her whip.

Shocked, Brod's sphincter relaxed. The Slave's tongue slithered, and entered. Despite his doubts, Brod's cock reared, half erect.

'That's it, my love,' the Mate encouraged. Kneeling beside Oania, she took Brod's cock, and rubbed its tip over her breasts. It twitched, and rose a fraction higher. The Mate lifted up one spike-tipped breast, and pulled back on Brod's foreskin. The engorged nipple and the slowly strengthening cock were brought together. With studied concentration, the Mate prodded her nipple's tip into the eye of Brod's cock.

'Kiss me!' the Mistress ordered.

Brod twisted sideways, and took the dominant Sister's lithe waist in the curve of his arm. She cupped his face in her two hands, and held it. Her mouth breathed spicy moist air into his. Her tongue lapped out. This kiss was different from any Brod had enjoyed before. Her mouth did not touch his; only her tongue stretched out, lapping. Brod parted his lips, and let his own tongue reach out. There was a perversion to this tongue-play, this deliberate teasing, that . . .

'Yes,' the Mate sighed. Brod's cock was rigid and burning between her palms. She stroked with long slithery grease-slick strokes. The Slave, behind Brod, wriggled her cord-bound body so that her nipples might graze the backs of his knees. The Mistress drank from his tongue. Oania gazed up, in adoring expectation. The Mate pumped harder. Her palms were slick along the hot flesh pole, slick and frantic.

It was impossible, after an entire night of endless coupling, but Brod felt his thighs begin to tremble. The Slave's panting breath tickled his scrotum. The Mistress was masturbating again. Brod could not see the feverish frotting of her fingers, but the liquid sounds were unmistakable.

'Yes,' he sighed into the Mistress's mouth.

'Yes,' the Slave whimpered.

'Give it to her,' the Mate urged, smoothing two oily thumbs across his glans at the end of each upstroke.

Oania stretched her mouth open to its widest. Brod's hips jerked, pulling the Slave's tongue free, and he came!

A great gout of creamy spending flopped across Oania's face. Grinning in delight, she scooped the precious fluids from her cheeks, and lapped it up out of her cupped palms. With her lips smeared with sticky strands, she lifted her eyes up to Brod and sobbed, 'Thank you, oh my Master. A million thanks, from your most devoted slave.'

JENNIFER'S INSTRUCTION

Cyrian Amberlake

The extraordinary novel, *Jennifer's Instruction*, features a young, bright and intensely curious girl whose Initiation into the mysterious world of ritualistic corporal punishment by a learned professor and his elegant wife, is documented in detail and with painful clarity.

She learns at first hand about the Devices of discipline, the Areas of her body on which punishment may be inflicted and the Positions that she must adopt to receive chastisement. An eager and willing pupil, she nevertheless makes frequent errors which earn her extra strokes, and cannot help but wonder whether the Initiation will never end. In this extract, Jennifer watches as Marion, the Professor's recalcitrant maid, is punished with the Hairbrush, knowing that a similar fate awaits her.

Cyrian Amberlake's debuts, *The Domino Tattoo*, has been hailed as a classic work of modern erotica, both by the readership and by numerous established and respected authors in the genre. All three titles in the *Domino* series have been reprinted and continue to enchant and arouse readers new to and familiar with erotic writing. *Forum* magazine said, 'Eroticism oozes from every page of Cyrian's books', and we sincerely hope that one day we shall see new work from this genuinely talented author of stories specialising in imaginative erotic punishment.

'The Plump Bottom tempts the disciplinarian to spank always by Hand,' the Professor said, regretfully, as the maid's sobs came under control. He fondled the bottom on his lap, as a contented person might fondle a pet animal. 'Well, you have seen what little good that did,' he said, picking up the brush again. 'Hold her legs, please,' he told me.

I reached tentatively for her ankles.

'No,' he said. 'Get down on your knees, on the floor, and put your arms around her feet. Place yourself where no detail will escape you.'

Obeying these instructions, I found the prescribed position and brought my face very close indeed, closer than I had ever thought possible, to the young woman's bottom. Her cleft was a dark valley ending in a tuft of soft hair as dark as a cocker spaniel's coat, around which the two swelling hills of her buttocks seemed to glow with many different shades of red: from shrimp pink to maroon. Marion, in that region, smelt rather noticeably of piss, and I hoped very much that wetting yourself was not the next stage after bursting into tears.

'A library out of order is an invitation to Chaos!' lectured the Professor, somewhere up above my head.

It was alarming how close the Hairbrush now whistled past the end of my nose. Although I could not help blinking as it smacked down, I squeezed Marion's round calves tightly to my breasts and proudly held up my head. It was exhilarating, like going for a ride at the fair, where your body instinctively feels in danger while inside you know perfectly well you are safe, protected by a mechanism of unerring accuracy. The Professor would not mind me thinking of his right arm in that way, I decided; and he would not miss Marion and hit me on the nose with the Hairbrush, no, not if he spanked the poor young woman until he could spank no more.

I hoped he would not have to do that; spank her for that long, I mean. I already felt a little sorry for her. Nasty as the Hairbrush obviously was, I could not wish it on her to keep it off my own bottom. Nor, I thought a little anxiously as Marion's spanking went on and on, would I like the Professor to become unable to fulfil his obligation to me because of having to see to her.

As if he had sensed my moment of doubt, the Professor promptly threw down the brush on the bed and, grabbing the little maid by the hips, lifted her up in the air. I let go of her at once, of course, swaying back out of reflex and grabbing at the bed to hold myself upright.

The Professor set the still wailing young woman down on her knees on the floor next to me, with only his right leg between us. She knelt there facing him between his own knees, which were now spread wide as the cut of his flannels would permit.

Though I was not as close to the site as I had been ten seconds previously, it was obvious to me that the Professor was once again – or more probably still, given the speed with which events had developed – afflicted with a very prominent erection. It became more than prominent a moment later: it became evident. The fly of the Professor's flannels was fastened with a zip, which he had opened, freeing the proud growth itself to breathe the air of its master's bedroom.

I could not restrain a gasp of admiration. How magisterially the phallus jutted from his groin! Uncircumcised, its shaft was as muscular and graceful as the neck of an antelope; while its glans, scarcely peeping yet from its fragrant sleeve, was the very shape and sheen of the helmet of Achilles, or some other hero of ancient renown.

'You may express your gratitude for this correction, Marion,' said the Professor in the most noble tone.

Sniffing only slightly now, the girl raised her curly head, and removed her hands from her vivid bottom, where they had fled. Her cap was hanging down over one ear and she reached up to reposition it. Clearly she had performed this service for her master before. How tenderly my hand itched to reach out and help her as she fumbled with her hair-grip!

The maid now approached her face, opening her mouth, not grossly wide, I noticed, like a child gobbling candy-floss, but in a decorous O just large enough to receive the Professor's swollen member. Yet dutiful as all her movements were, I had been close enough, my face on a level with her own, to notice the grimace of distaste she had to suppress as she received that gift. I was sad then, to think she was unhappy in her duties.

For a servant, especially a young, pretty, female servant, may be called upon to do many things, and must always be cheerful and willing. She must love her employment, since it is hers and no other's, and brighten the dull mops and dish-rags of domestic service with a ready smile. The Professor recommends a certain hymn of George Herbert's to be learnt by heart, exulting in housework and the spirit of devotion. Privately I imagine Mr Herbert in a skirt and pinny, trembling as he polishes the mistress's thigh-length boots.

With such a master and mistress, I thought, so eminent and yet so condescending, it should have been easy for Marion too to be devoted; to do at once and gladly all that she was bidden, even while, at this moment or that, she might have preferred to be elsewhere. To be found wanting and summarily spanked could of course never be pleasant, but discipline must always be taken in the spirit in which it is given, if the subject is to get the benefit of it. And then, after such a discipline, to be granted the sudden and overwhelming benison of the Professor's virile member to suck – should that not assuage all pain? Yet how she laboured over it, her cheeks red as apples with straining at it. To her it seemed as much of a chore as the spanking itself.

What a marvel the great man was. Was there no end to his resources, I asked myself dizzily. I was impressed beyond measure at the inspiration of his decision to relieve what I could only think must have become a very uncomfortable physical condition – and to relieve it in a way that sealed, so to speak, and reinforced the very discipline that had produced the condition in the first place!

Suddenly the Professor's eyes, which had been closed in dreamy intellectual meditation, opened and fell upon me: upon my eager face so close to the fount of his pleasure.

'Oh, no,' he said lazily. 'That won't do at all. In the corner, girl.'

I went at once obediently and faced the wall, my hands linked on top of my head. I was hardly sorry to be denied sight of such an awesome event. To be granted the opportunity – to be actually required and commanded – to perform such an intimate personal service for the Professor himself! To have his hands – his Hands – resting on your shoulders, caressing the back of your head while you worked! I doubted very much whether Marion appreciated the true honour that was being pressed upon her, into her, within her very lips, even now behind my back. How could she gobble him in such a heavy and ungrateful manner? Did she not know what a great man her master was? Had she never listened to him on the radio?

I heard a small grunt which I recognised immediately as signalling the Professor's delight.

In my mind's eye now, as clearly as though some convenient periscope had suddenly dropped from the bedroom ceiling, I seemed to see Marion's shoulders freeze and her bottom stop bobbing. Her mop of wild red hair would give five little jerks, or six – or more! – as though some invisible hand was spanking her still; and now the Professor would be withdrawing, glistening wet and perhaps already shrinking visibly. Silently I thanked him for directing my eyes away, for I could not wish ever to shame him by looking upon his mighty organ in detumescence. Behind me, a rustling sound announced, clear as any commentary, that the little maid had lifted her apron to envelop him and wipe him dry.

There was some shuffling of feet, the rustle of clothing being rearranged, the swift tiny buzz of a zip being fastened. Then I heard the words of Marion's dismissal.

'Now take my compliments to your mistress, girl,' the Professor said, 'and ask her will she please, as a matter of some importance, see that you learn the letters of the English alphabet, in the exact order which it pleased our noble ancestors first to arrange them.'

'Yes, sir,' said Marion uncertainly. She sounded a little subdued now, I thought. Then she asked: 'What about the PVC, sir?'

'Damn the PVC,' replied the philosopher succinctly. 'Attend to the ABC!'

I heard the hard little shoes hurry across the floor, and then the sound of the bedroom door closing. There had been no time for Marion to inspect herself in the giant mirror as she went; nor had she even asked the master's permission to do so. I could not understand how a woman could be so uninterested in the effects of a punishment that had seemed to me quite thorough. With more than a little pity in my heart for her, I thought perhaps young Marion was not altogether suited to her job.

The Professor sat, no doubt, on the bed still, laughing softly. I could almost see him shaking his head over the girl. Beneath his breath, he began to whistle a little tune.

Uncomfortably I realised that at some time in the last five minutes my vagina had began to seep again, all down my leg, while my heart was pounding like a sprinter's. My ears burned hot as match-heads as with shame I understood. I was jealous! So handsome was the Professor, so much already did I admire and wish to please him, I had even begun to envy his household staff! How stupid I must be. No matter how devoted and willing the pupil, no matter how ready to abase herself in the cause of learning, the simple domestic chores poor Marion had to perform would be forever beneath her.

'Jennifer,' called the Professor. 'Come here, please.'

'She will masturbate now,' said the Professor idly.

'She is young,' I said, instinctively impelled to excuse her.

The Professor snorted good-humouredly. 'She will do it whether she wants to or not,' he said, 'for my wife's pleasure.'

I was unsure how to respond to this. Was it a confidence he was imparting to me? What lesson did he mean me to derive from it?

'If she doesn't come off quickly, to use a suitably Lawrencian phrase, her mistress will do it for her.'

Now that startled me altogether. 'You're both so generous to her!' I exclaimed. Then I blushed slightly. It was wrong of me to make reference to the act he had forbidden me to witness.

'It is important,' the Professor said, toying with the Hairbrush, 'to give servants gifts and favours. That's the way you inspire devotion in them, you see.'

So it was as I'd suspected. The maid had neither the will nor the heart to aspire to discipline for her own sake. For the treatment she'd received, though she had thoroughly deserved it, her employers had to compensate her. She would not be satisfied with the wonderful gift of the Professor's emission, which she obviously didn't treasure, but had to have a clitoral spasm of her own.

'They have ways they use, to reduce the pain,' he said. 'Some go for anaesthetic, would you believe? Drugs and ointments of several kinds. Cold compresses have their adherents, who quote Victorian authorities, governesses' handbooks and the like. The daughters of the upper classes, and, no doubt, many a sly kitchen-maid, were formerly accustomed to rub themselves with butter.' He smiled indulgently at me where I stood before him, my hands still on my head. He knew I would appreciate this shocking extravagance.

'I myself,' he said, 'agree with my wife. She discovered the principle in her early years, and I have found it affirmed in memoirs of more than one brothel-keeper.'

He spoke this surprising phrase with nonchalance, but with his bright enquiring eyes still fixed upon mine as if to gauge the tenor of my response.

'Wisdom and good sense can appear in the strangest of places!' I said, rather faintly.

'It is orgasm that provides the most effective relief,' said the Professor, 'for the pain of corporal punishment.'

I felt my blush deepen. In my energetic and erratic fancies, I had rather missed the point again.

'I suppose it exercises the rigid tissue,' I said, in the rather off-handed way of someone who pretends to knowledge she doesn't actually possess.

'Oh, certainly,' said the Professor, to my gratitude. He put the brush aside and plucked at the knees of his flannel trousers. I was aware of the warm sharp reek of Marion's hind-quarters, perhaps tinged with the whiff of the Professor's own rich and creamy effusion, still lingering in the air.

'Wouldn't it be very wrong, though,' I asked, adopting the Socratic method, 'for a subject who had deserved punishment to try to relieve the pain herself?'

'Oh, doubtless,' said the Professor. For a moment I began to suspect he was making fun of me.

'The pain is the point, surely?' I said, stubbornly.

'Oh no, my dear,' said the Professor pedantically. 'The discipline is the point.'

I felt rather confused. I suppose that since I was still little more than halfway through my initiation, I could not expect to understand the mystery completely.

One thing, however, was clear in my mind.

'Professor?' I said. 'May I have permission to make a small – ' my blush, so newly cooled and faded, returned in force ' – exhibition of myself?' I finished.

'By all means, Jennifer,' the Professor said graciously.

'Thank you, sir.'

I took off my blouse again. 'I haven't got an apron,' I

said, 'but perhaps this – ' I wrapped the sleeves of the blouse around my waist ' – will be acceptable?'

I tied the sleeves together in the small of my back, then spread the blouse on the bed. I picked up the Hairbrush and put it on the blouse. Holding the blouse stretched out in front of me and curtseying carefully with bowed head, I offered the brush to my tutor.

'What makes you think I'd use that on you?' he asked, jocosely.

Startled again, I looked up.

'That's a Junior Hairbrush,' he said, taking it out of my makeshift apron and tossing it on the floor. I thought it looked quite senior enough to me. Then he pulled my blouse itself off me, bundled it up and threw it all the way over to the far side of the bed.

I was surprised that a gentleman who set such store by orderliness could perform such careless and cavalier acts. Then I realised of course that he had done them on purpose, to give Marion an extra task or two when she came to clean the bedroom next: tasks that could not help but remind her sharply of her punishment.

'Come downstairs,' said the Professor. 'That's where we keep the big girls' Hairbrush.' And he raised his eyebrows in a rather arch and unnerving way.

I said a silent, regretful farewell to all the other rooms on the top floor, whose doors had remained closed to me. At the same time, I felt that the study was perhaps where a new pupil more properly belonged; far away from the painful sight of such ignominious domestic mishaps as the bedroom had shown to me. If we had not gone up there in the first place, I reflected, the incident would never have occurred; and whatever its educational value, I felt sure Marion would have been happier to forego it.

I looked again at the paintings hanging on the staircase as we went down, and noticed that yes indeed, sexual arousal and satisfaction was an element of several of them, sometimes featuring in places and on occasions where the innocent spectator might be surprised to see it. I felt no less guilty for oozing as I had, sure that the properly disciplined young woman should aspire to a state of purity and clarity above such sordid bodily reflexes. I was sorry that the punishment of my bottom in particular, and then Marion's in addition, should have caused the Professor his own inconvenience. How calmly and gracefully, though, he had dealt with it!

We returned downstairs to the study, where the solemn tick of the grandfather clock welcomed us. The Professor threw another shovel of coal on the grate, reviving the ailing fire. I lingered by the notice-board in my bra, looking at my skirt and knickers, and wondering how I was to retrieve my blouse before I left the house. Perhaps the Professor's wife would let me pop up and fetch it; she knew what it was like for a woman to have to go around inadequately dressed.

'Sir?' I said, looking next at the Prospectus.

'What's that, Jennifer?'

'May I have permission to tick off Slipper, sir?'

'Oh, yes, girl, of course,' he said expansively.

I looked at the remaining words. 'But not Couch, I suppose, sir.'

The Professor straightened, wiping coal-dust from his hands. 'Couch?' he echoed.

Already I was wishing I hadn't mentioned it. 'Yes, sir,' I said, after a pause.

'Couch: Cushion or Couch: Knees Up?' he asked.

I still was not sure exactly what either of those might mean. 'No, sir,' I said. 'I don't know, sir,' I said.

'You concede that you have not yet experienced either of those Positions?' he asked, holding the palms of his hands to the fire.

'Yes, sir,' I said.

He feigned surprise. 'You have?'

'No, sir,' I said. 'I concede.'

He turned away from me. The dancing firelight gave his face a ruddy glow, and gilded the ends of his hair.

'Put ten more strokes on the list, Jennifer,' he commanded.

'Oh, what for, sir?' I cried, startled and dismayed. 'I'm

sorry, sir,' I said, before he could have a chance to reproach me. 'I mean, may I have permission to ask a question, sir, Socratically – ' I found myself playing with my hair, and took my hand away quickly ' – only I think a well-disciplined subject ought to do her best to understand her punishment, so as not to make the same mistake twice, sir.'

'You said no to me, Jennifer,' said the Professor, lightly.

I was appalled. 'When, sir?'

'In the bathroom,' he reminded me. 'I told you I would finish washing your nether parts with my wife's face flannel, and you refused me. Ten,' he said. 'I should take it, dear girl, and not try to argue about it. Refusals of all kinds can entail penalties much more severe than an extra ten, you know.'

Ten just for saying no! For sparing him trouble and, I had supposed, embarrassment! Of course I had not really been about to argue, but for a moment I could hardly think this punishment was just. Then I recognised that was only my pride speaking; the very pith of the wild, wilful quality in my character that the Professor had consented to subdue.

I took up the pen and drew the horrible strokes, trying not to wonder how they would be applied, and when. This third line of them stuck out beyond both the first two. I wondered how many there would be altogether, in the end. I wondered whether I would have to go on to a second column.

'What a picture you make,' said the Professor gently, 'standing there in your little white bra, dreaming of the future.'

I was not sure I would concede 'little': my bra was a few sizes larger than Marion's; several more than anything the Professor's wife might have needed to wear. But the merest mention of it seemed to make my nipples stir and my breasts swell with longing. It felt much, much worse to be condemned to stand naked except for a pretty little bra than naked except for a pretty little choker and button shoes.

'How is your bottom now?' the Professor asked me.

'Numb, sir,' I replied.

'Numb, Jennifer? Too numb to feel the Hairbrush, do you suppose?'

'I don't think anything could be that numb, sir,' I said.

'My dear,' said the Professor, as if patronising a public-spirited lady on *Any Questions*, 'I think you're right.'

I put the pen back on the small desk, while the Professor stepped behind his own desk and opened a drawer. I supposed it would be the same one where he kept the Rulers; I could not imagine that every drawer in the desk was full of Devices.

The Professor pulled out a wooden object nine or ten inches long and, smacking it down on his pale green blotting pad, slid it over for my inspection. 'What do you think of that, Jennifer?' he asked.

'Is that the Senior Brush, sir?' I asked, wanting to be absolutely sure before I committed myself to an opinion.

'One of them, Jennifer, yes,' said the Professor.

I knew as soon as I looked at it, the next lesson was not going to be easy. Marion's hairbrushing had been sharp and difficult for her, and I feared mine might be just as uncomfortable for me. Though I would approach it with a willing heart, still I knew my flesh would quail. I could feel it quailing already, even through the steady burn planted on it by the Hand and the Rulers and the Slipper.

A Senior Brush, for mature students. It was wooden, naturally: a very dark, dense-looking wood, set with thick clumps of stiffly spreading bristles. The head was oval in shape, no more than three inches across, all of a piece with its handle, which had been thoughtfully shaped in three dimensions to invite the user's hand. The bristles were quite yellow. I was slightly surprised. If the Junior Hairbrush had seemed masculine, the Senior one seemed almost feminine. I wondered if it might be very old too; if the wood had grown dark with time and use. Perhaps it was not unreasonable to imagine generation after generation of women lifting their skirts and lowering their knickers to make its acquaintance.

'I expect it's quite hard, sir,' I said.

'You may pick it up,' he informed me.

Willing my fingers not to shake, I took up the Hairbrush in my right hand, and, as if in unconscious imitation of what was about to happen to me, turned it upside down. I had been half afraid it would have a design in relief on the back: a monogram or family crest of some kind, which the Professor wished to print all over my bottom. To my relief, it was plain. It was heavier than it looked, and when I pressed my fingernail into it I found the wood was very hard indeed, the grain an almost invisible silver shadow, like the first hint of grizzle in a black dog's coat.

My hand started to shake in earnest then, so I had to bring the left one to support it as I laid the brush down carefully on the edge of the blotter. I realised I was handling it as though it was made of glass and likely to crack into a thousand pieces. 'I expect it works quite well, sir,' I said, trying to keep a quaver out of my voice.

'Careful, Jennifer,' the Professor admonished me. 'Levity is no part of a wise young woman's preparation.'

'No, sir,' I said. 'I think I am prepared, though, sir,' I told him.

'Are you indeed,' he said drily. 'And I suppose you are ready to take up a Position, too, are you?'

'No, sir,' I said, touching my hair and then forcing my hands back behind my back. 'Not quite.'

'Why not, pray?' came the relentless voice.

'Because you haven't told me which Position to take up yet, sir,' I said. I felt myself on firmer ground, saying that.

'What do you think, then?' asked the Professor, conversationally.

'Think, sir?'

'What Position do you think would be appropriate?' he elaborated, with menacing patience.

I was flattered to be consulted, but I would have to take a wild guess. 'Please, sir, Marion took her Hairbrush Spanking across your knee.'

'And you think that would be appropriate for you, Jennifer, do you?'

My nerve would not break. 'Yes, sir,' I said.

There was a short pause.

'To begin with,' I added.

The Professor squared the blotting pads on his desk, then set the Hairbrush exactly in the middle of it. 'Excellent, my dear,' he said quietly. 'An excellent answer. Let us put it into practice immediately. First, come and stand here, between my knees.'

He turned his chair and sat forward, his flanelled legs apart. I went to him and stood, with the slightest of shivers, between them. My thighs rested lightly against the edge of the chair-seat. I put my hands on my head.

'Put them down,' the Professor told me. 'Put them behind your back.'

As I stood there, looking into his face, the Professor began to brush my hair with the gentlest of strokes.

'Let's have you looking nice,' he said.

I caught my breath as the bristles swept across my head, and felt my nipples stiffen painfully inside my bra. Thank goodness he could not see them! I did not want him to think I was more feeble than Marion, requiring manual relief before a punishment even began. I did not want him to think I required relief at all.

I was overwhelmed at his unexpected kindness; tears sprang to my eyes. The great man was brushing my hair with the care and attention of a lady's maid, finding my long-lost parting and smoothing my tresses back to each side behind my ears. He turned me around and brushed the back. Soon my scalp felt itchy and uncomfortable no longer, but airy and light. I was amazed at his gentleness. It seemed to penetrate my skin like pain.

'Every hairbrush has two sides,' said the Professor after a while, in a rhetorical, quotational tone of voice. 'Shall we proceed to the other?'

'Yes please, sir,' I said softly, not knowing what else I might legitimately say at that point.

'You may adopt the Position you so artfully suggested,' he said.

Artfully! I was beyond all art, I thought. What did he

think I had meant by asking to be put back across his knee? I had meant nothing except to face the inevitable; or rather, to offer my bottom up to it.

The Professor helped me do so, guiding me into position. I found myself gazing once more at the dark brown floorboards.

The Professor's hand moved slowly, exploringly, across the bare cheeks of my bottom.

'Still numb?' he asked.

'A little bit, sir,' I said. 'Except when you touch it. Then it's quite – sore, sir,' I explained, catching my breath.

'Excellent,' he said again. 'You're quite red, you know. You colour very well: strongly but fleetingly. It must take quite a lot of work to get you up to full brilliance.'

He laid the backside of the Hairbrush to my own. It was quite cool. Helplessly, I felt my buttocks clench, as if they had been tickled. The brush would not stay cool for long, of that much I was sure.

'I want you to pay particular attention to this, Jennifer,' said the Professor. 'The Hand is natural, and extremely personal. The Ruler is scientific and precise. The Slipper is hearty and raises a good dust, and has a fetching symbolism of its own. But the Hairbrush, Jennifer,' he said, moving his arm around, stroking my bottom in circles with the brush, 'is the acme, the *ne plus ultra* of Spanking Devices. You might even think of it as the last actual Spanking Device on the Prospectus. Beyond the Hairbrush lies what, Jennifer?'

The blood was already beating dully in my temples from hanging upside down. 'The Strap, sir. Which is the last,' I said, just in case it had slipped his mind.

'Exactly,' he said gravely. 'The Strap: half spanking, half whipping. The Americans would no doubt insist on including their beloved Paddle, of leather or wood. In rural areas, it has sometimes been the whole of their education!'

The Professor moved, tilting me as his knees shifted. My breasts were pressed uncomfortably against his left thigh. My nerves were twisted to such a pitch that I thought I could hear them keening in my head. When would the punishment begin?

'Of course,' my tutor went on, 'we have several paddles here – souvenirs of lecture tours, gifts from exchange students and the like; but in this country we tend to think them too self-conscious, too whimsical for adult use. Matters of personal and domestic discipline do not require commercial, specialised equipment.'

Hearing the way he warmed to it, I recognised that the theme must be something of a favourite of his.

'For centuries, parents spanked their children and employers their servants in private, without the intrusion of industrial manufacturers, and often in extremely primitive conditions. A young lady might very profitably be set to binding her own birches, a young gentleman to carving a paddle of his own, or one for his sisters, but that was a matter of craft, not commerce. The attention of the subject can be wonderfully extended and intensified by making the very Device which he or she will subsequently receive. In addition, there is the value of craft itself: the discipline of producing a useful object. Idle hands these days are more likely to be pressing the buttons on some futile computer game!

'But I digress,' the Professor admitted, patting my back just below my bra and sliding his hand down around my buttocks to caress the region of my anus with a single fingertip. 'I intended, Jennifer, only to make the minor, semantic point that the Strap and everything beyond are not properly spanking Devices because they are manipulated in an entirely different way from everything you have experienced today. The Strap, the Tawse, Switches of various woods, the Cane, the Birch, the Martinet, Whips of all sizes . . .'

I was dizzy at this catalogue. Perhaps the drawers of the Professor's desk *were* full of Devices after all! Would I be expected to learn them all? How ever long would that take?

'All those, and others, lie beyond Spanking. The Strap

marks the upper limit of the Prospectus – a kind of Black Belt, you might say.'

'Yes, sir.'

'And below the Strap, the Hairbrush reigns supreme.'

I felt it coming through the air at me. After that I was not sure what I felt. Sharpness, like the Ruler, but with weight; weight like the Slipper, but rigid! Rigid! Rigid! How it snapped at a poor young woman's bottom, that horrible, hard, rigid piece of wood. This was what Marion had taken forty or fifty with, a lesser version of it for younger women, and it had made her cry. I was determined not to cry, though I shouted loudly and squealed without modesty or restraint.

'A good old-fashioned Hairbrush Spanking,' said the Professor, emphasising alternate syllables with quick whacks on my left cheek and on my right. 'Highly suitable for the lithe and lovely. Picture the scene, Jennifer. Perhaps a disagreement, on a Sunday afternoon walk in the country. The young woman is marched to the next suitable place along the route where she is confronted with the consequence of her own petulance. Her handbag is demanded of her, her hairbrush taken out. A convenient log or litter bin is designated The Place: then Mother, Father or Fiancé lifts the skirt and Sunday petticoat, and directs that the peach-trimmed knickers be lowered.'

He had paused, in the recollection of this improbable-sounding event. The Hairbrush hung suspended over me. I could feel its baleful shadow like the heat of a hurtling meteor. Now it landed, loudly, and my feet flew up in the air like any startled pony's.

'Your feet are kicking again, my dear,' the Professor pointed out. 'I shall have to spank your legs until they lie down and behave themselves.'

He introduced my left thigh to the Hairbrush, and then my right. Then came three more smacks on my left, closely spaced, followed by one savage one on the right. Then, while I was still sprawling, all hope of dignity fled, an almighty spank on my inner thigh landed, just where the skin is tender as a baby's. I shrieked so loud the Professor returned at once to the cheeks of my bottom, popping and smacking delicately around and about for a while. I could feel him restraining himself, lightening the force and tempo of my punishment out of consideration for my earlier sufferings and inexperience.

'At home the young lady or young wife always keeps a hairbrush on her dressing table: so handy for those private punishments, secure from the eyes of the rest of the family. A hundred years ago a "*Conversazione*" correspondent in the *Englishwoman's Domestic Magazine* famously suggested the purchase of two hairbrushes,' the Professor told me, 'one for the hair, the other for the purpose of discipline; "for reasons of hygiene", as she expressed it. As I recall,' he said, shifting my weight as though to ease the circulation in his thighs, though I feared it was more to improve the exposure of my lower regions and the accuracy of his aim, 'the correspondent was anonymous. Many of them were, you know. You can check that later,' he said in an aside. 'I have all the volumes for that period. Whether it was her own discipline or her children's, she also unaccountably failed to make clear. Perhaps in her mind there was no distinction.'

Through the delivery of this learned and interesting illustration, the spanking of the Hairbrush on my bottom had become very slow and almost languid, though neither light nor imprecise. The Professor still placed each tap of the brush smartly where it would most make me shiver and quake, and wriggle helplessly across his lap. It became apparent to me that while perhaps it was less cruel, and easier to endure, if handled with such expertise and care, the oval tip of this Device could wreak just as much deft damage among feminine curves as the sharper corners of Marion's model. There might be advantages after all to being granted the Senior Hairbrush.

'Oh, Jennifer!' exulted the Professor in a melodramatic whisper. 'How you shine! How lustrously you shine!'

With those words he slipped his fingers into my crotch. Squirming out of embarrassment as much as tenderness, I knew instantly he had discovered my shame: that I was wet enough there to float a boat. Yet he said nothing but only wiped the mucus smoothly and intimately down the inside of my thighs, as if to soothe the pain the brush had put there.

Wanting to assure him that, even though I couldn't conceal them from him any longer, my mind was still above such accidents of flesh, I tried to speak.

'Surely the Fiancé,' I squeaked tonelessly; and then again, making a bigger effort: 'Surely the young lady's Fiancé would not lift her skirts himself, sir, on a Sunday afternoon walk or any other time, sir? Surely only a Husband would have the right to do that?'

'True, Jennifer, true,' mused my historian; 'or a Parent, wishing to display to her Intended how his Dearly Beloved is accustomed to being punished, to set a good example for their married life. Such things used to happen more often than you would imagine, Jennifer,' he proclaimed, spanking me again.

There came another pause: quite a long and rather welcome one. I was not told to rise or move. Although it is extremely uncomfortable to hang one's head down for so long – and though the burning in one's bottom goes on and on regardless of actual strokes – when a spanking stops, it seems bliss itself. You feel you could lie like that forever, warm lap to warm lap.

'Do you know, Jennifer,' said the Professor in a smooth and even tone, 'I've just realised I'm still spanking you across my knee. And I did promise to vary the Position after a while. How frightfully forgetful of me, I do apologise.'

'It's quite all right, sir,' I answered valiantly 'though I must say it would be nice if we were still in the bedroom, so I could lie down for a moment or two, sir, and get my breath back.'

'You can lie on the floor if you like,' said the Professor, lifting me in his arms and carrying me over to the yellow carpet in front of the fire. 'You can lie there and be a bare-skin rug!'

And depositing me on the floor face down in a huddle,

the Professor stood and laughed at his own pun with sharp barks of laughter like the excited, high-pitched yapping of a happy dog. I was surprised to hear him forsake his customary gravity, and I wondered why it was. Rubbing my bottom slowly and thoughtfully, I remember thinking to myself: I hope he is not behaving oddly because of that new erection of his that has been boring into my belly for the last ten minutes.

ELAINE

Stephen Ferris

Stephen Ferris is, we have discovered, a man of many and varied talents, and we've often found ourselves wondering exactly how he finds the time, energy and inspiration to write such consistently engaging erotic fiction. Then again, we could just put our feet up and enjoy his books. With his next, *Captives of Argan*, scheduled for publication in March, and another, *Educating Ella*, coming up in August, Stephen's output now totals six books for Nexus.

His first book for Nexus, *Elaine*, centres around a young and beautiful bisexual woman. To help her aristocratic lesbian lover, Elaine sacrifices her innocence in the pleasure house of the mysterious Madam Max. Obliged to watch and then participate in acts of bizarre sex, bondage and discipline, she discovers a taste for domination.

In this extract, Elaine, recently arrived, is being taken on a guided tour of the house by Madam Max. Having witnessed the punishment of the Mistress' employees, she finds herself on the receiving end of some humiliating treatment. She also sees some of the bizarre facilities available for use by paying guests.

Stephen Ferris likes to write stories where pretty young women misbehave and find themselves wishing they hadn't! Usually there's a strict mistress not too far away who will be planning a suitable and painful chastisement and, inevitably, punishment will be inflicted in full view of onlookers – for extra shame. Stephen also likes to write erotic stories in mythical or semi-mythical settings. If you like the idea of a world ruled by leather-uniformed maidens who like to exercise total power, then *Warrior Women* is right for you. If, on the other hand, you prefer your ladies demure and corseted, check out *Captives of Argan* – due for publication in March.

The final table was occupied by a stunning redhead whose eyes, unlike those of the other girls, blazed anger and defiance at the approach of her tormentor. Her soft, pink skin complexion was typical of a redhead and any doubt as to the authenticity of that hair colour was dispelled by the huge thatch of red pubic hair. Elaine had never seen such a quantity. It marched up across the naked stomach almost to the navel, and was thick and curly enough to completely conceal the details of her sex, widely stretched though her thighs were.

'I have saved Mary until the last. She is a very, very special case and deserves the fullest attention. I seldom have to deal with my girls for slackness in their professional duties, but Mary seems to have a lot of difficulty in one particular area. She claims not to enjoy servicing our lady customers and several of them have complained about her lack of enthusiasm. This cannot be tolerated and I think I shall have to deal most severely with this little spitfire. As you have already seen, I select a punishment which blends with the crime and the personal attributes of the girl concerned. I want Mary to remember this lesson for some time, so I have decided to shave off all her body hair.' She reached down and grasped a handful of the red pubic curls, tugging viciously and eliciting a startled howl of anguish from the gagged mouth.

'With a thick, wiry growth like that, just imagine how uncomfortable the stubble is going to be for at least a couple of weeks, while it grows in again. The only alternative to that discomfort is for her to keep shaving and I know she is very proud of that hair. Well, my dear Mary; say goodbye to it now, because I am going to shave you as bald as a baby!'

Madam Max stooped below the table and produced a set of electric clippers, already plugged in. As she switched on and the clippers began to hum, Mary writhed, every muscle and tendon standing out as she sought to avoid the inevitable, but could do no more than watch helplessly, as Madam Max laid the coldness of the clippers lightly on her bare belly and took the first stroke across the uppermost part of her pubic hair. With calculated cruelty she made the torture last. Most of the time she just nibbled at the edges, but, now and again, she made a full scythe which sent red curls scattering to the floor and made Mary gasp. As the clipping went on, more and more bare, white belly was exposed to the view of Elaine and the unseen audience. Tantalisingly, just as she reached the beginning of Mary's vaginal slit, Madam Max stopped, leaving a small tuft there and moved on to the hairy inner part of the strained thighs, working upwards. Finally she started to work on the labia, clipping with loving slowness and making sure that the vibrating cutters were pressed well into the flesh in the area around the clitoris as Mary jumped and gasped in response.

Then, all that was left of the glorious red patch was a fine stubble; yet Madam Max had not finished. She produced a foam dispenser of shaving cream and a razor and proceeded to lather the redhead's lower belly, lingering with slippery fingers, rather longer than necessary around the vaginal area. While Mary moaned in misery, the razor removed the last traces of her hair from her, leaving the front of her body completely bald, the pink lips of her sex gaping slightly and clearly visible to any onlooker.

And still the torment was not over. At a sign from Madam Max, the black-suited attendants erected uprights and a bar. Mary put up much more of a fight as they unclipped her ankles, kicking and struggling, but she was overcome and her ankles secured to the ends of the bar so that she was doubled up with her legs widely spread and her naked, pink bottom sticking into the air, completely vulnerable to whatever might be coming next.

Madam Max leant over Mary and looked into her eyes. 'You thought I had forgotten the hairs down here, didn't you? No such luck, my dear. You are going to remember me for some time, every time you sit down.' She picked up the clippers again and set to work on the newly exposed area, scything away the luxuriant growth between Mary's bottom cheeks, until she met with the bald area already created. Then came the shaving cream, and this time Madam Max inserted a slippery finger into the girl's tight sphincter, which involuntarily tightened and puckered around it; gently easing it in and out to the accompaniment of infuriated howls.

Madam Max leant over Mary's face again. 'Now you realise that no part of you is sacred or private. As long as you work for me, I or anyone else I choose will look at you, touch you and use you in any way they like.' With that she took up the razor again and soon removed the last vestiges of hair. 'That will do for now. I'll have her depilated with a cream to make sure nothing has been missed, but that is a pretty perfect shave she has there and the real punishment can begin.'

Elaine gulped. This was not the end of it, then. There was more to come. Apparently so, for at another sign from Madam Max the guards lifted the uprights out of their sockets and moved them further down the table, placed the bar in a higher position and re-secured Mary's ankles so that her buttocks were just clear of the table and her legs, again, widely spread. They passed a wide leather strap around her body, just above the breasts, then repositioned her wrists, clipping them level with her hips. Two sections of table were removed on either side of Mary's head, leaving her with just a narrow strip for the back of her head to rest on.

On Madam Max's orders, the gag was removed, releasing a scream of abuse and threats. 'Bitch! Bitch! Let me go! I'll kill you!'

The gag was instantly replaced, muffling further words and Madam Max sighed in mock sorrow. 'Oh dear, Mary. You have such a lot to learn.' As the guards held Mary's head in a vice-like grip, Madam Max spread lather on each eyebrow and in a few strokes shaved them clean off.

'Now the gag is coming off again. Will you have any more to say, I wonder, or will you remember that that beautiful head of red hair you think so much of counts as body hair too? I have the clippers, the razor *and* the will to do it. If you think I won't you can abuse me again. If you think I will, you will be much better behaved this time.'

The gag was removed once more and Mary remained silent, though obviously seething. 'So much wiser my dear. Now you are going to service me and make a thorough job of it.' Madam Max stepped to the head of the table, slipped out of her black kimono and stood naked for a second, before mounting a couple of blocks and standing with one thigh either side of Mary's head, her black pubic hair almost brushing the available mouth.

'No Madam Max. Please don't. I don't like it. I'll do anything else. Please don't make me do that.' The tone was conciliatory and pleading, without any trace of the previous defiance.

Madam Max's eyes glittered and she passed her hands caressingly over her own breasts and down her stomach. The girl's helpless subjugation was obviously a complete turn-on for her. 'I can't tell you how glad I am to hear you say that, Mary. If there is one thing I like better than a good, tongue-induced orgasm, it is one which I have to force my server into. You know what you have to do. The sooner you start, the sooner the pain will ease and, if you please me very much, the pain may stop altogether, although I can't promise that because I get a little carried away and I enjoy inflicting discomfort on you.'

She took the little, padded quirt handed to her by one of her men and flicked it down in front of her body so that it landed squarely on Mary's unprotected left nipple. The next stroke fell on the right breast and then three in succession, right on the bald area of her pubic mound, just above the clitoris. Mary jumped and shouted, struggling to pull away down the table, but was restrained by the strap across her upper body, under her armpits. she twisted her head from side to side but was forced to return to staring up at the hairy lips, poised just above her face.

Madam Max grinned wolfishly. 'Take all the time you like, Mary. I am enjoying this. This is to be the pattern though. One on each breast followed by three on that lovely bald spot. When you think you can't stand it any more, you may begin your duties and when I begin to feel pleased I *may* ease off a little.' The ritualistic slapping of the leather pad continued and Elaine could guess, by the bright red colour of the tortured breasts and pubic mound, that the smarting was intense. Mary continued to groan and roll her head, trying to hold out against the pain. Finally, almost without her being aware of it, Mary's pink tongue emerged from between her lips. Glancing down without breaking the rhythm of her strokes, Madam Max observed the transition from defiance to compliance and smiled. 'Not good enough, Mary. I'm not going to come down to you. You have to come up to me.'

The slapping continued for a few more strokes before Mary's head lifted, slowly and reluctantly, and her tongue reached out to tentatively lick at the rounded surface of the outer labia. 'That's not doing a thing for me, Mary. I think we ought to put a little more sting into the whip to encourage you to do better.' The quirt rose and fell faster and with more bite. Coming as they did on already tenderised areas, the next few strokes broke Mary completely. She probed deeper with her tongue, inserting it between the inner labia and began to lap eagerly and quickly. A beatific smile spread over Madam Max's face and she began to manipulate her own nipple with one hand while the quirt slowed to become light and easy. Eventually it stopped altogether, leaving Madam Max with both hands free to reach between her own legs and spread herself for the attentions of that active tongue. Her eyes began to roll and her knees trembled. 'Find the place, Mary! Find the place! Oh God! That's right! Go on! Don't stop! Finish me! Do it to me!'

As orgasm hit her, her back arched and she raised a clenched fist to her mouth, biting furiously. Then she fell forward across the naked body beneath her, pressing her hot, wet sex tightly against Mary's mouth and clawing with both hands at the shaven area between the straining and widely separated thighs.

Presently she stirred and got up, slipping back into her kimono and tying the sash. As she rejoined Elaine she was obviously still struggling for composure; breathing a little heavily. 'Well. As you see my dear Elaine, that concludes this part of the show. The thing I want to impress upon you is that although these girls are temporarily restrained none of them are prisoners. Any of them could walk out tomorrow with no questions asked. They don't because they know when they are on to a good thing. Their accommodation is splendid. They are paid a great deal more than they could earn otherwise. They are well fed and their welfare is a prime consideration. In return for that, they agree to submit to my rules and my domination. It is on those conditions that you will be employed here.

'Before we go I have to tell you that there is always a final turn.' She gestured towards the mirror. 'Our audience would be disappointed to be deprived of their expected treat. Today *you* are that treat. Our friends behind the glass will want to look at you, as a new girl, in order to decide if and how they can make use of you – so just slip off your dress and I'll tell you what to do next.'

Elaine shrank away, blushing scarlet, her hands instinctively protecting her breasts and crotch. 'Oh no! I couldn't do that, Madam Max. I've never undressed in front of lots of people!'

'Then this will be a new experience for you. I promised you lots of new experiences. If you want to keep the job, you'll do it. If you refuse I shall simply get my men to strip you. I certainly don't intend to frustrate my clients because of your maidenly modesty. Make up your mind. Which is it to be? Strip or be stripped?'

With the greatest reluctance Elaine unbuttoned her dress, released the belt and drew it off over her head to stand in push-up brassière and flimsy panties. She was very conscious of her choice of suspender belt and stockings instead of panty-hose. Madam Max took her by the arm and pushed her towards the mirror. 'Stand here, on Number One, facing the mirror.'

For the first time Elaine noticed a row of brass numbers set into the carpet along the front of the mirror, about five feet from the glass, and guessed that they corresponded with the cubicles on the other side.

'Brush your hair back from your face, child! That's better. Now – hands on head!' Elaine did as she was told and Madam Max, standing behind her, reached around and folded down the top of her bra so that her breasts stood out even further and her pert nipples were fully exposed. She transferred her attention to the panties and, skimpy though they were, made them even more revealing by squeezing the crotch into a single cord and pulling up on the waistband, so that the material disappeared between Elaine's bottom cheeks and into the cleft of her sex, clearly revealing a bush of golden pubic hair.

'Now turn around. Hold it! Move on to Number Two. No. Don't take your hands off your head! Face the mirror. Turn. Hold it. Now to Number Three. That's right – you've got it. All the way down the line like that.' Mortified with embarrassment, Elaine did as she was instructed, finally arriving at Ten, the last number, with a sigh of relief. But Madam Max had not finished with her. 'Now a full strip. Everything off Come along, child. I haven't got all day. Get them off!' As Elaine hesitated Madam Max became impatient and crossing to where she stood, ripped her panties down to her knees in one swift jerk and unclipped her brassière so that her breasts, unencumbered and unsupported, flopped free. Trembling with shame, Elaine made the necessary movements to unfasten her suspenders, remove the belt and roll off her stockings. Standing, half crouched, she attempted to shield her body with her hands.

Madam Max picked up her little quirt and ran it menacingly through her fingers. 'I shall begin to think that you are being deliberately awkward. Perhaps you should have tasted this before we started?' Elaine hastily dropped her hands to her sides, very conscious that several pairs of eyes were examining her nakedness. 'Face the mirror. Flat on your back. Legs wide apart. Wider than that. Wider still. Now reach down with your hands and pull yourself apart so that the audience can judge the condition of your inner surfaces. Look, when I say "apart" I mean *wide* apart. That's better. Up on your feet! Turn around! Feet *wide* apart! Touch your toes! Now reach around behind you and pull your cheeks apart! Good. Up you get and repeat that at every number back down to One.'

In a daze Elaine obeyed. Could any shame be greater than this? Being forced to reveal her most private parts in this lewd fashion to unknown eyes. She lay down, got up, bent and showed off her body in a mechanical fashion at each position until at last she was back at Number One and the ordeal was finally over.

'You may dress now. I thought for a moment that I was going to have to have you table-topped, but I would prefer to reserve that pleasure for another time, after I have found out a little more about your likes and dislikes and had the opportunity to plan properly. Now follow me. There is much you have yet to see.'

Madam Max swept out of the room, so that Elaine had almost to run to keep up with her. Elaine's thoughts were racing. Maybe she had bitten off more than she knew. This job was not going to be an easy one and she wondered if she would have the nerve to carry it all the way through. She remembered the naked girls and she wished that she could have spoken to them, there and then, to find out whether she could recruit any allies to her cause. Better keep that for another day. They had other things to think about for the time being. The discomfort yet to come. Elaine shivered at the thought that she too might soon be naked, gagged, strapped down and at the mercy of Madam

Max's whim. She tried to put the thought out of her mind and followed Madam Max back to the drawing room.

Madam Max patted the place beside her on the large and comfortable sofa, in invitation. Elaine sat down wondering what was coming next.

'Would you like some tea, dear?'

Elaine, who had been expecting some further shock, floundered. The banality of the question had taken her by surprise, and it took a few seconds before she could say, 'Yes please.'

Madam Max rang the bell then returned. 'Such a nice custom, tea,' she said, and from there she led the conversation in her easy way, as if the recent, bizarre events had never happened. 'I'm glad I decided to employ you, Elaine. As I promised, if you please me there is a good chance of greater reward.'

'Thank you, Madam Max.'

'Not at all. I think you have natural talent and you are very, very beautiful.' She reached out and stroked Elaine's hair as she had done at their first meeting. This time, Elaine noticed, she did not ask permission, and there was something proprietorial in her manner, rather as if she were feeling the hocks of a horse.

The same maid came in with the tea and again Elaine was struck by a certain oddness about her. The maid stood by the trolley and waited to be dismissed. Madam Max, noticing Elaine's scrutiny, did not do so. 'You have noticed my maid?' she said. She beckoned to the maid who, finding herself in such prominence, was shaking with tension. 'Come here, Millicent. This nice young lady wants to examine you more closely. Lift up your dress.' The eyes pleaded but disobedience was out of the question. The dress rose slowly, revealing the tops of her black stockings, then the suspenders of a belt. 'Get it up, girl. Or must I lose my patience!' The skirt rose all the way to the waist, to reveal the genitalia of a man, except that the penis was encased in what looked like a steel sheath from which a chain passed around his scrotum causing his testicles to bulge forward. Another chain went about his body so tightly that it cut into the flesh and the whole thing was fastened together with padlocks. All the pubic area that Elaine could see, including the testicles, was shaved clean and Madam Max passed her hand across it, as though testing for smoothness, before getting up and going to a cupboard in the wall. The doors of the cupboard were formed from the same panelling as the rest of the room and, when open, revealed a large closet.

At this the man fell to his knees, his hands clasped, as though in prayer. 'Mercy! Please! Not again!'

Madam Max was exasperated. 'Get up, girl. For goodness' sake pull yourself together and stop that whining. When I am ready to cane you, you will know all about it. And pull that skirt up again. Who said you could let it down!' He did so and stood, exposed again, obviously in acute embarrassment and fear.

Madam Max came back with a duplicate of the fearsome gadget he wore and showed it to Elaine. 'This is a penis restraint. They are widely used here, and one of the things you must learn is how to put one on. Not now, of course, that can come later. I just want to show you that it is lined inside with sharp bristles. It is uncomfortable all the time but, when an erection comes to mind, the discomfort quickly puts a stop to those thoughts. I think I can demonstrate that best by asking you to stroke the shaved areas. Make your touch nice and soft and gentle.'

Elaine reached out and stroked him as ordered, running her fingers over the extended testicles as well. After just a few seconds the man's knees buckled. He groaned in misery and screwed up his face, as though with intense concentration, as he fought to turn his mind away from what was being done to him, so as to stop the further swelling of his organ.

'How long has it been on now, Millicent?'

'Two hours, Madam.'

'Very well. I think another two hour period is called for.' Then, as if it was an afterthought, she added, 'At least!'

The man groaned again. 'You may drop your skirt and go now.' Thankfully, he did so and hobbled from the room.

Elaine could not restrain her curiosity. 'Is that one of the fantasies you were talking about?'

Madam Max smiled grimly. 'It could easily be but, in this case, it isn't. He was foolish enough, whilst in my employ, to try to steal a great deal of my money. I offered him the choice. A very long period in prison, or a short period of my own particular brand of punishment. I'm not sure now, that he thinks he made a wise choice. He is, or was, a very egotistical, arrogant, macho-man. I needed a servant and it pleases me, for the time being, to humiliate him as much as I can.'

'How long has he been . . .? I mean . . .'

'A few weeks. I am getting bored with the game, so I shall not keep him much longer, but he does not know that.' Elaine shivered, aware that in trying to match wills with this woman, she was playing with fire.

Madam Max said, 'I allowed you to see that because it will be a part of your education to see other men treated in the same way. Men who pay handsomely for the privilege. Yes, it is incredible, isn't it?' she continued, noticing Elaine's expression. 'But that is their dearest wish, and I am happy to make it come true, at a price. I enjoy domination of men or women. It may be that you will find that you have talent in that direction. It so happens that I have such an appointment this afternoon. You can help me with that and then we shall see. For the time being, we will see if we can give you a flavour of the delights which make my clients come back, time and again.'

She conducted Elaine along the corridors again and they went into a side-room. It was completely curtained along one side. There was a drinks cabinet, a table and some comfortable chairs. What was remarkable was that there were two TV cameras on stands, some distance apart, pointing at the curtain. Madam Max dimmed the lights and going to the curtain pulled part of it aside. The wall behind it was transparent and gave a full view of what appeared to be a small dressing, or changing room, softly carpeted and equipped with a large shower.

'We have just a little while to wait,' Madam Max said. 'Let's have a drink.' She went to the cabinet and poured drinks for both of them, then settled herself in a chair and indicated that Elaine should occupy the other. Seeing that Elaine was very curious, she explained. 'All the fantasy rooms, and a few of the others in the house are equipped like this, with another room alongside. The other side of that glass wall is a mirror. I'm sure you will remember the one you saw earlier.'

She smiled sardonically as she saw that Elaine remembered very well. 'From here, I, or any other privileged person, can watch what goes on in the next room. The TV cameras are operated from a central control room. The wall is soundproof. Concealed microphones on the other side relay sound to these loudspeakers in this room and direct to the cameras. To put that in a less complicated way, we, and the TV cameras, can see and hear everything that happens next door. Neither the cameras, nor the occupants of the other room, can hear what we are saying. Clear?'

Elaine nodded and sipped her drink, conscious that a lot of money and effort went into the running of this establishment. Just then a green light glowed and there was an electronic 'ping' as the door of the dressing room opened and two women came in. Madam Max crossed to the nearest camera and pressed a button beneath it, waiting until the red 'on' light appeared before returning to continue her observation of the women. They were both elegantly dressed in evening clothes and both had dark hair. One appeared to be about 25 or 26, the other older – Elaine judged her to be in her late thirties. They kissed one another on the mouth – a lingering, hungry kiss which went on for a long time. Their hands groped and fondled at each other's bodies, then they began to undress each other.

It wasn't easy for them to do that without interrupting their long kiss, and they had to do that from time to time, but returned to it immediately. They stripped one another naked and Elaine saw that the younger one had a magnificent body, tanned all over, without marks of clothing; beautifully muscled and perfectly proportioned, reminding Elaine of the sleek qualities of a leopard. Her breasts were large, but taut and firm. The older woman was a little heavier. Her breasts were also large, but swung and joggled just a little, with her movements. In spite of that, or perhaps because of it, she was sexually exciting; the whiteness of her skin and the rounded contours of her haunches exuding the same qualities as the lusty women in a Rembrandt or Rubens painting.

They stopped kissing at last. Laughing, they picked up bathing caps, which were provided along with the towels, and put them on, tucking their hair inside with great care. Elaine thought that they were going to take a shower together and was puzzled when they moved to a door which led to whatever was behind the rest of the curtain. She followed Madam Max as she moved along the glass and drew it back. The red light on the second camera glowed red. The other room, thus revealed, was a little larger than the first but carpeted in the same way. It was completely devoid of furniture. In the centre of it was a thing which resembled a child's portable paddling pool, except that it was much larger, about eight feet square, and had rounded edges padded with matching carpet, so that it looked as though it was built into the floor. Elaine looked to Madam Max for an explanation.

'These women met at one of my parties last week and were mutually attracted. They were able to get together only briefly then, but decided that they would like to return together, for this session. This is one of our more popular fantasies – popular with heterosexual couples as well – very simple in itself, but complicated and expensive if they tried to arrange it themselves. The pool is about six inches deep. It is not filled with water but oil; vegetable oil to which a subtle blend of aromas has been added. It is, believe me, a most pleasant sensation to bathe in it.'

The two women stopped beside the pool. The elder

waited while the younger got down on hands and knees and crawled in. 'They have been cautioned against standing up,' said Madam Max. It would be extremely difficult.'

As the tanned girl moved, Elaine watched the swing of her muscular, bare buttocks and was again reminded of a big cat. When she reached the centre she turned over and sat down, obviously enjoying the sensation of the oil on her body and between her legs. She cupped her hands and lifted oil to splash on her face. It ran down over her breasts and stomach in a glistening stream and she rubbed her slippery hands over her shoulders and arms. 'Come on, Peggy. It's lovely. Just slightly warm.'

Peggy got down on her hands and knees and crawled into the pool. She stopped by the younger woman, but remained on her hands and knees, her breasts dangling and swaying. 'I'm not ready, Jane. I might slip. Don't rush me,' she said nervously.

'Fraidy cat!' said Jane, and crawled around her, splashing oil up underneath her, wetting her breasts and belly and then, as she turned away defensively, scooping handfuls to splash her thighs and bottom. Peggy let out girlish screams and splashed back as best she could with one hand.

'Come on. Get it on your face, like me,' said Jane and crawled towards her menacingly.

Guessing her intention Peggy backed away. 'No, Jane. You're not to. No, Jane. I'm serious!'

She shrieked as Jane hurled herself on her and tried to knock away her supporting hands. For a while they remained locked together, like two wrestlers, Jane trying hard for a grip but finding it difficult with the oil. Then she was on Peggy's back, holding her tightly with interlocked arms, distorting her ample breasts. Her strong thighs wrapped around her stomach, squeezing tightly, heels digging into her pubic hair. For a second or two as Peggy bucked and jumped to dislodge her, she rode her like a horse, until with a sudden outward, scything movement, Jane knocked her arms away from under her. She fell, face first into the oil, squirming and wriggling as Jane, still on top of her, dunked her head under for a second. She came up gasping and blowing and wiping her face, then the action slowed as they came into one another's arms and lay pressed together, breast to breast, belly to belly, with pubic hair intertwined.

For a long time they just lay there, their lips pressed together in a passionate, open-mouthed kiss. The only movement was a slight undulation of their bodies, as each sought – by rubbing and sliding – to maximise the feel of the naked oiliness of the other. Their hands also moved constantly, feeling the texture of the oil as they slid them up and down, massaging and fondling each other's backs and buttocks.

Elaine had seen bodies massaged with oil before, but only with small quantities, which gave the skin a certain shine. Not with these virtually unlimited amounts. The bare, intertwined bodies of these women glistened and shone with oil. She found that, and their movements, incredibly erotic. She felt herself lubricating and wanted to touch herself and, glancing across at Madam Max, noticed that the display had had the same effect on her. She was leaning forward, staring intently. Her hands were inside her kimono – her left massaging her breasts and her right between her legs. From the subtle movements Elaine could tell that she was masturbating.

Her movements increased as the women parted slightly, so as to permit their hands access to the fronts of their bodies, then massaged each other's breasts and bellies before kissing again, each with a hand between her partner's thighs. They stayed like this for a long time until, apparently by mutual consent, they crawled to the side of the pool and got out, their bodies as sleek as seals, and went back to the dressing room. Peggy turned on the shower and adjusted the temperature and they went in together. The shower was large and the entrance faced the transparent wall. There was no curtain or door, so everything they did could be seen.

They took it in turns to soap one another, seeming to

take as much pleasure in soaping as they did in being soaped. Jane stood behind Peggy and reached around her, rubbing suds into her breasts, lifting the weight of them and irritating the nipples with her fingers. Then she transferred her attention to her stomach and worked up a good lather in her pubic hair before plunging her slippery hands between her legs to slide her fingers to and fro along her sex. Peggy moved constantly under this treatment, her whole body twitching with excitement.

Then it was Jane's turn to receive the same treatment from Peggy and she raised her arms and stretched back, placing her hands behind Peggy's head, in order to lift her superb, brown breasts to maximum prominence and stretch the skin tighter around her nipples to increase the stimulation they were receiving.

When they came out of the shower, they removed their bathing caps, spread fluffy towels on the carpet and, without bothering to dry, got down on to them. Jane lay on her back with her head towards the camera, raised her knees and parted her legs wide. Peggy got astride her in the classic sixty-nine position, kneeling and facing her feet. She bent forward, arching her back down so that her pendulous breasts brushed Jane's naked stomach, then began to kiss and lick between the parted thighs. In this way, her plump, white, bottom cheeks were displayed to Jane and to the camera, her sex stretched apart so as to reveal the excited, swollen entrance to her vagina. Jane put her arms around Peggy's bottom and pulled herself up so that her tongue could work on the area so invitingly exposed, lapping and sucking, then biting gently on the spread labial lips, before searching out the clitoris and concentrating on that.

Peggy came to orgasm first, with a great sigh and a frantic wriggling of her buttocks. She kept up her work and Jane soon followed, showering kisses on the bare, white flesh above her as she did so. Elaine thought that Madam Max came to orgasm with them, but she could not be sure and suspected that the woman was not going to reveal that to her, if she could help it.

Elaine took her lunch in her room, which was luxuriously appointed with every conceivable requirement, and where she had only to lift the telephone to have food or drinks brought to her. The one thing she could not have brought to her was Stewart, and she found that she needed the comfort of his presence very badly. She would have to find a way to see him, at least, even if those meetings had to be formal and businesslike.

She found her opportunity after lunch when she reported again to the drawing room. 'Madam Max. I have been thinking about what you have shown me and it seems to me that I shall become useful more quickly if I learn as much as I can about what goes on here. Visiting different rooms with you is the best way, of course, but you are not always available and it occurred to me that if I spent some of my time in the TV Control Room, then I could monitor what is going on in several rooms at the same time. What do you think?'

Madam Max was gratified at this display of enthusiasm by her pupil. 'An excellent idea, my dear. I will tell Stewart to be as helpful as he can. Now to this afternoon's business. I think this will be interesting for you and you can help me. First I have to change.' She went to the closet in the panelling and opening it, brought out a large box. She set it on the sofa and removed some clothing from it. Then with complete unconcern, slipped out of her kimono and shoes and stood naked. 'Help me to dress, dear,' she said. Elaine did so.

First there was what could best be described as the bottom half of a black, shiny, leather bikini. The triangle at the front was covered in metal studs. At the back there was merely a thong which submerged itself between her bottom-cheeks and disappeared, leaving her buttocks completely uncovered. Instead of a thin waistband it had a broad, studded belt with a heavy buckle. Next came a pair of shiny, black boots, which reached to just below the knee and had incredibly high heels. Elaine helped her to pull them on and zip them up.

The bodice of the costume was a collection of leather-straps held together by rings. When fitted, just about the whole of her upper body was clearly visible, including her bare breasts, the straps against her white skin serving only to emphasise her nudity. A pair of elbow-length gloves completed the outfit and she posed for Elaine. 'Like it?'

Elaine felt a sudden surge inside her which reminded her of the time she had first seen a naked woman, bound and hanging, helpless. She was a little breathless as she answered, 'Yes,' and meant it. This was pure fantasy and it was exciting.

FALLEN ANGELS

Kendal Grahame

When we asked Kendal Grahame for permission to include an extract of his work in this collection, he said he'd be honoured. It goes without saying that we hold this author in the same high esteem. His books all share an element of the fantastic and an exuberance which no doubt stems from the vast amount of kinky sexual activity his characters engage in.

In *Fallen Angels*, Janet and Lisa – two very special girls with astounding good looks and libidos bordering on nymphomania – set out to enjoy as much varied and abandoned sex with as many different people as possible. They are, however, in the thrall of a powerful and mysterious guardian. Certain conditions must be fulfilled and rules observed.

Here, Lisa's exhibitionist behaviour almost spells disaster for a peeping Tom. She also begins to have misgivings about the pact she's entered into with her guardian, but refuses to let her doubts spoil her enjoyment of some very strenuous and salacious group activity.

Fallen Angels was Kendal Grahame's first book for Nexus. He has also written *Demonia*, a tale of vampirism and unquenchable lust set in modern-day London, and *The Cloak of Aphrodite* – an exceptionally well-written and very erotic adaptation of the Jason and Medea myth. His fourth book – *Pyramid of Delights* – was published by Nexus in November 1996 and explores the strange, exotic sex rituals of life in the time of the pharaohs.

Lisa rushed over to the window, opened it and helped the hapless voyeur into her room. 'Are you all right?' she asked, forgetting her near-nakedness for a moment. She held his arm with genuine concern.

'I'm sorry, I . . .' was all the stranger could say. He was staring at her now, gazing at her lovely body, savouring the view.

She pretended embarrassment, turning from him and grabbing a small item of clothing, holding it uselessly against her body, knowing she was hiding nothing. 'Oh my God, I didn't realise . . . I'd better put something on!'

'Don't trouble on my account.'

Lisa smiled and kissed him lightly on the cheek. Then she looked deep into his eyes, willing him to take her. For a second he seemed to waver, but the intensity of her will began to work on him, the little resistance that he held fading with the increase in his lust.

Their mouths met, their tongues immediately darting licking, tasting. He ran his hands down her naked back to her bottom, making her press her crotch against his. He felt hard through the rough material of the boiler-suit, its very coarseness thrilling her. She unbuttoned the garment slowly from the top as he moved his rough hands to her breasts, feeling their size, their firmness, running his thumbs over the hard nipples, teasing them to button-hard erection.

When she had unbuttoned his overall to the waist she pulled it off his shoulders, revealing a strong, naked torso

One more button and she was able to pull the boiler-suit to his ankles, leaving him wearing just a pair of brightly coloured boxer-shorts. Lisa pulled these down in one quick movement, thrilling at the sight of his long, thick penis as it sprang up to meet her admiring gaze. She took hold of the firm tool with both hands and kissed him lightly on the lips. 'Who's a big boy, then?' she said, sultrily. He didn't answer, still obviously unable to believe his luck.

Lisa knelt down and took his hardness into her pouting mouth, running her tongue deftly around the thick, bulbous end, tasting the erotic flavour of his excited state. Then she took it from her wet mouth and licked up and down the full length, occasionally rubbing it quite vigorously with her free hand; her other fingers were busily engaged in fondling her own sex, bringing her almost to the point of orgasm.

She stood up slowly, kissing his hairy stomach and chest, licking his nipples and finally kissing him hard on the mouth, whilst at no time letting her hand leave his hard erection.

Finally, without a word, she pulled him by his cock to the bed. 'Lie down!' she commanded. He did as he was told, his face holding the expression of a schoolboy about to be caned. Lisa removed the rumpled clothes from around his feet, followed by the heavy, workman's boots and rather tatty socks. He just lay there as she took in the sight of his strong body, a little too hairy for her taste but nevertheless beautiful, his manhood large and ready.

She climbed astride him and took his sex in her hand, guiding it to her wet opening. The thick end found its target and he pushed upward a little as Lisa sat down on the superb length, taking every inch inside her in one, graceful movement. She remained still for a moment, then began to slowly move up and down, screwing herself on his lovely stiffness, taking full control. This seemed to suit the stranger, who lay with his hands clasped behind his head, watching this vision of beauty impaled upon his hard stalk.

Lisa started to move with more urgency now, tightening her vaginal muscles as she felt him slide in and out of her body, maintaining wet contact with every inch. His hips began to thrust involuntarily upward in time to her movements, and his breathing became heavy. She didn't want a long session, she just wanted to drain this stranger, to feel him come inside her, and to bring them both to orgasm when *she* chose.

She was riding him quickly now, leaning forward so that her pendulous breasts swung against his face. His breathing became sharper, his hands grasped her thrusting bottom and the fingernails dug painlessly into her flesh. She revelled in the knowledge that he couldn't hold back any longer, that she had taken charge, that she had seduced and then fucked a man under her own terms and now brought him to orgasm at exactly the right time to suit he needs.

He groaned and started to thrust violently into her. She matched his movements, leaping up and down on his body, ramming herself on to him as she felt the magic waves of her own orgasm approaching. With a cry she came, feeling at the same time the pumping of his sex as the sperm shot deep into her body. She bit him hard on the shoulder as her orgasm took hold of her, almost crying with the sheer pleasure and ecstasy of her release. Finally, she collapsed exhausted on him and they lay still.

'I really shouldn't have done that,' the stranger said nervously, 'I only got married this month. I don't know what came over me. I didn't seem able to stop myself.'

Lisa smiled, kissing him on the tip of his nose. 'It'll be our little secret,' she said, reassuringly. This was how the power should be used, she thought to herself. To seduce unsuspecting or even unwilling hunks in order to satisfy her own carnal lust.

The young man dressed quickly and left by the front door, still looking bewildered. Lisa returned again to the bathroom, and used the hand-held shower head to rinse herself between the legs.

The force of the warm spray soon had an effect and

she found herself directing it unconsciously on her erect clitoris. She closed her eyes and gritted her teeth, feeling that another orgasm was near.

'Put that down!' The suddenness of the shouted instructions caused her to drop the showerhead, allowing it to clatter into the empty bath. Lisa looked around her, terrified. At first she saw nothing, then she glanced into the small mirror on the bathroom cabinet. The evil features of the old man glared out at her.

She trembled visibly as the disembodied face broke into a heinous grin. 'You know the rules, my dear,' cackled the foul voice of her benefactor, 'this is your last warning. No self-stimulation!'

'I-I'm sorry, sir,' she stuttered, 'I wasn't thinking. I won't do it again.'

'See that you don't,' the old man barked, his image beginning to fade in the mirror, 'or you know what will happen.'

He was gone as quickly as he had appeared. Lisa sat down heavily on the edge of the bath and caught her breath. Her suspicions were gradually being confirmed; she was dealing with something that was very wrong, very powerful and she felt afraid.

Lisa arrived at the Grand Hotel on time, the taxi-cab pulling up outside the main entrance. Janet was standing by the doorway, wearing a thick, full-length fur coat, looking very elegant and totally in keeping with the expensive surroundings. She smiled and waved when she spotted Lisa, beckoning her to come inside the building.

They walked together into the plush bar and sat at a small secluded table by the window. Janet had already ordered drinks, which were delivered by a rather overly familiar waiter, who had obviously deduced the nature of their business. He stooped as he placed the glasses on the table, pointedly staring at the way Lisa's breasts forced her coat forward almost ludicrously.

'Can I get you ladies anything else – food, or perhaps some company?'

Janet glared at him. 'Fuck off,' she said quietly, through clenched teeth. The waiter bowed in mock subservience and returned to his place by the bar.

'That was a bit strong,' said Lisa, a little embarrassed.

'No, it wasn't,' Janet replied, still angry, 'he thinks we're hookers; common prostitutes.'

Lisa looked uncomfortable. 'Well, we . . .'

Janet caught her roughly by the elbow. 'No,' she hissed, 'we are *not*. We do this for our own pleasure, OK?'

Lisa nodded, pulling her arm from her friend's grip. She wondered if Janet was quite so sure that their role was as innocuous as she supposed.

There was a silent pause. Janet unbuttoned her coat revealing a high-necked, full-length black evening gown. Lisa looked at her with some surprise.

'I thought you said we had to dress erotically?' she said a little perplexed. Her own choice was such that she didn't dare unfasten her own coat in the hotel bar, for fear of being arrested.

'I did,' said Janet, with a grin, 'you wait till you see the back of it.'

Lisa smiled, happy that the conversation had turned light again. 'I can't even open my coat at all!'

'I can't wait,' said Janet, with genuine lust in her eyes.

'What happens now?' They were alone in the bar, except for the smarmy waiter.

'A car will be sent to collect us. It should be here at any moment.' Janet peered out of the window into the brightly lit street.

Lisa sipped her drink thoughtfully. Despite her misgivings she was looking forward to the night ahead, wondering what sort of deviations the Ambassador might indulge in. She also knew that she couldn't wait to show herself to him and to Janet for that matter, certain that her outfit would have the desired effect.

'I think that's them,' said Janet, looking at a large, black car that had drawn up outside the hotel entrance, 'yes, yes there's Frank. Come on.'

The two girls quickly drained their glasses and headed

back to the reception area. Frank was waiting for them holding open the large glass door to the hotel. He ushered them outside and opened the door to the car.

He was dressed in formal, evening attire, complete with black bow-tie, a sight that Lisa found most appealing. She smiled sweetly at him as he helped them into the back of the sleek limousine, willing him to join them and have sex with her, but to her surprise the powers she had learnt to use so effectively in the past were lost on him, his handsome, rugged features showing little emotion other than a polite smile.

She sat on the large, white leather seat in the rear of the car next to Janet, her disappointment obvious as she watched Frank sit in the front, next to the driver.

'It doesn't work on him,' Janet whispered in her ear, 'you can only have Frank under his terms.'

'Pity.'

'Tell me about it. There are times when I could fuck him rigid. Still, don't worry, we should be there soon.'

Lisa looked longingly into her friend's eyes. 'I need a feel. Give me a feel, please.'

She was almost begging. 'You randy cow,' said Janet, pushing her hand between the folds of Lisa's coat, her fingertips making immediate contact with her friend's pussy, finding her already damp. Lisa sat back in the plush seat, her legs wide open as Janet expertly fondled her sex, dipping her fingers deep into the welcoming honeypot, her thumb rubbing swiftly against the hard clitoris.

Lisa began to moan, pushing her hips forward to meet the probing fingers. 'More, more, push more in,' she said, opening her legs even wider, lifting her bottom off the seat. Janet did as instructed, filling the eager pussy with her hand, the thick, wet lips gripping her wrist. 'Yes, that's it, more!' said Lisa, feeling her friend's fist deep inside her body, loving every second of the new sensation. Janet used her arm like a giant penis, pushing in and out of Lisa, faster and faster.

Lisa began to cry out in time with Janet's steady thrusting, knowing she was about to come. With a sudden, deafening scream she let go, one of her feet accidentally kicking the back of the front seats, knocking Frank forward with the force. He turned and scowled, but she was past caring. 'Oh, God, yes!' she cried, as the waves of extreme pleasure began to subside, 'that's the most amazing feeling!'

Janet smiled and kissed her friend lightly on the mouth, pulling her arm gently from between her legs. 'I hope the Ambassador's got a big dick, or you won't feel a thing after that treatment!'

Lisa struggled to compose herself. Frank turned to face them again. 'Right, ladies,' he said, 'we're here. Sort yourselves out.' His tone was almost dictatorial, as though talking to very minor underlings on his staff. Lisa wasn't sure she liked it; he may have been the most gorgeous man she had ever seen, but he needed to learn some simple manners.

The door to the Embassy was huge; heavy, dark oak, carved with various medieval designs that suited the overall gothic appearance of the building. It reminded Lisa of a scene from an old Hollywood horror movie; she half expected it to be opened by a twisted dwarf named Igor.

Instead, the door swung slowly open to reveal the delightful form of a young black girl of about sixteen or seventeen, dressed in a tiny maid's outfit which revealed more than it hid. The beauty of the girl almost took Lisa's breath away. She looked like a tiny version of her friend and lover Sonia, her dark eyes large and hypnotic, the whites shining in stark contrast to her flawless, ebony skin. Her nose was tiny, her mouth large, with thick, pouting lips which jutted forward markedly, as though purposely made for nothing more than sucking cock.

She wore a white, frilly maid's hat and pinafore, the latter small and totally see-through, tied with a thin piece of material at her back. Her only other clothing was a pair of tiny white panties, suspender belt and white, lacy stockings. Her breasts, small but firm, thrust arrogantly against the flimsy material, the long, almost jet-black nipples erect, seemingly begging for attention.

The maid welcomed the three guests and turned to lead them through the great hall. As Lisa watched the girl's near-naked thrusting buttocks as she walked ahead of them, she couldn't help but wonder why the Ambassador needed the services of herself and Janet, with such delicate loveliness at his command.

They were led through another pair of heavy oak doors into a large, brightly lit room. In front of them stood a giant of a man, also black, naked but for a red leather posing pouch which strained to contain obviously huge genitals. He stood, unsmiling, holding out a muscular arm. 'May I take your coats, ladies?' he said, in a clear, booming voice that seemed to echo around the building.

Lisa was suddenly reminded of the way that she was dressed. She waited with nervous excitement as Janet removed her heavy fur, draping it over the servant's muscular forearm.

She saw what her friend had meant as she looked at her gown; her back was completely exposed from her head to her feet, the material held together with thin strips of black lace, the gap in the dress being about four inches. Needless to say, Janet hadn't worn underwear, the resulting view being both beautiful and erotic in its tantalising subtlety.

Lisa began to wonder if she'd perhaps gone too far this time. Subtlety wasn't the word that would be used in her case, she knew. The massive African stood waiting patiently for her coat, which she unbuttoned slowly, gradually revealing her outfit. Finally, she removed the coat and draped it with Janet's, and stood back nervously as she waited for some sort of reaction.

Apart from her black stockings and suspenders she wore a pair of tight, black shorts in shiny PVC, split wide at the crotch, the puffy lips of her sex fully exposed. The shorts were held up by braces of lightweight chain, the silvery links straining on either side of her mountainous breasts, which jutted naked and unfettered before her. The outfit was completed by another, much thicker chain drawn tightly around her waist, the surplus links of this savage belt hanging loosely by her side, almost to her knee.

Frank whistled appreciatively and Lisa breathed a sigh of relief. She looked at the giant servant's face, but he remained impassive, probably used to such sights.

Janet breathed in her ear, lustily. 'No wonder you couldn't open your coat in the hotel!'

'You look pretty sexy yourself!'

'You both look wonderful,' said Frank, speaking with some gentleness for a change. 'I'm sure the Ambassador will approve.'

'The Ambassador *does* approve!'

The voice came from behind them, the girls swinging round to meet their host. He was a small man, quite chubby with dark hair and complexion, a thick, bushy moustache over his broadly grinning mouth. Lisa reckoned that he was about forty years old, but couldn't be too sure, his Latin looks maintaining an attractive youthful appearance.

'Welcome to my home, young ladies,' he said, holding his hand out in greeting. Lisa clutched his sweaty palm first and he gripped her small hand tightly with both of his, kissing her on the cheek. He greeted Janet in the same way, then warmly shook Frank by the hand, betraying affection for an old friend.

'You will have drinks, yes?' he said, motioning to the young maid, 'and then we will have some fun. Now, let me see you more closely.'

He caught Janet by the arms and turned her around, his eyes glinting as he examined her naked rear. 'Such a perfect arse,' he said, as though inspecting a fine piece of livestock, 'I will have much pleasure with that.' He ran his podgy hand over Janet's smooth buttocks, allowing his middle finger to probe gently between them. 'Yes, much pleasure.'

He turned to Lisa. 'And you now, my dear,' he said, 'such a sexy outfit. I can see where you want me to touch you.' His hand went straight for her sex, which was still wet and puffy from her experience with Janet in the car.

'Ah, she is wet for me already!' he boasted. 'You have done well, Frank.'

Frank just smiled. The little maid brought a tray of drinks and stepped back next to the other servant, his bulk dwarfing her, making her look extremely vulnerable. 'Now,' said the Ambassador, eagerly, 'before we start I will give you a little show, to get you in the mood, although I don't think the lovely blonde needs any help.' He leered at Lisa. 'Come, everybody sit.'

The four of them sat together on a large settee, Lisa and Janet on either side of the Ambassador. Once settled, he clapped his hands and the two servants walked in front of them, their faces showing no emotion whatsoever. The Ambassador leant over to Lisa and spoke into her ear, 'You watch these two; I could watch them for hours!'

The little maid stripped off her skimpy uniform and panties and stood before her audience, her fingers rubbing quickly at her hairy pussy, her eyes staring into Lisa's. She then turned to face the other servant. So small was she, and so large her partner, her face came level with his lower chest, which she kissed gently, before running her tongue sensuously down over his powerful abdomen to the leather pouch which covered his obviously rising manhood. Although fully bent over she kept her legs straight, her perfect bottom thrusting provocatively in the air.

'Don't you just want to have that pretty, black ass?' said their host to Frank, who grinned in agreement. 'You will, my friend, before the night is over, but first, see what he does.'

The maid ran her tongue wetly over the straining pouch, chewing hungrily at the bulge, her hands groping the stiff sinews of the man's buttocks. Slowly, she drew the tiny garment down, pressing her mouth to the exposed flesh, concealing his secrets from the curiosity of the seated guests. She nuzzled at his sex, still hiding it from them, teasing them until suddenly she threw her head back, allowing his penis to thrust into view.

The size of his sex matched his enormous bulk and for a moment Lisa feared for the young maid, knowing that she was probably about to take it inside her, but then surmised that such an event was probably a regular occurrence. For herself, she yearned to feel the big, black phallus forcing its way within her, filling and stretching her to the limit. She also remembered that they were there to please the Ambassador and not themselves, although she secretly hoped that a session with this huge man was part of the night's agenda.

The maid had clamped her thick lips over the end of the exposed cock now, unable to take more than a couple of inches inside her little mouth. She pumped at his steel-hard length with both of her hands as though trying to milk it, and occasionally paused to grip his heavy balls or stroke his firm bottom. The Ambassador, meanwhile, had started to probe at Lisa's pussy with one hand, whilst fondling Janet's bare backside with the other, an inane grin of self-satisfaction on his face

After a couple of minutes the maid stood and walked over to the far side of the room, leaving her partner standing alone, his tool jutting ridiculously in front of him. Lisa wanted to rush over and clamp her mouth over it; to suck on him and taste his flesh. She was sure that Janet must be feeling the same way, but they had to stay where they were, as playthings for their host.

The tiny servant returned, carrying something by her side. Lisa's eyes shone with mounting lust as she realised that it was a long, vicious-looking whip with three or four strands of harsh leather. The maid drew back the weapon and cracked it hard against the thigh of her lover, causing him to cry out in pain. She repeated the action over and over again, whipping his back, legs and buttocks with a wild ferocity, until he fell to his knees, whimpering. Lisa noted with incredulity that, throughout this vicious treatment he remained fully hard; clearly he was enjoying every stinging blow.

He fell on his back now, his manhood lying erect on his stomach, the thick, bulbous end resting against his navel. His young tormentor whipped him across the chest, then the stomach, dangerously close to the stiff erection. She then played the strands around his cock, teasing him with them as he quivered in anticipation.

Suddenly she threw the whip to one side and leapt astride the prostrate figure, grabbing at his stiff tool desperately. Finding it, she guided the head to her tiny sex and sat down hard on the mammoth length, its hugeness slipping with impossible ease into her receptive sheath.

'Where the hell does she put it all?' mused Lisa, watching in astonishment as the big, black stalk disappeared into the young girl's wildly-stretched sex-lips as she forced herself to take every thick inch.

With cries of lust and pain, she rode her lover in the same savage way that she had beaten him: hard and without mercy until, with a bellow worthy of a rampaging bull, he threw his hips up to meet her downward pumping thrusts, coming inside her frail body with all the power he held.

As soon as he had subsided, the maid pulled herself from him, allowing his shrinking shaft to flop noisily on to his belly. She squatted over his face, forcing him to lick at her inflamed clitoris until, with a loud groan she orgasmed, grinding her sex into his mouth as his tongue flicked at her erect bud. Finally she collapsed at his side, sated and exhausted.

The Ambassador stood up and applauded. 'Did I not say that they are wonderful?' he said, proudly. He turned to look at his guests, as the two servants slipped quietly from the room. 'And now, for our pleasure, I will take you to my special room.'

'I will stay here,' said Frank, 'perhaps, when your maid has recovered . . .?'

'I'll send her to you. You will find she knows many tricks.'

'I'm sure she does,' said Frank, casually squeezing the prominent bulge in his trousers. 'Now, you girls, remember, do whatever His Excellency wishes.'

The girls smiled to indicate their acquiescence, and followed the Ambassador from the room.

He led them back through the great hall and to a small

door at the far end. Opening it, Lisa saw that it led to some sort of cellar, the steep steps disappearing into the darkness. Their host turned on a light and bade them follow him as he proceeded down the staircase.

At the bottom of the stairs was another, smaller hall, the stone walls lined with many heavy, barred doors, reminding Lisa of a prison. She wondered what secrets lay beyond these portals, what terrible events took place within the cell-like rooms. She felt the excitement mounting inside her, sexual desire mixed with uncertainty and fear, a powerful combination.

Their host took a large bunch of keys from a hook on the wall, unlocked one of the doors and pushed it open, indicating to the girls that they should enter. Janet walked in first, Lisa following, her eyes peering into the darkness. The Ambassador joined them, closing the door with a thud before switching on a light.

Lisa gasped at the sight that met her eyes. The room resembled a medieval torture chamber, filled with all manner of wooden benches, shackles and strange instruments. Heavy chains were hanging from the walls, their purpose unclear. She looked anxiously at Janet, but her friend seemed untroubled by the scene, an expression of sheer lust and excitement playing across her face.

The Ambassador walked to the centre of the room, holding out his arms with pride. 'Welcome to my special playroom, ladies,' he said, smiling broadly. 'We will have much pleasure, I think.'

Janet stood by a large, rack-like bench, her fingers stroking one of four manacles attached to the sides by thick chains. Lisa trembled, remembering the force with which the young maid had laid into her lover, wondering if she was to undergo similar experiences. At the same time though, she felt the arousal increasing in her sex, her lust for the unknown coming to the fore.

The door opened, the sudden noise making her jump with shock. The massive form of the male servant entered, his head stooped slightly against the low ceiling. He was still fully naked, the thick phallus she had seen plunge into the maid just a few moments previously now hanging limp, but nevertheless still fearsomely large between his heavily-muscled thighs. He stood by the door with his arms folded, as though awaiting instructions.

The Ambassador threw off his robe, revealing his extremely hairy, rotund nakedness, his small cock firmly erect against his fat belly. 'Come, ladies, be naked with me,' he cried, licking his lips in anticipation of joys to come.

Janet removed her dress quickly and stood naked but for her high heeled shoes, her hands on her hips, her legs slightly apart. Lisa followed suit, leaving on her stockings, suspender belt and the thick silver chain around her waist the latter touch seeming to her to match the circumstances and environment.

The Ambassador walked over to them and firstly caressed Janet's breasts. His jutting penis pointed directly at her hairy sex, while his thumbs teased her nipples to erection. She breathed heavily, shivering with excitement as one of his hands moved on to her back, down to her pert bottom, then round to the front, pressing his palm over her pussy.

'So wet, so ready,' he said, through clenched teeth, his eyes blazing with lust. 'Go, amuse yourself with my manservant, I will take your friend first.'

Lisa watched with not a little envy as Janet smiled and went to join the huge, black stud, seeing her clutch his rising stalk with both hands, kissing and licking his massive, sweating chest. The Ambassador came over to her and took hold of the chain that hung by her side, pulling her to him. She trembled as the fingertips of his other hand fluttered over her breasts, then gasped as both hands cupped them, lifting them high.

'Lick your nipples,' he commanded, 'lick them hard.'

Lisa pushed her head slightly forward and stuck out her tongue, the tip easily touching her nipple, which became immediately erect in response. She repeated the exercise with her other breast, until both nipples jutted upward, each over an inch long and very hard. The Ambassador let her huge breasts fall gently back and clutched her waist, staring appreciatively at her heaving bosom.

'You have the biggest tits I have ever seen on such a slim girl,' he said without taking his eyes from her thrusting mounds. 'They are superb!'

Using the chain around her waist again, he turned her round so that her back was to him. 'And such a perfect arse!' he said, his hands now rubbing her soft buttocks. 'Truly, an arse like this was made to be fucked!'

He knelt behind her and pressed his face against her bottom, his tongue lapping greedily between the cheeks. She opened her legs and bent forward a little, enjoying the sensation, allowing him to taste the saltiness of her anus, feeling the tip of his tongue prodding at her tight hole.

Suddenly he stood up, wiping the saliva from his chin. 'Enough!' he cried, 'I must have this girl!' He took hold of the chain and dragged her over to a large 'X' frame, fastening first her wrists and then her ankles to the heavy, metal manacles, so that her back was to him. He stood back for a moment, admiring his captive, then she felt him run his hands delicately over her shoulders, down her back and again on to her bottom, the fingers kneading her soft flesh.

She pushed her buttocks out as far as her restraints would allow, desperate to take him inside her. She felt him probe with his podgy fingers into the wetness of her pussy, drawing her juices on to her anus, lubricating the tiny sphincter; preparing her.

She felt one of his fingers snake inside her bottom, the feeling almost making her come with its suddenness. Then it was withdrawn, to be replaced with the thicker intrusion of his cock which, although small, still filled her tight hole adequately.

She sighed with pleasure as he began to pump in and out of her, the constraints of the shackles increasing her enjoyment, the knowledge that he could do to her whatever he pleased driving her mad with lust. She'd become used to taking the dominant role; this feeling of total vulnerability and submission was wonderfully erotic.

She heard Janet cry out and turned her head, just in time to see her friend accommodate the manservant's huge black stalk inside her pussy as she squatted over his reclining body. The sight must have attracted the Ambassador also, for he pulled himself away from Lisa's body and almost leapt towards the rutting couple, and quickly rammed his hard little prick straight into Janet's backside, making her squeal with shock and pleasure.

Lisa watched as her friend was double-fucked, frustrated at her inability to move, to join in. The Ambassador's fat thighs humped furiously against Janet's bum, eventually knocking her from the huge stalk that was impaling her pussy. The servant pulled himself from under her body, leaving his master to hammer away to his heart's content and walked towards Lisa, his manhood jutting proudly in front of him, causing her to gulp with terrified anticipation.

She prayed that he would not take her in the way preferred by his master. She knew there was no way she could painlessly accommodate such a monster anally. It was to her relief, therefore, that she felt him fingering her sex opening the wet lips for his invasion. She braced herself as she felt the thick end of his knob touch her tender lips and his steel-hard shaft begin to slide inside her.

She was amazed at the ease with which he entered her, his hairy crotch touching her bottom almost immediately. He pumped into her with long, slow strokes – the urgency taken from him by the session with Janet – filling her, stretching her in every way. She felt every nerve-ending; every sensation in her body was centred on his perfect tool, his steady shafting exciting her with its insistent demands.

He seemed to sense her need, the pace of his thrusting increasing, his hard thighs bashing against her lovely bottom as he plunged into her greedy honeypot. Lisa felt the sensations tearing at her sex, and the waves of pleasure shooting down her legs to the tips of her toes as she struggled against the tightness of the manacles; so eager was she to wrap her arms and legs around her lover, to take him inside her body as deeply as possible.

The final surge nearly caused her to shout out involuntarily, as the orgasm ripped through her with a ferocity that even these days she rarely experienced. The servant pumped heavily into her, the speed incredible, thrusting his gigantic stalk in and out like the piston of a well-lubricated engine. With a roar he pulled out of her, and she felt the spray of his come soaking her back and bottom. She began to cry with the sheer exhilaration of the moment, her ravaged pussy aching but sated.

After a few minutes, Lisa was released from her shackles, and fell to the stone floor, still weak from the screwing she'd just undergone. The Ambassador was lying on the bench; Janet was busily fastening his wrists to the iron restraints, his small tool glistening and erect. The manservant joined her, fastening his master's ankles, then stood over him, seemingly glaring at the reclining figure, holding his still large black penis in his hand.

Suddenly, he began to pee, the urine spraying all over the Ambassador's face and body. The flow seemed to go on for ages, the girls watching in astonishment as the chained man's cock grew even harder, his pleasure apparent.

Janet took the hint and climbed on to the bench, squatting over his face. With some effort the pee began to trickle from her, then gushed in a torrent, the effusion soaking her victim.

The manservant finished, and motioned to Lisa to take his place. Following Janet's example she squatted over him, this time aiming to soak his genitals. She strained hard, and with some difficulty began to piss on him, just as Janet finished drenching his face. She felt a sort of perverse pleasure, an unusual sensation of power as she peed, happy that she had discovered another sexual practice to add to her repertoire.

Suddenly, with a mighty cry, the Ambassador came, straining and struggling against his shackles, his seed pumping high into the air, soaking her. She had never seen or imagined such a copious amount of sperm from one ejaculation, his orgasm continuing for easily a full minute. Lisa watched as he pulled harder at the chains, his teeth gritted as he enjoyed his strange release; the sight of this powerful man in complete subjugation was oddly arousing.

Eventually, the Ambassador was finished. He lay exhausted as the girls unfastened the manacles, then meekly rose and followed them as they walked out of the room to return upstairs. The servant remained, already starting to clean up the remnants of their mutual pleasure.

Back in the large drawing-room they found Frank curled up on the floor with the little maid, obviously recovering from a long bout of sex. He looked meaningfully at the girls, saying nothing. They knew what they had to do.

Gently, they sat the exhausted Ambassador down on the settee, and sat themselves either side of him, stroking his head and kissing his fat face gently. Lisa could feel the powers building up within her, knowing she was transferring a hypnotic command of capitulation to the unsuspecting man. His eyes became heavy and he drifted off into a deep sleep.

Frank got up from the floor and motioned for the girls to leave. The maid lay asleep, unlikely to wake before the morning, so he could question the Ambassador as much as he wished.

Lisa and Janet left the room, to be met by the manservant in the hall, who was clearly aware of what was going on. He handed them their clothes and coats and led them to a sumptuous bathroom where they showered and dressed in silence.

The girls took their coats and left the Embassy, happy with the memory of some good sex, but both feeling a little uneasy. The limousine waited, ready to take them home.

THE TRAINING GROUNDS

Sarah Veitch

Whether forbidding and austere or hedonistic and opulent, worlds within worlds – self-governing societies isolated from the mundanity and petty rules of everyday life – provide the ideal setting for a Nexus novel. A modern mistress of bondage and corporal punishment fiction, Sarah Veitch has set her books in locations as diverse as a corrective institute for young female offenders – *Serving Time* – and an exotic, tropical island presided over by a strict, mysterious master – *The Training Grounds*.

Charlotte, the heroine of *The Training Grounds*, is taken for two months' holiday in the sun by her rich, handsome boyfriend, Vernon. She is more than a little surprised to find that their destination is in fact a vast correction centre, and further shocks are in store, when she discovers that she is there not as a guest, but as a pleasure slave.

In the following extract, Charlotte, who has deliberately and wantonly flouted the rules, is punished by the Master, only to rebel again. Can he ever bring this feisty young woman to heel?

Many Nexus books feature scenes of corporal punishment. Some Nexus books feature little else! The potent combination of arousal and shame, and defiance and discipline, is an aspect of erotic fiction which has appeared in some of the best-known books in the genre. Sarah Veitch is a specialist in such material and has been published not just by Nexus but by magazines devoted to the popular art of spanking. *The Training Grounds, Lingering Lessons and Serving Time* are full-length novels. *Different Strokes* is a collection of short stories – twenty-two of the best! – which will delight anyone who takes pleasure in a well-disciplined bottom.

'The Master will see you now.'

'Will he, indeed?' Charlotte stretched out on the chaise 'And if I don't go?'

Staring at her unsmilingly, the guide undid the leash and collar tied round his waist.

'All right! All right!'

She could at least walk there with some dignity. Swallowing hard, Charlotte followed the youth down the corridor and out of doors. 'Where are we going anyway?'

'To the Medical Centre,' the youth said.

Maybe they were just going to give her a check up. She swallowed harder.

'Why . . .?'

'The Master will explain.'

Charlotte didn't doubt it. Someone here was always explaining something. She only hoped he wasn't going to explain with his hands or his belt!

They walked on in silence. Her legs felt tremulous. They reached a tall blue building and walked in. Her bare feet sank into thick carpets. The cool evening air had been warmed by coal-effect fires. Guy had explained days ago that they had their own electricity generator here.

Vast amounts of money obviously went into this place. And power. Charlotte felt the man's power as she was led into a small white room in which the Master sat. The room held the chair he was sitting in, a wall-mounted cabinet and a long low massage couch with straps. Seeing the couch – and its punishing potential – Charlotte got ready to bolt.

But the youth was barring the door, looking at her nude body appraisingly.

'Sit down,' said the Master, indicating the couch.

Uncertainly Charlotte sat, just resting her bottom against the edge of the thing. When they relaxed their attention she would make her move.

The Master stared at her.

'You remember yesterday's somewhat painful inauguration?'

'Yes, sir.'

'And what were you told after it?'

She thought back, choosing her words carefully: 'That I should stay in my cell for the remainder of the night.'

'More specifically?'

'That I should never enter a building without permission.'

'So what were you doing eavesdropping in the Artist's Studio today?'

So they *had* seen her – or someone had! At a loss for words, Charlotte stared nervously at the ground.

'You admit you've been disobedient, girl?' the Master said softly.

'Y . . . yes.'

'And what happens to slaves who are disobedient?'

'They . . .'

She couldn't say it! She couldn't! With a half-sob, Charlotte dashed towards the door.

She managed six wild steps before the Master's hand grabbed for her and gripped her shoulders.

'Who did this to you?' she heard him ask, his fingers prodding at her back.

'What'? Oh . . .' She remembered the incident with the paintbrush, 'One of the girls I was painting with. I said something which offended her. It doesn't hurt.'

The Master nodded towards the guide, and he slipped out of the room. Charlotte felt too weak to resist as the Master pushed her back against the couch. She whimpered slightly as he turned her over on to her belly. She knew what was coming next.

'What do you think we should do to someone who spies on others?'

'Spank them,' she whispered, and felt the heavy leather straps being fastened over her ankles and wrists.

'How hard should we spank them, Charlotte?'

'Till they promise they won't do it again.'

She was, she told herself, just asking for a spanking to avoid a whipping. Babs in the Artist's Studio had asked for three strokes and had ultimately received five. If you didn't ask for something they simply disciplined you more soundly. She was beginning to learn . . .

With exquisite slowness, the Master palmed her buttocks. He felt the crease at the top of her thighs, and moved endlessly up to cup the swell of her helpless rear.

'To think we trusted you to be obedient,' he said regretfully. 'To think I'm having to chastise you further on your second day.'

'Please. I won't do it again,' Charlotte whispered.

'I'm going to have to teach your bottom a lesson so that it doesn't,' the Master said.

He lifted his hand up and brought it down with a moderate slap against the swell of her rear end. Charlotte tensed, then relaxed: this wasn't so bad! For a while he punished her at this level; the strokes firm but bearable. She could feel her buttocks heating up; she was hugely aware of each separate cheek; of the dividing cleft; of the swelling leaves of her quim . . .

Suddenly the Master stopped and palmed her arse some more. 'Now we've prepared this wicked little posterior for punishment,' he murmured, 'how many blows do you think your proper spanking should contain?'

Opening her eyes, Charlotte stared at the white sheet which covered the massage couch. She might have known he'd find a way to prolong her humiliation and make her suffer anew.

'Ten,' she said, glad that she wasn't Babs, receiving the tawse on her upturned rear end.

'Ten seems fair,' said the Master, raising his hand again. He brought it down with all the force he could muster, and she screamed and kicked her legs.

Or tried to, for the strong restraints held them. As she moaned and writhed the Master planted three more full-force slaps on her smarting rear. Charlotte cried out and wriggled; her eyes watering. An inarticulate stream of words and sounds issued from her lips.

'The ten whacks aren't negotiable,' the man said, teasing the tormented flesh, 'so save your promises.'

He continued to toast his heavy palm against her throbbing rear. Charlotte sobbed as he quietly counted each correction. Five. Six. Seven. Eight. Nine. Ten.

As the sound of the tenth slap echoed round the room, she twisted her head to one side and cried: 'I hate you!'

'I think not,' said the Master amicably, putting his middle finger in her clamping buttock cleft. He ran his finger slowly down till she tightened further, then moved it round to rest between her soft fleshy lips.

'You're a wet little girl.'

She closed her eyes again. This couldn't be happening!

'An excited little girl. A girl who played with herself earlier today.'

Charlotte gritted her teeth; she tried to imagine herself somewhere else, and couldn't. Someone had seen her bringing herself off. No one had ever seen such things except him . . .

'What were you thinking about when you came, Charlotte – about Babs's poor bottom? Did you imagine it was *your* bottom, Charlotte? Did it make you hot like it's making you hot now?'

'No,' she said. 'No! You're mistaken . . .'

'If you say so,' said the man, taking his hand away.

Damn him, his hand had got her started – she needed to come desperately! She couldn't do anything with her hands and legs tied like this.

'Untie me,' she muttered, trying to push her swollen mound against the couch top. She could go back to her cell and bring herself some urgent release.

'Not yet,' said the Master slowly, returning his attentions to her bottom. He stroked it thoughtfully. 'Did you enjoy your breakfast this morning, my dear?'

'Yes, Mas . . .' She choked back the word. God it must be catching, living in this place. 'Yes!' she snapped, writhing as he continued to touch her, both hands lightly massaging her burning bum.

'And lunch and dinner were equally satisfactory?'

'Uh huh.'

'And you enjoyed a refreshing bath, and a good night's sleep?'

'Yes. Thank you.'

She couldn't fault these aspects of his hospitality.

'And yet you repay me by abandoning your work.'

Again Charlotte felt caught out, helpless. 'I . . . I'm sorry.'

'We're going to have to make you sorry,' said the man.

Charlotte felt the almost familiar lurch in her lower belly. Her groin felt hot and large, and was throbbing needily.

'You've failed at the first task we set you,' continued the Master, running his flattened hand thoughtfully over her punished globes until they tingled further. 'Do you know what happens to workers who fail at their allocated tasks?'

'Don't tell me – you spank them!' muttered Charlotte, awkwardly.

'No, they become pleasure slaves. Though, of course, the guests like punishing them with more than spanks . . .'

He paused.

'I think, in a round about way, you'll enjoy it, Charlotte. You can learn a lot about yourself as a pleasure slave. Of course, most slaves have at least a year to learn the job's . . . er . . . refinements. You'll have to learn within six weeks.'

Charlotte moaned. 'But I'll only be here for eight weeks – it isn't worth it!' She wished the man would stop doing such exquisite things to her arse.

'I'm sure the men who push their cocks between your lips will think it's worth it, Charlotte. I'm sure there'll be no complaints from whoever receives this virgin prize.'

So saying, he touched the entrance to her bottom very gently. She wriggled further. She couldn't take much more! As if reading her thoughts he murmured: 'You'll have to take all I can give you, Charlotte.'

She twisted her head round to see him dipping his middle finger in the contents of a pottery jar.

Oil – it was obviously oil! He put his finger against her anus, confirming this. His finger felt warm and gelatinous. As she whimpered he slid it in a quarter of an inch.

'You've never had a finger in there before, have you Charlotte?'

'No, sir.'

The sentence was out before she had time to bite back the 'sir'.

'Nor anything larger, like a man's cock?'

'No.'

'Such a waste. We must teach you to ask for one nicely,' murmured the man. His finger invaded further. Charlotte groaned softly. This was terrible, yet wonderful. Sensation was building like a pressure cooker between her legs.

'Please. I can't bear it,' she whispered pitifully.

'I've bared it for you, you bad girl,' the Master said.

He slid in a little further, and put his free hand on her pudenda. She pushed against it. And pushed and pushed. He finger-fucked her base as she rubbed herself against his fingers. She came and came; the pleasure starting at her quim, spreading out across her belly and coursing through to her newly invaded arse.

The Master went on teasing her after her orgasm had ended.

'Too much!' she gasped, but he continued to finger the over-sensitive bud's outer contours with feather light strokes.

'That's for me to decide, my dear,' he said, conversationally. 'If I want to play with you for another hour, I will.'

'No! Stop!' Despite her pleas, he continued to torment her. She knew some more humble response was needed,

'Yes, sir. You must finger me for as long as you see fit, sir,' she gasped and he moved his cruel hand away.

'There, that wasn't so difficult, was it?' he asked, calmly.

She shook her head. He squeezed her buttocks hard.

'No, sir. Thank you sir.'

She panted out the words as his fingers threatened to stimulate her throbbing sex lips again.

'You're too tight, though. That's unfortunate.'

Her tummy churned further.

'I'm sorry.'

'Don't be sorry, Charlotte. Just help us make it right.'

Walking over to the cupboard he extracted something, brought it over and held it in front of her.

'An anal plug,' he murmured. 'The smallest size.'

He walked towards her feet, and she felt him undo the ankle straps.

'Spread your legs wide.'

She spread them, feeling wetness pool between her thighs.

'Good girl.'

She felt more oil being poured in the cleft between her buttocks. She felt his fingers probing and opened her legs wider still.

'Good. Good.'

She sensed he'd placed something at the entrance to her anus, and tensed automatically. He slapped both her buttocks hard. The oil seemed to intensify the pain, and add to the ongoing throbbing. She yelped and jerked, then used all her will-power to keep her bottom relaxed.

'That's better. We can do it when we try, can't we, Charlotte?'

'Yes, sir.'

She heard the smile in his voice.

'You'll call me Master one of these days, my dear.'

'Never!'

'Taste my whip on your arse before you say never, my pretty bitch.'

How could he talk down to her like this? How could he!

Her lower belly felt strangely excited again. The plug was now against her arsehole and being pushed forward. She cried out as he slid it in place; not that it stretched her much – it didn't. It was just so alien, so strange.

'I'm being gentle with you, Charlotte.'

She shuddered: 'Thank you, sir.'

'I could have had you fitted with a much thicker plug than this.'

At the prospect she closed her eyes, feeling both horrified and breathless. The Master rotated the plug till she squirmed. 'You won't let me down?'

'No, sir.'

'Silly girl – you don't even know what you're agreeing to!'

He stroked her firmly, reminding her of how sore her bottom was.

'Don't fail me this time. Only take this plug out to answer a call of nature. Then wash it yourself and put it straight back.' She sensed him smile. 'Think of me as you're pushing it back into that cute little rump, Charlotte. And think of the men to come.'

Leaving her still tethered by her wrists, he pressed a button on the wall and the guide who had brought her to the Medical Centre reappeared again.

'Our failed little painter has repented of her ways,' the Master said.

Charlotte closed her eyes, ashamed that the youth was staring at her scolded flesh, her invaded bottom.

'Shall I take her back to her cell, Master?' he said.

'Yes. Her bath has been run. A light supper awaits her.' He spoke as if Charlotte was no longer there.

'And can I . . .?' asked the youth, stroking his erection before laying his cool hand on her hot little derrière.

'No,' said the Master. 'She is reserved for the guests.'

But not for him? Biting back the thought, Charlotte lay quietly as the boy untied her ankles. She got up stiffly without looking at either of the men. As she moved towards the door, she found the presence of the plug meant she had to keep her thighs slightly further apart than usual. She was sure her walk must look ungainly and strange.

'Sweet dreams, Charlotte,' said the Master, as she walked from the Medical Centre. 'You'll probably want to sleep on your tummy tonight.'

Charlotte had orgasmed mainly from having her bottom spanked! Vernon stretched out in his armchair recalling last night's session, feeling himself grow hard. He'd sat behind the one-way mirror at the Medical Centre with Suki; a welcome, purring burden in his lap. He'd seen Charlotte stretched out, tied, her buttocks warmed, and her arse invaded with the little plug. He'd wanted to fuck her there and then, whilst she was still hot and wet. He had started to signal to a guide . . .

'Wait a few hours,' Suki had whispered, obviously reluctant to let go of him. 'She'll be wider by then. The plug will have begun its work.'

'And will you watch behind the mirror, my sweet, as I fuck the belligerence from my horny little girlfriend?'

'If you desire it, sir,' murmured Suki. Blushing, she hid her head in his armpit, and wriggled against the arm of the chair.

He'd stroked her hair, then guided her head down to his surging hardness. She'd sucked him off a few times now, her sure lips siphoning off his juice. He came all the more, imagining it trickling down her throat and into her belly. He'd come between her buoyantly bouncing breasts, and he'd exploded whilst rubbing himself in the tight hot cleft of her bottom. He was still being faithful to Charlotte in not going all the way.

Not that he wasn't tempted! Gorgeous as the feel of her velvet tongue was, he couldn't help but be drawn to her other fleshy attractions. He had found himself staring with increasing lust at that coffee coloured Mount of Venus, and that tempting rear. Suki didn't help his self-control; continually rubbing her pubic bone against the bulge in his trousers; bending over to straighten the mattress so that he was treated to the sight of those luscious dusky folds . . .

Now, as he reminisced, she returned from her bath and knelt at the foot of the bed. She smiled gently, and kissed his feet.

'Sir, what are we going to do today?'

'We're going to see Charlotte, my little beauty. The Master has promised we can check on her progress for ourselves.'

'And will you . . .' Suki trailed off, obviously realising she mustn't ask personal questions. 'She will want you back,' she said sadly. 'She will plead for you to take her away to the outside world.'

'That's where you're wrong.'

With some regret, Vernon pushed her head away as it planted little kisses up his calves, his thighs, his stirring scrotum .

'She's to be blindfolded. I'm to wear some of your island essence. She won't know who's pleasuring her unless I speak.' He watched as the native girl relaxed a little. 'Come and watch,' he said, staring into her face, noting how she flinched at the humiliating prospect.

'Yes, sir. Whatever you say, sir.'

'I'll be ramming my cock right up her,' he said with deliberate cruelty. 'She's been missing it a lot.'

He showered and breakfasted, then a guide came and took him and Suki to one of the lounges behind the Pleasure Suite. 'Enjoy,' he said, handing Vernon his favourite drink.

Enjoying himself already, Vernon settled himself on a low couch behind the one way mirror, with Suki by his side. They could see through the glass into the suite; the Master was visible, already seated in one of its many chairs. After a few seconds Charlotte walked in behind a guide, her eyes downcast. Hesitantly she walked up to the Master and stood facing him.

'You have bathed, Charlotte?'

She nodded.

'Your body is ready to receive a man?'

'I . . .?' She shrugged, her mouth twisting helplessly. An excited gleam had come into her eyes.

'He may want to touch all your private places.'

Charlotte swallowed hard.

Vernon watched as the man's hand moved to her arsehole, pushing gently at the obstruction then turning it. Charlotte was just standing before him, like a well-trained dog.

There was a pause. Vernon saw Charlotte shudder slightly. What was she up to?

'I hope you've been keeping your anal plug in place, Charlotte?' the Master said.

'I . . . yes.'

'Because it's time to have an inspection.'

'Oh.' Charlotte looked awkwardly at the floor, and studied her feet.

'Bend over that settee, Charlotte. That's right – legs wide open.'

Vernon pushed Suki away from him so he could get a better view. The man was sliding his hand up Charlotte's inner thighs, making her wriggle. 'Steady,' he kept saying. 'Dear me, we're going to have to teach you some control, girl. You're like a bitch on heat.'

He concentrated on caressing her thighs for long moments. 'Now push your arse out towards me. Right out. Push your legs apart as far as they'll go.'

She did so, and he put his fingers against the divide between her spread cheeks. He palpated the plug, and pushed it in slightly further. Charlotte flinched away.

'Bad girl. Stay still!'

The man struck her twice on her posterior. She flinched again, then kept her bottom in its hugely exposed state. Again the Master played with the plug, pulling it half out, then twisting it round. Charlotte whimpered.

'Are you sure you kept that plug in all night?'

'Yes!'

Her voice was a half sigh. She stared at the settee cover.

The man pushed the plug back in fully and turned her round. 'Come and watch a film, Charlotte, a very special film. Perhaps it'll take your mind off how stretched your poor bottom feels.'

The viewers saw her body relax and watched her cross to the settee and begin to lower herself on to it.

'No. Lie over my knees,' the Master said, sitting down on one of the armless chairs and invitingly patting his lap.

'I won't – you can't make me!'

Charlotte turned and sprinted across the enormous hall. Seeking an exit, her gaze darted about wildly. Shaking his head slightly, the Master signalled to the guide. The boy raced after her and caught her, and sadistically took his time in bringing her back.

'Such impetuousness,' the Master murmured, smiling as the guide tied her wrists together before her. The boy then fastened a leather collar round her neck, added a lead to it, and tied the lead to a ring in the ground. Charlotte thrashed around on the floor as he did so. Only her feebly kicking legs were left free.

Vernon gulped and Suki sighed softly as the boy held her, and stretched her over the Master's lap. Now her pale heaving bottom lay helplessly beneath his roving hands.

'This is nice, now, isn't it?' he murmured, teasingly. There was no answer from his blushing lap girl, though the writhing of her buttocks showed how humiliated she was. As the viewers watched, the Master pressed a button for the film to begin.

Charlotte looked at the video before her, obviously trying to take her mind off the ignominy of her position. As Vernon stared at the screen he saw it was of Charlotte entering a lounge; of Charlotte wanking herself, her fingers moving like crazy; of Charlotte coming, her mouth opened in a drawn out cry.

Charlotte blushed even more hotly as she saw the film. She wriggled on the man's knee, then wriggled further. The screen showed her being led into a golden cell. She was walking with her thighs spread apart, her buttocks pink and glowing.

'Sleep well,' said the guide on the film, closing and locking the bars which made up the door.

On the screen Charlotte made a face at his retreating back, then lay down on the chaise and stared at her chastened globes. Lightly. she touched the plug that protruded an inch from her arse. After a moment she shifted position, and grimaced. She moved some more, then reached a hand back and removed the plug. For a second she studied it; studied her liberated anus. Then she threw the plug childishly on the floor.

She slept then, a smile playing about her face intermittently. A clock in the corner of the screen helped the watchers keep time. They saw the film fast-forwarded on to 8 a.m., where she wakened and returned the plug to her arsehole. Seconds later a guide with a trolley appeared.

'So you heard the girl coming and pretended you'd done what you were told,' the Master whispered, stroking Charlotte's recalcitrant bottom. 'Why are you so relentlessly bad?'

'It felt strange! I didn't like it!'

'You didn't give yourself time to like it. You didn't like being naked at first.'

Silence. Charlotte's eyes were closed, her mouth open. Her backside was moving convulsively, her nude stomach rubbing against his trousered lap.

'Such a simple request – and you fail me! I'll have to punish this stubborn young derrière,' the Master said.

'Please, no! It was only punished yesterday!'

'You merely received a spanking,' murmured the man. 'It obviously wasn't enough.'

He moved his thighs so that her bottom was raised further; an inviting target.

'What are you going to do to me?' whispered Charlotte, trying to push her posterior back down.

'What do you think I should do?' the Master replied, coolly.

'Belt her,' said Vernon, softly. Suki shuddered and licked his arm. The guide in the lounge looked over at him.

'Sir, should I tell the Master that?'

'Yes. Ask him to take a light belt across her disobedient little bum.'

Suki took the zip of his trousers between her teeth and pulled it down.

'Sir. I can bring you much more pleasure than the Charlotte woman can,' she said, closing her mouth round his flesh.

The way he was feeling now, he could come with both women! Vernon sat back and enjoyed Suki's tongue on him; enjoyed the scene taking place in the Pleasure Suite. He stared as a whimpering Charlotte was pushed down on to her hands and knees by the Master, and made to walk around like a dog led by her collar and lead.

He saw the guide enter and say something to the Master, who then indicated one of the many cupboards lining the walls. Smiling, the guide approached the largest one, rifled through its contents, and brought out a belt.

'Where should we bind this wicked young pup?' asked the Master, casually. He looked around. 'I think we'll tether it to the four-poster bed.'

As the guide pulled and a sorrowful Charlotte barely resisted, the three of them made their way over to one of the huge four-posters in the Pleasure Suite.

'Spread-eagle her,' said the Master, lightly. Soon Charlotte's arms and legs were scissored far apart and tied to the posts of the bed.

'Now, tell me you deserve to be disciplined,' said the Master, stroking the belt lightly over her buttocks. Charlotte said nothing. The Master teased the belt across her arse. 'Tell me you – '

'I won't say it!'

The man gave her a light taste of the belt.

'Please. Can't I retain some dignity?' The words were half enraged, half sobbed.

'*What* dignity? You're naked. We're all staring at you. You came when I spanked you. You got wet when I forced a little plug up your butt.'

Charlotte was slithering around even more at his words. Vernon looked at Suki, who was growing wetter beside him.

'She holds on to her pride,' whispers Suki. 'She doesn't understand.'

'Tell me you deserve to be disciplined.'

A second leathering.

'Tell me . . .'

'All right! All right!'

'Say it. Say the words, my pretty dear.'

'I deserve to be disciplined. Satisfied?'

The words were there, but it was easy to sense that she was still holding back.

'What do you deserve exactly?'

'To . . .' She buried her face into the pillow, and closed her eyes tightly.

A third stroke, firm and fast.

'Oh, you bastard! I deserve to . . . to feel your belt against my arse!'

'Dear, dear. We mustn't call our Master a bastard. I believe it's not the first time, either. Some more indiscretions to be chalked up in the punishment book,' he sighed. 'But for now, we've got you to admit that you've been wicked, that you had to be taught.' He fondled her twitching rear. 'It really hurt, didn't it?' he whispered.

'You know it did!'

'Hurts almost as much as the pleasure you receive when you're good. Think about that . . .'

He touched her tits.

'What was our deal, Charlotte?'

'I'm to become a pleasure slave.'

The words were half-defiant, half-whimpering. The guide sighed.

'Exactly. A *pleasure* slave. And one of our friends wants to take pleasure from your sex right now.'

The guide's cock straightened; Vernon's cock straightened. Suki frowned and took both of his hands.

'Please, sir. I am as hot as she is,' the native girl whispered.

The guide grinned at them both, then turned to Vernon: 'Your woman will be ready for you in five minutes, sir.'

Five minutes – he could hardly wait! Vernon settled

down to watch the mirror, noting the Master was still teasing Charlotte's fiery posterior.

'Such a sore little butt,' he murmured sorrowfully. 'I do hope we're teaching it to be good.'

'Yes, I'll be good. So good.' Charlotte was writhing, perspiring.

'I hope you'll please our rampant male friend.'

The Master continued to knead Charlotte's buttocks with varying degrees of severity. When she was subservient he released the pressure; when she was arrogant he increased the force of his grip.

'Untie me, and I'll please your friend with my fingers,' murmured Charlotte, beseechingly.

'No, no, dear. We can't trust you yet not to put a consoling hand on that chastened rear.'

'I won't! I promise.'

'More obedient girls than you have promised. But the temptation to protect those tender globes, to put a cool hand on that well-warmed flesh is just too much.'

The Master smiled.

'In fact, my friend likes bad girls to remain tied up. And he likes them blindfolded. So we're going to tie this scarf over your eyes. It helps concentrate the mind.'

So saying, he took a black cotton square from the nearest guide, and tied it round Charlotte's head, knotting it at the back, checking that she couldn't see anything through it.

'Now await your pleasure, slave,' he said, and pressing a button, the Master nodded.

'He's ready for us,' said the guide. Suki made to follow them, but Vernon kissed her lips, then pushed her back gently in her chair.

'Keep the seat warm for me,' he said softly. 'Watch, and you may learn.'

Breathing hard, he followed the youth through two sets of doors till they entered the Pleasure Suite. It looked even larger inside than it did viewing it from behind the glass.

'Here is your first owner,' said the Master to Charlotte

standing back a little. 'Show by your wetness and your words that you are happy to receive him,' he ordered, before taking a seat at her head.

There was a silence. Vernon stared down at Charlotte's helpless, staked out body. Her rear end was red, and he touched it, revelling in the heat.

'Please sir. Please untie me,' whispered the spread-eagled Charlotte.

Vernon looked at the Master and shook his head.

'Ask only for cock, slave!' warned the Master. 'This man does not waste his time in idle words with his inferiors.'

Charlotte said nothing. Vernon returned his palms to her arse. He stroked round and round till she whimpered. He slapped down on one buttock, then again and again.

'Oh! Oh!'

She wriggled until he made both sides symmetrical. Then she pushed her bottom back the little she could in her bonds.

'I think she's begging to be fucked,' the Master murmured. 'Say it, Charlotte. Beg for a fucking.'

'No!'

She spat the word out angrily into the pillow and pulled at her bonds.

'Your cunt wants it. Your guest knows you want it.'

He indicated to Vernon to check how wet she was. Gently Vernon slid his finger between her closed sex lips. They felt dry on the outside but opened to reveal a cup of gelatinous wetness.

'All that heat rushed to your bum, and some of it reached your pussy,' murmured the Master. 'And now the pussy wants a tom cat to make her come.'

Charlotte buried her head deeper in the pillow, though her buttocks tightened. Vernon slid a hand down the cleft, which was slick and hot.

'You're about to be fucked tied down over a bed. Can you imagine?' murmured the Master. Charlotte moaned quietly. Vernon's cock throbbed within his briefs.

It was strange, the Master watching – the guides watching. He thought of Suki watching from behind the mirror, and his balls felt as if they'd explode. It was lucky he'd allowed his little naked native girl to tongue him to full pleasure twenty minutes before. It meant he could hold out longer now, and make Charlotte writhe against his rock hard cock.

He touched the puckered mouth of her anus, noting the slight redness.

'You've displeased our friend by taking your plug out,' the Master said. 'He has the right to punish you for such misdemeanours. Imagine, Charlotte, if he takes off his belt . . .'

'No. Please. I'll give him such a good time. I'm wet for him.'

'How wet?'

'So wet I can't bear it. I need to come!'

'Only if your owner wishes you to come, you realise.'

'Yes, sir.'

'Yes, *Master*.'

Charlotte refused to repeat the word.

'Teach her manners with your masculine accoutrements,' the Master said, lightly.

Unzipping himself, Vernon placed his cock against the entrance to Charlotte's canal. Tethered and wet as she was, she was easy to enter. He slid in fully, and she gasped and tried to push her hips back to enjoy more cock.

'Greedy,' said the Master. 'Our friend may grow annoyed with you. He may not want to fuck some cheap little tart who's so desperate for his tool.'

'Please . . .' Charlotte's voice was a sigh. The covers were wet beneath her. Vernon half pulled out, before thrusting forward again.

This was exquisite – wonderful! The heat of her arse, of her cunt; her snuffling half-cries. He leant forward, slid his hands to her front, and cupped her mammaries. The nipples felt hard and tumid; unusually hot.

'More!' whimpered Charlotte again, trying to fight her bonds, to take him in deeper. He slid one hand down her flat belly, and brushed it against her bud. She half-screamed with desire, then squirmed even more desperately. Her clit felt swollen to twice its usual size.

Grinning, Vernon moved his cock out by degrees till just the tip was inside her. Then he played with her sex lips and pussy hair, enjoying her urgent cries.

'Maybe we'll leave you tied up all day,' the Master whispered, 'so you can't touch yourself like a dirty little girl.'

'Please – I need to come! I'll do anything!'

'Like keep your anal plug in overnight?'

'Yes, fit it back now! Stick it in hard! Do anything, any way, but let me come.'

'Wicked,' murmured the Master. Vernon palmed Charlotte's arse and made her writhe some more.

He rammed into her again and she sighed with relief. 'Please sir, do it to me, sir,' she begged throatily.

'Beg for cock, specifically, Charlotte,' reminded the Master, sounding impressively calm.

'Please, sir. Put your cock inside me, right up me, and fuck me hard.'

'How hard?' asked the Master.

'As hard as he can.'

As aroused as he was, that was *very* hard! Vernon gripped her belly and pulled himself deeper into her quim.

'And how deep?'

'So that he shoots his load right up inside me.'

'She's got a filthy mouth on her,' said the Master quietly. 'She's a dirty little bitch.'

Charlotte cried out, obviously approaching nirvana. Vernon continued to thrust, his own ecstasy drawing near. His balls were getting that incredible almost-almost-almost feeling. The rhythm was speeding up in his hips and in his head.

'We're recording this on film, Charlotte,' the Master said, almost conversationally. 'You'll see yourself taking my belt across your arse.'

Charlotte squirmed and sighed and lifted her hips the little she could in her tied-down position.

'You'll see the way it wriggles. You'll see it going from pink to deepest red.'

Vernon thrust and thrust.

'You'll watch yourself beg for a stranger's cock,' added the Master. Orgasmic yells half-muffled by the pillow, Charlotte came.

Jesus! That sound always finished him off! Muffling his cries into her back, Vernon exploded inside her. He licked her shoulders, pleased that they still tasted the same. Her hair was wet, though, her hairline slicked with perspiration. When he pulled out he saw the river of desire between her legs.

'It's amazing what a good talking to can do,' said the Master, smiling. 'We'll just leave her there for a bit to reflect on her sins.'

Dazed, Vernon stood up and put his well-milked manhood back into his trousers. Staring in the direction of the mirror and wishing he could see through it, he winked towards where he thought Suki would be sitting, and gave her the thumbs up. He was about to thank the Master when the man smiled and indicated the tied-up and blindfolded Charlotte, putting his finger to his lips.

'If sir will accompany me to the lounge,' he said, calmly, 'Sir can relax with a drink.'

A double whisky awaited him behind the mirror, though Suki, as a slave girl, had to make do with a soft tangerine-like drink. Vernon lay back in his chair and sipped the malted spirit. He watched covetously as the maid servant anointed Charlotte's arse. The tumult was abating in his emptied balls; in his sensation-stick. Suki crouched on the floor beside him, her lips to his trousered calves, nuzzling. He could sense her large eyes pleading for attention, but he refused to meet her gaze.

Staring into the mirror he felt a perverse sense of enjoyment. Both women wanted him now; both wanted him to pleasure them hard! He gazed out at his girlfriend's well-oiled softness. Already he wanted to touch her fevered flesh again . . .

As he watched, a guide came in and undid the bonds which held Charlotte's arms and legs to the bed's corners.

After a moment of flexing each limb, she crawled into a kneeling position on the bed.

'You've done well,' said the Master, striding through the hall towards her.

The watchers noted her flush of pleasure.

'Thank you, sir.'

'You can go back to your cell and rest till after lunch. I'll send a maid to wash your hair – another bath awaits you.' He paused and winked. 'A *cool* bath, of course!'

Charlotte blushed.

Sighing, Suki curled her hands round Vernon's ankles. Then she tugged off his sandals and licked his soles. Her tongue slid insistently between each toe, and he sighed with satisfaction as her wetness teased each cavity. Then her teeth nipped gently at his lower legs.

She traced her kisses behind his knees, slipping her tongue into each hollow. Her lips moved closer and closer to his hirsute thighs. He was vaguely aware of her hands beginning to ride upwards as he watched the Charlotte he'd just fucked to orgasm being led from the room.

BEATRICE

Anonymous

First published in Paris in the 1920s, it is likely that Beatrice was written in Britain at the end of the nineteenth century. Thus the novel is not, strictly speaking, 'new erotica', but merits inclusion in this collection on all other counts.

Its twenty-five-year-old heroine flees from her loveless marriage and, together with her equally attractive sister Caroline, seeks comfort and a new beginning in the disciplined household of her uncle and his lascivious second wife. The novel is remarkable both for its explicit subject matter and for the superior, often subtly poetic quality of the writing. Bizarre though their experiences may be, the characterisation of Beatrice, Caroline and their equally sensual cousin Jenny renders them infinitely more believable than most other heroines of Victorian literature.

Here, Beatrice and Caroline find themselves providing part of the entertainment at a debauched gathering, and then enjoy a riding lesson with a pleasurably painful difference.

Much erotic writing produced in the early part of the twentieth century is populated by flagellants, servants, errant maids and strict governesses. Although contemporary life is less hierarchical, the allure of these archetypes is strong, and one can find their like gracing the pages of popular, mass-market erotic fiction. Our Victorian ancestors were a kinky lot, for all their displays of respectability and manners. If this extract from *Beatrice* intrigues you, look out for the books in Nexus's *Eroticon* series: anthologies of genuinely old erotica featuring extracts from classic Victoriana such as Walter's *My Secret Life* and the scandalous *My Conversion*.

There were crumbs around my mouth. I wiped my lips delicately with my napkin and yawned. After the meal which the servant had brought to my room, I had sipped my liqueur. It had not been taken. The servant who brought the tray was the young girl who had curtsied to us when we had been taken to the stable that morning. Her name was Mary. She was unlearned but pretty. It pleased her to wait upon me. The flush of pleasure lay on her cheeks.

She appeared not surprised to find me naked except for my stockings and boots. On her coming back for the plates, the wine bottle and the glasses, I took her wrist and sat up. I swung my legs over the bed.

'M'am?' she asked. The housekeeper had not called me M'am. I sensed ranks, classes within classes, initiations. I drew Mary down beside me. 'I dares not stay,' she said, 'they will punish me.'

'With the strap?' I asked.

She gazed at the floor. Her feet were shod in neat black boots. Small feet. I would lick her toes perhaps. No. Crumbs of dirt between them. My nose wrinkled with distaste. My hand slid from her wrist and covered her hand. She trembled visibly. Her rosebud mouth was sweet. Such gestures are fatal. They have meaning – like commas, dashes, question marks. I have walked between words. I know the dangers of the spaces between them.

I passed my hand up the nape of her neck and felt her hair. It had not the silkiness of mine, but it was clean. I turned her face, moving my lips over hers. She started like a fawn. I held her. There was a taste of fresh bread in her mouth.

'Tell me,' I said.

'There are no answers,' a voice said. It was Jenny. She had entered quietly. I neither moved nor sprang up as perhaps she wanted me to. Instead I pressed my mouth again upon the girl's. She trembled in her freshness, a salty dew between her thighs. I felt intimations of boldness. Jenny's hand fell upon my shoulder.

She drew Mary up from my embrace. The girl turned and went, leaving the plates. I made to rise when Jenny fell upon me, spreading my legs by forcing hers between them. The hairs of her pubis were springy to mine through her thin cotton dress. It was a new dress. Small mauve flowers on a blue background. I wanted it.

'There is a wildness in you,' Jenny said. Her tongue licked suddenly into my mouth and then withdrew.

'Let me kiss your thighs,' I begged. She laughed and rose, pushing herself up on her forearms slowly so that her breasts bobbed their juicy gourds over mine.

Bereft I lay. Would she seek my tears – kiss the salty droplets? At Christmas Eve I had been carried upstairs with my drawers down. The sea-cry, the wind-cry. Jenny turned to the window and looked down. The darkness now beyond – the mouth of night.

'The stations are all closed – the people have gone. The ships have sailed,' she said. I began to cry. She turned and shook me roughly. 'The reception will begin soon, Beatrice – get dressed stand up!'

Words stuttered in my mouth but knew no seeking beyond. I wanted my nipples to be burnished by her lips. Instead I obeyed quietly as she told me to remove my boots and stockings. In place of the stockings I was to wear tights such as dancers do on the stage. They were flesh-coloured. The burr of my pubic curls showed through. They bulged. A top of the same material was passed over my shoulders. It hugged my waist and hips, fitting so tightly that my nipples protruded into the fine net.

'Longer boots,' Jenny said. She pointed to the wardrobe. I padded to it. They had been made ready for me, polished. Sleek-fitting, I drew them on. The heels were narrow and spiked. 'Brush your hair – make yourself presentable,' Jenny said, 'I shall return for you in a minute.'

I had not then seen the house except for the back stairs and the entrance hall. There was buzzing of voices as I was made to descend with Caroline – she dressed as I. The grooves between our buttock cheeks showed through the mesh. A piano played. It stopped when we entered. People in formal evening dress gazed at us and then turned away. Gilt mirrors ranged the walls with paintings between them – one by one around the room. Mary and another girl moved among the visitors with champagne. On sideboards there were canapés in numerous colours. They looked as pretty as flowers on their silver trays.

The piano played again. Mozart, I thought. Men looked at my breasts and buttocks. Their eyes fanned Caroline's curves. The high heels made us walk awkwardly, stiffly. The cheeks of our bottoms rolled.

To the one blank wall farthest from the doors Jenny led us, a hand on each of our elbows. There were clamps, chains, bands of leather.

Caroline first. Her legs were splayed, her ankles fastened. Her arms above her head.

'Hang your head back – let your bottom protrude!' Jenny snapped at her. I wanted to be blindfolded. I knew it was good to be so. Black velvet bands swathed our eyes. In darkness we stood, our shoulders touching warm. The manacles were tight.

I had seen a distant relative of ours. He watched upon our obedience. I heard his voice. There was silence in the room. The last chords of the piano tinkled and were gone. A wink of fishes' tails and gone.

Caroline first. I heard the intake of her breath as he passed his hands up the backs of her thighs and squeezed her bottom cheeks. 'My doves,' he breathed. He placed a broad, warm palm on each of our bottoms. People clapped. The room stirred again, came alive.

We were left. Knuckles slyly nudged our bottoms from time to time. Were we forbidden? Female fingers touched more delicately. With the protrusion of our bottoms and the splaying of our legs, our slits were at pillage. Mine wettened into the mesh of the tights as slender fingers quested and sought the lips. And found. I tried not to wriggled my hips.

Champagne was passed between our lips from goblets unseen. I absorbed mine greedily. I could hear Caroline's tongue lapping. There was dancing. I heard the feet. The plaintive cry of an oboe accompanying the piano. If it were a girl playing I would know her by her slimness, her tight small mouth that only an oboe reed would enter. Her face would be oval and pale, her breasts light and springy. She would speak little. Her words would be dried corn, her days spent in quiet rooms. At the high notes I envisaged her on a bed in a white cell. She would not struggle. Her stockings would be white, her thighs slender.

Laid on her back, she would breathe slowly, quietly, fitfully through her nose. Her dress would be raised. Knees would kneel on the bed between her legs. Her knees would falter, stir and bend. Her bottom would be small and tight. Hands would cup and lift. She would wear white gloves of kid. I had almost forgotten the gloves. They would be decorated with small pearl buttons spaced half an inch apart.

No words. Her mouth would be dry. A small dry mouth. Her cunny would be dry. A small dry cunny. A tongue would moisten it – her fingers would clench. She would close her eyes. Her eyelashes would have the colour of straw.

Her knees would be held. The knob-glow of a penis three times the girth of her oboe would probe her slit. A small cry. A quavering. In her dryness. entering, deep-entering it would enter. Lodged. Held full within. The tightness there. In rhythmic movement it would move, the lips expanding around the stem.

Silently he would work, upheld on forearms bared, gazing down upon the pallor of her face.

Her buttocks would twitch and tighten. A crow would alight at the window. Pecking at stone it would be gone.

The penis moving, stiff. A small bubble of sound from her lips, suppressed. The tightening of her buttocks would compress the sealskin walls that gripped him. In his oozing he would groan. Deep in him he would groan. His face would bend. His lips would move over her dry eyelids.

She would not stir. There were no words to speak for her. In the white cell of her room a rag doll would smile and loll against the wall. Through her nostrils now her breath would hiss. Music scores would dance through her mind. The oboe of flesh would play in her.

'Pmmffff!' Her breath explodes, mouth opens. He ravages her mouth, she struggles, squirms. His loins flash faster. Faint velvet squelch between their loins. Her cuntlips grip like a clam. He clamps her bottom, draws the cheeks apart. Mutinous still, her tongue retreats, unseeking to his seeking.

The sperm boils. In the itching stem the lava rises. The bed rocks. Music of lust. There is dryness here in the lovelust dry. The curtains falter and wave. Her bottom is lifted, back arched. His pestle pounds.

She receives. The squirting she receives – the long thin jets. Spatter-tingling of sperm. Their breath hush-rushes. Her arms lie limp. Long-leaping strands of wet. The oozy. Last jet of come. The dribbling. The last tremors. Bellies warm. A weakness, falling. The strong loins of his urging are paper now. Strengthless he lies, then moves from her.

Her face is pallid. She awaits his going and rises. Her dress is straightened. A vague fussing of hair. Quiet as a wraith she descends.

'You will have tea now, dear? You have had your lesson?' she is asked. She nods. Her knees tremble. A warm trickling between her thighs. The oboe, yes. The tall ship sailing.

I emerged from my dreams. We were loosed and turned

about, our bonds replaced. My bottom bulbed to the wall. I waited.

There was quiet again. The music ceased again. I had not liked it. Its feebleness irritated.

The Lady Arabella was announced. I turned my head, though I could not see.

'Let her enter and be brought here,' I heard my uncle say. There was a sound as if of a heavy table moving. Jenny's hands moved about my face. I knew the scent and taste of them. Her fingertip bobbled over my lower lip. The blindfold slipped down an inch beneath my eyes.

'Look,' Jenny said. I saw the woman enter. Her coiffure was exquisite. A diamond choker, a swan neck. Her curves were elegant beneath a swathing white gown of satin flecked with red. The collar of her gown was raised slightly at the back, as one sees it in portraits of the Elizabethans.

She wore a look of coldness and distance. Her lips were full, her nose long and straight. Her eyelids were shadowed in imitation of the early Egyptians.

She made to step back as my uncle reached her. Her fingers were a glitterbed of jewels. Behind her entered a man of military look, impeccable in a black jacket and white trousers, as was the evening fashion then. I judged the years between them. She was the younger.

'Not here. It is unseemly,' she said.

Jenny covered my eyes. Did she then uncover Caroline's? I heard not a sound beside me.

'No,' the woman said in answer to some muttered remark. There was movement past me. I felt it. As the air moves I felt. Hands touched my thighs, caressed. A finger traced the lips of my quim which pressed its outlines through the fine mesh of the tights. It was removed quickly, as if by another. I heard the jangling of bracelets.

'Not here,' the woman said again. I felt her as if surrounded, jostled. They would not dare to jostle, but they had touched me. Was I an exhibit?

'B . . . Beatrice. . . .' A croaking whisper from my sister. I ignored her. I heard her squeal. She always squeals. She was being fingered. Her bonds jangled. The girl with the oboe would be tight. The sperm would squirt in her thinly. Would she feel it?

Jenny favoured me. Once more my blindfold slipped. The chandeliers danced their crystal diamonds. The Lady Arabella was moving forward. As if through water she moved. An older woman moved beside her, a hand cupping her elbow. The older woman wore a purple dress. Her vulgarity was obvious.

'Arabella, my sweet, you will come to dinner tomorrow night? The Sandhursts are coming.' Her voice cooed.

'I do not know. Perhaps, yes. I must look in my diary, of course.'

Arabella's look was constrained, her lips set. Behind her, as I felt, the man who had escorted her in was nudging her bottom. It was of an ample size, though not too large by comparison with her stately curves. Her face turned to her escort as if pleading. He shook his head. I saw the table then. It had indeed been pushed forward. Upon its nearest edge was a large velvet cushion. Her long legs appeared to stiffen as she approached it. Her footsteps dragged. Her shoes were silver as I saw from the occasional peeping of her toes beneath the hem of her gown.

Jenny covered my eyes again. I had not looked at Caroline. Her veins throbbed in mine. Her lips were my lips. We had been bound together naked. I had sipped her saliva.

There were murmurings, whispers, protestations, retreats. The doors to the morning room opened and closed, re-opened and closed again.

'It is private,' I heard my aunt say to others. The room was stiller. I heard a cry as from Arabella.

'Lift her gown fully,' a voice said, 'hold her arms.'

'Not here. . . .' She seemed unable to say anything else. Not here, not here, not here, not here. A rustling sound. Slight creak of wood. A gasp. Plaintive.

'Remove her drawers.'

'She was unseemly? Is she not betrothed to him?' It was

my aunt's voice. To whom she spoke I knew not. I guessed it to be the escort. His voice was dry and thin.

'Improper,' he replied. The word fell like the closing of a book. 'Take them right off. Do not let her kick,' he said.

'No! not the birch!' A wail from Arabella. The modulations of my aunt's voice and the military gentleman's amused me. They were tonally flat – courteous. Would he have her bound, my aunt asked. It was not necessary, he said, but her wrists should be held.

I envisaged her bent over the table, the globe of her bottom gleaming. Her garters would be of white satin, flecked with red. The deep of her groove – the inrolling. Her breathing came to me, filtering its small waiting sobs. The dry rustling sound of a birch. I had never yet tasted the twigs. It was said that they should be softened first.

'Not bound,' my aunt said. Her voice sounded almost regretful. 'Hilda – you will hold her wrists tight. Stretch her arms out.'

'Noooooo!'

The long, sweet aristocratic cry came as the first swishing came. It sounded not as violently as I thought. I wanted to see. My mind groped, grappled for Jenny. Perhaps she had been sent with others to the morning room. Beside me Caroline uttered a small whimper. Did she fear the birch? She would not receive it. I would protect her. I ran through tunnels calling Father's name. Edward had used his stepmother's first name. She had permitted it. He had lain upon her.

'Na! Naaaaah!' A further cry. Her sobbing rose like violins. A creaking of table. Beneath her raised gown, her underskirt, her chemise, the velvet cushion would press beneath her belly. There was comfort. I comforted myself with the comfort.

The sounds went on. The birch swished gently but firmly as it seemed to me. First across one cheek then the other. no doubt. The bouncy hemispheres would redden and squirm. Streaks of heat. Was it like the strap? I did not like the stable. Did I like it?

'Ask her now,' the man's voice came. There was whispering – a quavering cry. A negation. Refusal. 'Three more,' he said, 'her drawers were down when I caught them together.'

My aunt tutted. The small dots of her tutting impinged across the sobs, the swishings. They flew like small birds across the room.

'Whaaah! No-ooooh! Wha-aaaaah!' Arabella sobbed. I felt her sobs in my throat, globules of anguish swelling. They contracted, slithered down. There was quiet. Her tears would shine upon the polished wood of the table.

'Ask her again.' The same voice, impassive, quiet. The sobs were unending.

'Have you before?' my aunt asked. It was her garden voice, clear and enquiring. The lilt of a question mark that could not fail to invite.

'Twice – but she resists. What does she say?' He asked as if to another.

'I cannot hear. Arabella, you must speak, my dear, or take the birch again.' It was undoubtedly the voice of the woman holding her wrists. Who held the birch?

'I c . . . c . . . cannot. No – yes – oh do not. Do not let him!'

I saw nods. Through my blindfold I saw nods. I envisaged. There was a shuffling. Wrists tighter held. A jerk of hips. The arrogant bosom out-thrust, burning.

'No! not there! *Ah!* it is too big! Not *there!'*

The floor drummed in my dreams. His penis extended, fleshpole, thickpole, entering. Smack-slap of flesh. The chandeliers glittering with their hundred candles.

Her sobs died, died with their heaving groans. 'N . . . n . . . n . . . n . . .' she stuttered from moment to moment. At every inward thrust the table creaked. Was she still being held? I needed voices, descriptions.

'Work your bottom, Arabella! Thrust to him!'

My aunt spoke. Their breathings flooded the room. A gulping gasp. A last sob. Silence. 'Have her dress,' my aunt said at last. 'Hilda – see to her hair, bathe her face, she has been good. Have you not been good, Arabella?' A mumbling. Kissing. 'So good,' my aunt said. Bodies moved, moved past us and were gone. The doors to the morning room were re-opened. A flooding of people, a flurry, voices. Enquiries. My aunt would not answer. The deeper voice of my uncle said occasionally, 'I do not know.'

My limbs ached, yet I was proud in my aching that I had not struggled. I was free in my proudness, my pride. We could speak but we had not spoken. Our minds whispered. We were wicked.

A chink of light. Our blindfolds were removed. Caroline blinked more than I. She had not seen before. People stared at us more strangely now. They were of all ages. Eyes glowed at the bobbing of our breasts.

'You must go to bed. A servant will bring you supper,' Jenny said.

I moved carefully, cautiously – wanting to be touched, not wanting to be touched. My hips swayed. I thought of Arabella.

As we reached the bottom of the stairs she began to descend. We waited. I wanted to be masked. Accompanying her was the older woman in purple. I knew then that it was she who had held her wrists. Their eyes passed across us unseeing.

'And there will be a garden party – for the church, you know,' the woman in purple said.

Arabella's eyes were clear, her voice soft and beautifully modulated.

'Of course – I should love to come,' she replied. They entered the drawing room together as we went up.

'Did you see?' Caroline asked me the next morning.

'There was nothing to see. People were making noises,' I replied. I wanted her to sense that I was more innocent than she.

'That man felt my breasts,' she said.

She looked pleased.

I like the mornings, the bright mornings, the sun-hazed mornings.

It was so when we sat in the breakfast room that

morning, Caroline and I. The chairs had been taken away save for hers and mine.

'You will breakfast alone. in future,' our aunt said. 'Eat slowly, chew slowly. Have you bathed?' We nodded. Jenny passed the door and looked in at us. Her face held the expression of a sheet of paper. There was a riding crop in her hand. It smacked a small smacking sound against her thigh.

The drawing room had looked immaculate as we passed – its doors wide open, announcing innocence. The walls against which we had been bound were covered with mirrors, paintings. Perhaps we had dreamed the night.

There would be riding, Aunt Maude said. We were not to change. Our summer dresses would suffice. Katherine passed the window, walking on the flagstones at the edge of the lawn. She wore a long white dress that trailed on the ground. The neck was low and frilled. The melons of her breasts showed. Her straw hat was broadbrimmed. There were tiny flowers painted around the band. She carried a white parasol. Her servant walked behind her in a grey uniform.

When we had eaten Jenny came again to the door and beckoned us. We followed her through the grounds and beyond the fence into the meadow. Frederick stood waiting, holding the reins of two fine chestnut horses. They were gifts to us, Jenny said. The leather of the new saddles was covered in blue velvet.

We were told to mount. The servant looked away. He studied the elms on the high rise of the ground in the distance.

'Swing your legs over the saddles. You will ride as men ride. No side-saddle,' Jenny told us. The breeze lifted my skirt, showing my bottom. We wore no drawers. I exposed my bush. Frederick had turned to hold the reins of both horses. The stallions stood like statues. The velvet was soft and warm between my thighs. The lips of my pussy spread upon it.

Jenny said we were to ride around her in a tight circle, I clockwise, Caroline counter-clockwise. The servant turned my horse. I faced the house. It looked small and distant. A doll's house. When we returned and entered it we would become tiny.

Jenny clapped her hands and we began. The movement of the velvet beneath me made my lips part with pleasure. Caroline's face was flushed as she passed me, the flanks of our steeds almost brushing. Our hair rose and flowed outwards in the breeze. We kept our backs straight as we had been taught. No one could have reached up so high to smack me.

'Straighten your legs – lift your bottoms – high!' Jenny called. She stood in the middle of the circle we made. The breeze lifted our skirts, exposing us. The hems of our skirts curled and flowed about our waists. The sky spun about me.

'Higher!' Jenny commanded. Our knees straightened. Frederick had gone. I was pleased. In profile the pale moon of Caroline's bottom flashed past me. I heard her squeal, a long thin squeal as the crop caught her, light and stinging across her out-thrust cheeks. And then mine! The breath whistled from my throat. I kept my head back. In the far distance near the house two figures were watching. Our relative was watching. Katherine's head lay on his shoulder, her parasol twirling.

Again the crop. It skimmed my naked bottom cheeks, not cutting but skimming as if it were skittering across the face of a balloon. Who had taught her that? It stung, lifting me up on to my toes in the stirrups. I leant forward, clutching at the horse's mane, breathing my whistling cries to the far-deep empty sky.

At the twelfth stroke of the crop upon each of us, Jenny raised her hand. We slowed, we cantered, we reined in. Panting we fell forward, exposing our burning bottoms to the air. The breeze was cool across our pumpkins hot.

'Dismount!' Jenny called. Frederick the servant was returning. He carried things. 'Stable them!' Jenny ordered him. She referred I thought to the horses, but he ignored them. My bottom tightened as he approached. The ground would receive me – surely it would receive me. I would bury myself in the longer grass and hide until I was called in to tea. I would be fifteen again.

The leather collar bonds that I now saw in the servant's hands were broad and thick, studded with steel points on the outer surfaces. My eyes said no but he did not look. I wrote a question silently on my lips. The servant could not read. He fastened the first collar around my neck. A chain ran down my back. The tip tied in the outcurving of my buttocks. From behind me then where Caroline stood I heard a small cry.

'No, Caroline, be still!' Jenny hissed. 'Walk forward to the barn now!'

Behind us the servant held the chains one in each hand like reins. We stumbled over the grass, the rough hillocks.

'Why?' Caroline asked. It was only to herself that she spoke, but Jenny answered her. She walked beside us, ushering our steps.

'Love is firmness, Caroline. You are the privileged ones. Halt!'

We had neared the stable doors. They were open. The darkness within yawned upon the meadow, eating the air that came near it. Katherine was there. She closed her parasol and leant it against one of the doors.

'Leave this – I will see to them,' she told Jenny.

'Yes, Madame,' Jenny answered Was she not queen? Who was queen? The chains snaked against our backs, urging us forward. And within. In the flushing of Caroline's cheeks I could feel my flushing.

'Over there,' Katherine said and pointed to two stalls – too narrow for horses. The dividing wall between them was but a foot high. I saw the chains again, the wall rings. Caroline wilted and would have stepped back. She was prodded forward. The manacles, ankle rings and chains all were secured. We stood side by side, the low wall between us. I wanted the back of my hand to touch Caroline's hand, but it could not.

'Their dresses, you fool – raise their skirts,' Katherine said. I felt Frederick's hands. They were strong but delicate. Not touching my legs or bottom he bared me to my waist. Caroline quivered and bit her lip as he repeated the action with her.

'Wash their flanks,' Katherine said.

I heard a clink of bucket. The sponge attended to us both. Water trickled over our buttocks and thighs. It ran down into the tops of my stockings and lay in rills around the tight rims. Patted roughly, we were dried.

'They are fair mounts. What do you think, Frederick?'

'Yes, Madame.'

His voice was stiff, expressionless. I relaxed my bottom, feeling its glow – the aftermath of the cropping. The out-curving cheeks above my dampy thighs were roseate. I could see them in my mind. I wished I could see Katherine now in her white dress, but my back was held to her. She is very beautiful. Her dark hair flows down over her shoulders.

'Display, Frederick!'

Her voice was curt. She waited. I could hear her waiting, the sound of her waiting, like a bell that has stopped tolling and waits for the rope to be pulled again.

'Madame?'

His voice was a croak. Was he afraid? I felt not afraid. The day lay upon me, soft of the morning. My flesh bloomed. The damp upon my flesh was warm with my flesh. The tops of my stockings chilled. Caroline breathed through her nose. There were noises, shufflings, small metal noises, cloth noises.

Cloth makes noises like fog.

Display? What was display?

'Turn them!' I heard Katherine say. Ah, it was strange. He held his loins back as he obeyed so that the wavering crest of his pintle-pestle would not touch us. It was long and thick. I like long and thick now. The chains rattled. We were turned. I saw through the barn doors as through a huge eye. The world outside disenchanted me. There was an emptiness. Katherine sat on a bale, her legs crossed. Her skirts were drawn up to show her knees. She smiled at me a light smile, a wisp of a smile. Caroline's face was scarlet. The servant was naked. His balls were big. His penis was a horn of plenty.

We stood side by side still – children waiting to be called to the front of the class. For punishment or to be given prizes? Frederick's body was slender, muscular.

'Come!' Katherine said to him. He turned and moved to her. His back was to us, but he did not look at her. I could feel he did not. His glance was high. Above her head. In homage high. There was a trestle close – two pairs of legs shaped in a narrow V with a bar across. He moved to the front of it and stopped. His back touched the bar. Then he bent – a backward bend – so that his spine arched over the bar, his palms flat on the floor beyond. His penis stuck straight up.

Katherine moved her long wide skirt with an elegant gesture and slipped down off the bale. She came to us. We had kept our legs apart. She was pleased.

'Caroline will lie with her face between my thighs tonight, Beatrice. I shall wear black stockings – pearls around my neck. My thighs will clench her ears. Will you see? Do you wish to see?'

My eyes pleaded. She laughed. She squeezed my chin until my lips parted. 'You can see his cock,' she breathed. Her tongue snaked within my mouth. I tasted the breath of her, warm and sweet as Benedictine. She twirled her tongue, then moved to Caroline.

'Put your tongue in my mouth – *Caroline!*'

Oh, the fool – she should have obeyed immediately. Katherine slapped her face. The tip of Frederick's prick quivered.

'I shall commence exercising you soon, Caroline. Do you understand?'

'No.' My sister's voice was small as if she were hiding behind a pew in church.

'You say, "No, Madame." '

'No, Madame.'

Caroline can be dutiful. I like her body. It curves so sweetly. Her breasts and bottom are plentiful.

'You will learn,' Katherine said. Then Jenny entered. It

was a play – a private play, I felt. She stood in the doorway, hands on hips, observing us. Was she jealous? When Katherine turned, Jenny's hands dropped immediately to her sides. There were words yet. It was a mime.

'Let him rise,' Katherine commanded. Jenny smiled. She walked forward and flicked her crop against his straining tool. He groaned in his rising. His eyes were haggard.

'You may choose,' Katherine told her. Jenny tossed her head. She looked from one to the other of us. She strode – strode to Caroline and pulled her forward.

'Please no,' Caroline said. Her feet skittered, dragged. Her free hand pleaded to the air. The chauffeur had turned to face her. He had tucked our dresses up sufficiently tightly for them to remain so. He said he wanted to kiss Caroline's bottom. The cheeks are firm and plump. Her pubis pouts.

'Bend her over the trestle,' Katherine said.

Caroline shrieked. Jenny had hold of the chain from her neckband and pulled it tight, forcing her over. Caroline's shriek dropped like a fallen handkerchief and lay there, crumpled and used. Her back was bent until she was forced to place her palms on the floor. Her bottom mounded. The sweet fig of her slit showed.

The servant waited. His erection remained as stiff as ever. There was excitement.

'Dip!' Katherine said.

There were new words. I was learning them. Display – dip. His eyes burned. Caroline's hips were high. He took them, gripped them. Rebelliously she endeavoured to twist them but he held her. His lips moved. I wanted words to come – a revelation – but no words came. His loins arched. The crest of his penis touched, probed.

'Caroline! Do not move or speak or you will be whipped!' Katherine said.

She stood observing, as one observes. It was so in the drawing room the night before when my aunt watched the waiting penis enter between the cheeks of Arabella's bottom. I could see now only the servant's haunches, his balls hanging below. Caroline bubbled a moan. Was it speech? His shaft entered – slow, but slow – the petal lips parting to receive it. The straining veins, the purplish head, the foreskin stretched.

Caroline's head jerked up and then was pulled back down by the tensioning of the chain in Jenny's grip.

'*No,* Caroline!' Jenny said softly.

Four inches, five. Caroline's mouth opened. Perhaps she had not, as I thought, sucked upon the penis. Her love-mouth gripped. The ring of truth. Cries gurgled from her lips. Six inches, seven. The fit was tight. I saw her buttocks squeeze, relax. His hands moved to the fronts of her thighs, suavely gripping them. A burr of stocking tops to his palms.

'*No-ooooh!*'

A soft, faint whimper. *In!* Ensconced. Buried to the hilt, his balls hung beneath her bottom.

A second ticked. Two. Three.

'*Out!*' Katherine snapped.

Gleaming, his shaft emerged. I saw his face in profile, the lines etched as by Durer. She jerked her head. He moved towards his clothes. Caroline blubbered softly, her hips wriggled as if she still contained him. Jenny drew her up by the chain. Caroline's eyes floated with tears. Her face suffused.

In the house – not until in the house – were our neck halters removed. We stood in the morning room. We waited. Katherine moved to Caroline and stroked her cheek.

'Are you learning?' she asked. There was summer in her voice.

'Madame?'

Caroline's voice was blank, soft as the sponge that had laved us. Katherine shook her head. 'It does not matter,' she said. We shared secrets, but I knew not what they were. The secret between Caroline's thighs tingled. I could feel its tingling like a buzzing on my lips. Caroline was wicked. I felt certain that she was. Her containment had been too great. She should have cried. Would I have cried? Kathy turned away.

'You know I will whip you if you do not tell me, Caroline.'

Caroline's lips moved, burbled, hummed. 'M . . . m . . . m . . .' Her thighs trembled. Kathy turned back to her.

'That is better,' she smiled, 'you are naughty, Caroline, you know you are. I have to train you. Edward is trained. Do you not think he is well trained?'

Caroline bent her head. She was alone. Each of us alone except when we are kissing, touching. Sometimes when I am being touched I am alone. There was a small cloud around her lips, pretty lips. It said yes. Katherine was pleased again. Aunt Maude entered. There was movement. Unspeaking she took my arm and led me out.

Upstairs in my room she removed my dress. I saw the bed and it was not my bed, not the bed I had slept in. The headboard was different. Wrist clamps hung from the headboard. She made me lie down. She straightened my stockings and drew my legs apart. I waited for my ankles to be secured. I was passive. She drew my arms above my head and fastened the wrist straps. Her face bent over mine.

'It is for your good, Beatrice. Are you happy?'

I said yes. I wanted to please her. Proud in my bonds I lay. My belly made a slight curve.

'Perhaps,' she answered. It was a strange word. 'You will grow happy. Edward was weak for you, was he not?'

I nodded. The morning light grew and bloomed over my body. I had fine breasts, good haunches, a slender waist, Aunt Maude said. Was Jenny nice to me, she asked. I thought yes, no. I wanted to be kissed. I parted my lips as Jenny had told me to. I was not sure, Aunt Maude said. I would be sure soon. She bent over and kissed me and laid her fingers on the innerness of my nearest thigh. Her mouth was warm and full.

'Flick your tongue a little, Beatrice. Quick little flicks with half your tongue.'

She was teaching me. Our mouths fused together. Her

forefinger brushed my button – too lightly. My hips bucked. My aunt stopped kissing me and smiled. She sat up. Regarding me, she unbuttoned her dress and laid it back from her shoulders. Her breasts were heavy gourds, the nipples dark brown and thick. Brown in their darkness brown. The gourds loomed over my face, brushed my chin, my nose. My aunt purred a purring sound. Her breasts swung like bells across my mouth. The nipples grew and teased between my lips. I wanted to bite.

Katherine entered. She waited and my aunt rose.

'He has not whipped her yet?' Katherine asked. Aunt Maude shook her head.

'Soon, perhaps.'

'Yes,' Katherine said. She removed her dress, the filmy folds. Her stockings were silver, banded by black garters of ruched silk. Her drawers were of black satin, small, such as a ballet dancer wears. Her breasts jiggled free. She sat at the dressing table beside my bed. Aunt Maude stripped off her own dress and stood at Katherine's back, brushing her hair. They smiled at one another in the mirror. The smile would stay there for a moment like the impress of my lips when I used to kiss myself after a spanking.

Katherine rose. My aunt looked superb in her stockings, bootees, a waspie corset, frilled knickers. They exchanged sentences with their eyes as if they were posting small, personal notes. My aunt nodded. Katherine mounted the bed over me at my shoulders, facing my feet. The moon of her bottom loomed over my face.

'Her legs,' she said.

The board of the bed to which my ankles were now tethered and spread moved forward, making my knees bend. It was an ingenious device, as I later discovered. The upright board was fixed to the legs which rested on heavy castors. Being slightly wider than the bed itself, the legs and the board were able to be moved at will. My knees were bent up, splayed. The globe of Katherine's knickered bottom brushed the tip of my nose. It descended. In a darkness of bliss it squashed upon my mouth, my eyes, my face.

I tasted her.

'Do not move your lips, Beatrice – it is forbidden!'

I could not breathe. The fleshweight of her hemispheres was upon me. The impress of the lips of her slit in their silken net were upon my mouth. Her bottom bloomed its bigness over me. I panted.

Her bottom moved, ground over my face. It lifted but an inch. I gulped in air. Smothered again, I grunted, gasped. Aunt Maude had a feather. The tip of it, the tickling tip of it, passed upwards in my cunny. I gurgled, choked. The feather twirled, inserted and withdrew. Air whistled through my nostrils and was squashed again. My loins shifted, jerked.

The agony of ecstasy was intense at the feather's touching. A wisping of wickedness, it passed around my clit, tickling and burning. My bottom thumped. The bed creaked. The sides of my face were gripped tight between Katherine's silken thighs. Long tendrils of desire urged their desire within my cunny. My bottom lifted, pleading, in my smothering. Musk, perfume, acrid sweetness – I knew them all.

Let me be loved, in my desiring.

No – Katherine swung off me. Her panties were wet. Sweat glistened on my brow, my cheeks. My loins itched, stung. My mouth was wet with her. I closed my eyes and whispered with Caroline behind a pew. We wore candy-striped blouses, pretty bonnets. We chewed bonbons. I wanted one.

They turned me quickly, unloosing the shackles swiftly. Once on my belly the bonds were refastened. The board at the foot of the bed pressed farther up, forcing my knees up almost to my breasts. The cleft of my pumpkin was exposed.

Something nosed between my cheeks. A velvet touch, a thin dildo of leather swathed in a velvet sheath. The oiled nose of it probed my rose, the tight puckering of my secret mouth, the O of my anus.

'N . . . n . . . n . . . n. . . .' I choked. It penetrated sleekly, entered. My mouth mouthed in my pillow. In the heat of it, the ice of it, I felt it, slender, long, like Edward's penis. Edward had never attempted my bottom. He did not know it had been smacked.

'Oooooh!'

One should not cry out. Should one cry out? I am quieter now. I accept. I am given, loved, I submit. In my moods. It was different then. My bottom mouth gripped it in a grip of treachery – the sleek black velvet of my velvet love. The pointed nose oozed in and twirled. My bottom was riven. In the wild twisting of my face and hips I saw Katherine's legs. Thighs of ivory splendour. Rotating, it withdrew. I was opened. I bit my pillow. The stinging sweetness tremored in my loins. The oil which had been smoothed upon it made it slippery. I grimaced, cried. Katherine laughed.

'Enough – it is enough. How sweetly she sobs – how her bottom bulges to it.'

'It was so when she was spanked. She should be whipped now,' my aunt said. A faint succulent *plop* and it deserted me. I was hollow, empty. I needed. My O was a bigger O. I dived beneath sandcastles of shame. My toes wriggled. *Foutre.*

Was Father's ship sailing back? It would beach at Eastbourne. People on the beach would run screaming, the pebbles sliding beneath their feet. My father with a cutlass would descend.

They released me. The board moved back. My legs straightened. My wrists and ankles were freed. I sank down, curling up. I would become a hedgehog. Gypsies would catch me.

'Shall we go out now, Beatrice?'

It was Katherine's voice. I turned. She was putting on her dress. My aunt was putting on her own dress. She buttoned it with the air of someone who had had it accidentally removed, or by a doctor perhaps. I hid my eyes.

'Yes,' I said. I felt shy. Katherine clapped her hands with pleasure. She reached down and pulled me up.

'Come – get dressed you silly girl. How old are you?'
'Twenty-five,' I said. I had said that to Father. They all knew. Why did they ask? Aunt Maude scolded me to brush my hair.
'Don't be a naughty girl, Beatrice,' she said.